I0587033

The Miracle Royal

Cenarth Fox

The Miracle Royal
Copyright © 2023 Cenarth Fox

The real events, places and people in this novel are used fictitiously as a way of telling an invented tale. All other characters are fictitious and any resemblance to real persons, living or dead is purely coincidental.

All rights reserved. No part of this publication may be reproduced, transmitted or stored in a retrieval system in any form or by any means without permission in writing from the publisher.

Cenarth Fox has asserted his right to be identified as the author of this work in accordance with the Copyright Act 1968.

First published in 2023 by Fox Plays
Melbourne Australia

www.cenfoxbooks.com
www.foxplays.com

ISBN 978-0-949175-72-4

Cover design by oliviaprodesign

Book 1 *The Miracle Railway*
Book 2 *The Miracle Branch Line*
Book 3 *The Miracle Royal*
Book 4 *The Miracle Terminus*

Acknowledgements

With grateful thanks to

Mike Bootman
GER and LNER Societies

Andrew Watts
Norfolk Disused Railways

Richard and Amy Brown
The Royal Station, Wolferton

Michael Petch
St Peter's Church, Wolferton

Dedication

To Tom Rigg
Station master extraordinaire and railway historian

Front cover

Station master's house, Wolferton
Photography: Andrew Watts

Chapter 1

George Miracle saw his mother brutally taken hostage by desperate, armed men and dragged away. His heart screamed. She screamed and struggled but landed in the back of the gunmen's stolen car. What could George do?

Inside the car stuck on the crossing, a revolver shot shattered the calm of a quiet Sunday morning. George lost it and screamed, 'Ma!'

Unarmed—how many station masters carry a weapon?—he knew the danger but his mother, the woman who brought him up to always do the right thing, who loved him as only a mother can, and who now may have died or is dying a shocking and violent death, meant he didn't stop to think. Ignoring the pain in his wounded hip, he ran.

Reaching the car, George grabbed the handle and flung open the door. In the back seat the robber boss, the brains behind the vicious raid, used his hostage, Connie Miracle, as a shield.

George never saw such an expression on his mother's face. He'd seen her cry, weep even when her husband, his father, suffered a terrible work accident and died on George's 12th birthday. He'd seen her angry and annoyed, and seen her laugh with eyes sparkling, but right now her facial expression appeared brand new, unique.

'Ma,' blurted George who reached in and grabbed her arm.

'I shot him,' she gasped, retching, ready to vomit.

George heaved his mother out of the vehicle and onto the Up line. With a train due in four minutes, George forgot trains. He knelt beside his mother who collapsed on the ballast between the rails.

'Are you hurt, Ma?' croaked George cradling his mother.

'I'm sorry about your breakfast, son,' she said as the panicking but now much relieved station master helped Connie to her feet.

Everything happened at once. Porters arrived, villagers too. Stephen Fitzsimons came running. Madge poked his shotgun inside the car. Signalman Monty's earlier phone call to emergency services meant the police and ambulance screeched to a halt minutes apart.

Helping his mother home, George shouted. 'Eric's been shot. He's in my office.'

Not to put too fine a point on it, this Sunday was not your typical day of worship in the sleepy village of Whittleton, East Anglia.

With an arm around his mother, George walked the 20 odd yards to the station house and helped her sit in the kitchen. He put the kettle on the stove.

'There's brandy in the back of the cupboard,' she said pointing. He made the tea.

Someone banged on the front door. 'Go,' said Connie. 'There's no chance it'll be the gunman.' George took off.

Connie should know. As the criminal controlling her raised his gun to shoot Connie's onrushing World War 1 hero son, in a split second she grabbed the robber's wrist and pushed down. As she did, he pulled the trigger with the revolver now pointing at his groin. Ouch! The robber struggled to deal with the pain made worse by the fact a woman made him shoot himself. Staring at both barrels of Monty's shotgun didn't help matters.

'Stephen,' said George opening the door to the young Lord Fitzsimons.

'How's your mother?'

'Come in, come in,' said George leading the visitor to the kitchen.

Connie suppressed the urge to stand and curtsy.

'Mrs Miracle, how are you? Do you need a doctor?' Stephen turned to George. 'Brandy, George.' It appeared.

'Here's the tea,' said George.

Stephen ignored the tea, picked up an empty cup and added a splash of brandy. 'Take this dear lady, slowly now.'

Anyone would think Stephen served for years in the Friends of the Ambulance tipping brandy down the throats of dozens of wounded soldiers on the Western Front. He did so again, albeit gently.

Connie swallowed and nodded. 'Thank you, I feel much better.'

Another person knocked on the door although with less enthusiasm. 'I'll go,' said Stephen, departing.

'What happened to Eric?' asked Connie.

'He copped a bullet in the shoulder.'

As George continued helping his mother, an ambulance officer and a policeman arrived. The medical man attended to Connie.

'Are you hurt, madam?'

'I'm fine. How's Eric?'

The policeman knew. 'He should be okay, a flesh wound and they've taken him to the hospital.'

'And the robbers?' asked George.

'Arrested and being taken away as we speak, sir,' replied the constable. 'One's in a lot of pain. Are you injured, sir?'

'And the money?' asked the station master now thinking only of the consequences of losing such a sizeable amount.

'We have it, sir, and when you're ready, we should like you to deal with the matter.'

George wanted to go but couldn't leave his mother. He changed his mind when his mother's friend from the church, a worried John Beckwith entered in haste.

'Connie, are you all right? I heard you were kidnapped.'

'I'm fine, John.'

'Would you like a brandy?' he asked.

Connie held up her cup. George decided.

'Ma, if Mr Beckwith can stay with you, I might slip away.'

'Of course,' said the middle-aged fiancé. 'You go, George.'

The SM took off with Stephen and the officials following only using less energy. George burst into his office and saw his two fit porters and a policeman guarding a large canvas bag sitting on his desk.

It took ten minutes to open the bag, remove the money and count it twice. George took the relevant paperwork from the safe and showed it to Gordon and the officer.

'Well done, sir,' said Gordon, happy with the result and this time not being part of any skullduggery.

'You've been lucky, sir,' said a constable. 'My sergeant will want a statement but I suggest you secure the cash first.'

George did but panicked when he realized he'd forgotten the trains. 'What about the 8:24 Up and the 8:32 Down?'

'Monty's held all trains, sir, waiting for your all clear,' said Gordon.

George rushed onto the platform. Monty stood outside the door to his home away from home. The SM waved and yelled. 'Monty, it's all clear, let the trains proceed.'

Monty waved and disappeared inside his signal box. Desmond sprang into action and closed the gates to the road, the stolen car having been pushed off the tracks. George realized his hands were shaking and probably had been for the last 20 minutes. The sound of a locomotive on the Up gave him a massive sigh of relief. He watched as the train pulled in. The guard, Henry, leant out.

'What's your game, George? Did you sleep in—again?'

George moved to the guard and spoke in a quiet voice. 'Three armed robbers tried to pinch the takings and shot Eric.'

Henry thought this a leg pull. Of course he did. He and the young station master constantly played tricks on one another over the years.

The train set off and Henry called. 'Nice story, George, you almost had me there.' When he later discovered the truth, Henry became dumb for all of five seconds then muttered one word, 'Blimey!'

Stephen returned to Ripley Hall where the residents were anxiously waiting. The gunshots, particularly the shotgun exploding against the grill of the getaway car, made a dreadful sound. Nerves jangled. Stephen explained the story with everyone mightily relieved.

Louisa swam in her anxiety. Last night, having told the station master she loved him and having kissed him with passion, now in an instant she thought something terrible may have happened.

Stephen gave more details of the armed robbery with only the senior porter being harmed and with a flesh wound.

'And Mr Miracle?' enquired Lady Fitzsimons.

'Again the hero,' said her son and Louisa sighed being unable to stop a tear or two. She wiped them quickly and went upstairs to tell her friend Valerie the news.

'I'm so pleased, Lou. It's a small hiccup in your romance and once life settles, the station master will arrive to tell you he's fine before asking the all-important question.'

She didn't finish as pain exploded in her abdomen. She yelled, she screamed. Not due for nearly a month, this second pregnancy proved a challenge.

Louisa rushed to Valerie's side clasping her hand. 'Try and be still. I'll fetch George. Will you be okay for a minute?'

Valerie nodded not wanting to speak in case she screamed again. Louisa disappeared and, as the men heard the scream, she met the

Lords Carruthers and Fitzsimons heading upstairs with George limping as best he could. They burst into the room and their cursory examination convinced them remaining here was not an option.

'I'll ring for an ambulance,' said Stephen and left.

Beside his wife, George spoke gently. 'Hold on, my darling.'

Louisa said what she thought. 'Would it be quicker and better if we left now and went in Lord Fitzsimon's car?'

'Brilliant, Lou, please go and ask him,' said George who squeezed his wife's hand and called after the nanny, 'Thank you, Louisa.'

Valerie stared at her husband. 'I'm sorry, my Lord,' she said and George Carruthers remained calm, well hardly calm but as restrained as such a tricky situation allowed.

'It's a funny old partnership this creating a new life,' he said struggling for something to say. She forced a weak grin. 'We chaps do our bit taking all of a few minutes and for the next nine months you ladies go through bloody hell on a daily basis. Whom should I blame?'

'It's only eight months and a bit,' she replied gritting her teeth.

He rubbed her arm, continuing to feel helpless.

'At least Louisa is okay,' said Valerie explaining the finer details of her friend's love affair. Husbands are always the last to know. 'She thought her true love might have been injured or worse.'

Carruthers now understood as Louisa returned with Stephen.

'I agree,' he said. 'The car's coming around now. I'll drive, George, you and Valerie sit in the back and Louisa can have wee George in the front. Agreed?'

George and Valerie nodded. The station master's sweetheart took responsibility for the SM's godson, as Carruthers helped his wife downstairs.

Five minutes later they drove along the Ripley Hall drive and headed for London. Valerie seemed in less or at least more tolerable pain, and so they decided to head to the private hospital where she received treatment by a resident doctor and an on-call gynaecologist.

Long after they left and the station returned to a semblance of normality, George Miracle told Gordon and Pip the lad porter he wanted to check on the people at Ripley Hall. The Sunday timetable displayed decent gaps, and particularly with the branch, so George hurried to the manor house.

Memories of his meeting on the Down platform last night with the woman he loved still whirled in his brain. He needed to see her, desperately wanted to see her in the daylight and reassure her of his love. He hurried along the drive as his shrapnel hip complained.

The front door opened and the family retainer greeted him. 'I'm sorry, Mr Miracle, but Lord Fitzsimons has driven the visitors back to London.' George struggled to understand. 'There's an emergency with Lady Carruthers and I believe they've taken her directly to the hospital.'

'*All* the visitors?' said George, asking the wrong question. He should have first enquired after the health of the pregnant visitor.

'Yes sir, all of them. I imagine Lord Fitzsimons will have news later today. Can I take a message?'

George struggled with embarrassment and shame. 'Thank you, no. But please tell his Lordship I called. Good day,' said George and set off back to work.

News of the daring and dangerous robbery soon spread. Of course it did. The station master with the platform gardens and the Druid tourist site now had others adding "dashing hero" to his CV.

Ever since the publicity promoting the station, the Pickling Halt and the manor house continued to receive punters. Word of mouth spread the benefits of a trip on the local branch line, and wine lovers headed to Ripley Hall. How long this would last remained to be seen but right now, about an hour after the botched robbery, George counted passengers on the island platform keen to board the Crabbie.

'All clear here, sir, said Gordon, 'and young Pip is doing a grand job on the Down.'

'Is there any word on Eric?' asked the SM and Gordon shook his head. 'Then you go and help Pip; I'll take care of matters here.'

Gordon nodded and crossed the tracks.

George needed another porter, news about his mother and Eric, and news about Lady Carruthers and especially her companion. He'd never been in love before and it overwhelmed him in its depth and power. He couldn't stop thinking about his girl.

Chapter 2

In 1862, the Prince of Wales, Albert Edward Saxe-Coburg and Gotha, and known as Bertie, earned a reputation as a bit of a ladies' man, a Jack the Lad. Many said his reputation continued for much of his life. His parents, Queen Victoria and Prince Albert, wanted their son to fly the nest but a pad in London might bring temptation too close for comfort. To encourage the young man to take up healthy outdoor pursuits, a possible solution appeared; snap up a chunk of Norfolk in what became known as the Sandringham Estate.

It consisted of about 20,000 acres with various houses, woodland, wetland, pasture and tenant farms enabling produce to be sent to London and elsewhere, and provided plenty of space for the Prince of Wales and his chums to go riding, hunting and fishing.

The main residence on the property did not ooze charm and in time was demolished to be replaced with a far more stately building still standing today.

At first the Royals reached the estate by train from London St Pancras. At King's Lynn, called Lynn by the locals, they travelled towards Hunstanton, called Hunstan by the locals and Sunny Hunny by holidaymakers, alighting at Wolferton. In time, Wolferton became known as the Royal Station.

Members of the Royal Family and their friends and dignitaries would alight at Wolferton. From there horse-drawn carriages would transport the first-class travellers a little over two miles to Sandringham. The return journey to London happened in reverse.

Now a so-called Royal Station must provide the best for the Monarch. You couldn't expect Queen Victoria and later, her heirs and successors to rough it on a bench on the Great Eastern Railway's Wolferton platforms. Like Sandringham House, the attractive Tudor style station was built to the highest standards. It was at most times a quiet country station in a quiet country village but constructed for its important passengers.

The station buildings were architecturally glorious with the station master's house and the signal box a thing of beauty and the station platform lamps were topped with a crown. But within the station, the pièce de résistance was not the public waiting-rooms but the retirement-rooms, exclusively for Royal passengers. Quality decor, exquisite carpentry with oak-panelling and fashionable furniture oozed style fit for a Queen. The lavatory became a convenience of class with accoutrements Thomas Crapper would have approved. After all, the plumber installed 30 lavatories in Sandringham House.

And everything, the buildings, the grounds and the regular visits by Royal and other VIP passengers, meant an appointment as station master to Wolferton became a plum job. When George Miracle ran the Whittleton station, the current Wolferton SM prepared to retire. Harry Saward approached forty years of service at the Royal Station.

George didn't know retirement loomed large for Harry or much if anything about the Wolferton station other than its Royal status. George beavered away in his own little world, his heart bursting with love for Louisa McClaren, the girl of his dreams.

Two other major issues popped in and out of his mind. His most experienced porter lay in a hospital bed with a non-life threatening gunshot wound, and his widowed mother wanted to re-marry.

Close to retirement and being shot on duty helped Eric decide enough was enough. George called to see him, encouraging him to stay on but failed. Over Eric's back fence lay his allotment on which he tended a spectacular vegetable garden, and the shed in his back yard housed his much-loved racing pigeons. The marrows and feathered friends could now enjoy his full attention.

The LNER sent a new porter to Whittleton. Twice as old as George, bachelor Fletcher Drum showed no interest in being promoted. He sang in an all-male choir and the local parish church welcomed him with open arms. George found him as reliable and as po-faced as Eric. Fletcher boarded with a widow, Mrs Rough, the lady in charge of the flowers in the Whittleton church.

Stephen Fitzsimons arrived late in the afternoon with news of his visitors now all returned to the capital. He called at the station.

'I dropped them at the hospital and I'm sure your namesake will telephone tonight and give me the latest.'

'Please give my best to George and to Valerie.'

'Of course,' he said before hesitating. 'But not to your girl?' Immediately embarrassed, Stephen apologized. 'I'm sorry, old man; uncalled for and impolite.'

George smiled. 'No apology needed but I admit to feeling disappointed not being able to say goodbye to the lady in question.'

'Never fear, my friend. Remember absence makes the heart grow fonder. Now I'll be away but will telephone once I have news.'

George told his mother about the sudden return to London of Louisa and her employers.

'Lady Carruthers will be in the best of hands, George. You wait; life usually comes good.'

'But with a new baby at Tudor House, Louisa will be required even more. I can't ask her to marry me when my friends really need her.'

Connie saw his dilemma and she too felt pressure. How could she marry John Beckwith and leave her son in the station house to do his own washing, ironing, cooking and cleaning? Further discussion on the subject moved to the back burner although the Carruthers phone call the next day from London kept George thinking about his girl.

Next week he received a letter from Head Office asking him to attend a meeting to discuss the armed robbery. He advised his porters of his future absence.

The night before the trip, he went over his notes on the robbery to better answer the questions from his superiors.

On the Wednesday, his appointment was at 11. He worked on the Up and looked across the tracks to see the Crabbie arrive. He saw Freda and her dog Rufus alight and head his way. He girded his loins for the barrage of kissing and licking from human and canine.

Freda approached but with no real enthusiasm. In fact she appeared downright miserable. 'Good morning, George,' she said without any attempt to kiss her favourite SM. Even Rufus refrained although his tail worked overtime.

'Good morning, Freda. Are you unwell?'

She headed to a bench on the platform and their meeting began.

'It's Danny,' she said. 'He's gone overboard.'

George knew about the awkward behaviour of the farmer on whose land tourists walked to see the rocks supposedly used by the Druids.

'What's happened?' he asked.

'He's scaring the tourists, George, really scaring them. Numbers are dropping anyway but if he keeps behaving like a madman, he'll kill the business which'll mean the end of the Crabbie.'

'What's he done?'

'You mean what *hasn't* he done? I think he should be sent to your old station in London.' George squinted, confused.

'My old station? What do you mean?'

'They built Liverpool Street station on the site of the mental hospital called Bedlam.' George stared in disbelief which surprised Freda. 'Didn't you know?'

'No,' he said now worried even more. 'I'll have a chat with him.'

'You know I catch the first afternoon train going home so I can come with you.'

'Not today, Freda, I have to go to London. But tomorrow, I'll be on the 9:17 arriving at Pickling at ...'

'9:38,' she said without boasting. She stood. 'Okay, see you tomorrow morning.'

She stepped forward and kissed him sweetly on the lips. Rufus went one better only with tongue.

New porter Fletcher Drum witnessed the exchange and needed his fellow porters to explain the unusual relationship the SM enjoyed with the passenger, the woman dressed in homemade clothes and accompanied by an Irish wolf hound, some believed also homemade.

George left his porters in charge and headed for London. The meeting at Head Office went remarkably well. George explained the robbery, received praise for his actions including congratulations for not losing any of the company's money.

'We're a new company, Mr Miracle,' said one senior LNER manager, and making a profit is proving difficult. Making money is excellent but not losing any is as good. Well done, sir.'

George departed feeling the best since the Whittleton raid. Rather than go straight home, he found his way to the former site of the

Bethlem Royal Hospital otherwise known as Bedlam, and knocked on the SM's door at Liverpool Street. Jack Rogers beamed.

'George Miracle, as I live and breathe,' cried the man George worked with when first he joined the railways.

They enthusiastically shook hands. George explained his London visit with Jack wanting to hear everything about the failed robbery.

'Your uncle would be so proud, George, and no wonder the company's delighted. But they're right about not making money. I think being big doesn't necessarily mean being successful.'

'The LNER men reckoned the company will never make a profit.'

'It could be true.' Jack wanted to move on. 'So what's happening with your career? When are you going to take my job here at Liverpool Street?'

They laughed and chatted until Rogers shocked the young man.

'I think you need to move, George.'

'Me, move? But why?'

'You were talked about when promoted to SM so young, and after this armed raid, the gossip will increase. People will look at Whittleton to see if you fail. I know you, young man; you're not fond of the limelight. Consider moving, search for another post where no-one knows you. If I hear of anything suitable, I'll let you know.'

They shook hands as George pondered his colleague's suggestion.

Valerie suffered constant distress with her baby not due for a fortnight. The best doctors in one of the best London hospitals examined her and discussed the situation. Their plan involved having the baby come early praying it would be healthy.

They explained the situation to Lord Carruthers who asked many questions. 'We're not sure, my Lord,' became a constant reply.

George Carruthers rarely left the hospital which kept Louisa at Tudor House to care for toddler George in Hampstead. The father-to-be brought a camp stretcher into his wife's room where he slept fitfully during the early hours. A nurse shook him awake at a minute past 4am.

'Lord Carruthers,' she spoke as quietly as possible.

Having slept in a trench in France in the Great War, waking instantly happened easily for George Carruthers. Attaching his prosthetic limb took time. His wife's crowded room meant he moved to a "back-row" position. His heart ached as his wife's cries were like a dagger being thrust in his chest. He wanted to hold her hand but knew she was in the best place with the best people. The birth seemed to go on forever.

The medical people were experienced but all knew the unique nature of each birth meant the possibility of injury even death.

George was guided to a position close to his wife but her pain meant she paid him no mind.

'Push, my Lady,' became a constant refrain with George trying to interpret their tone of voice. Valerie screamed as much from pain as determination and George heard a sound which made him weep. A newborn cried, screamed even.

'Congratulations, my Lord,' said a doctor. 'You have a daughter.'

The good news travelled fast. Stephen Fitzsimons rang the Whittleton station at 7.15am and, unsurprisingly, George Miracle was on duty.

'Congratulations Mr Miracle, your godson has a sister. Mother and baby are doing well and the little one's name is Annie.'

George rejoiced. 'Wonderful news, Stephen, thank you for letting me know.'

His Lordship's voice changed tone. 'Because the little one has arrived early, George 1 believes she'll remain in hospital until the doctors are happy with her feeding and such.'

'I understand,' said George 2. 'My mother will be delighted.'

The call ended and one issue dominated the SM's thinking.

Louisa will be extra busy caring for little George. She can't and wouldn't desert the couple who employed her which means she won't be available until the new baby is home and doing well. Any plan for us to marry will have to wait. And the knock-on effect means my mother won't leave her son and marry as she so dearly wants to do.

Once the new porter, Fletcher Drum arrived, George slipped home and told his mother the news. Connie rejoiced as all mothers know what it means and how difficult it can be to give birth. George mentioned the fact the premature birth meant the baby would remain in hospital for the foreseeable future. Connie had questions but said nothing. She knew both their marriage plans could be delayed.

George caught the first Crabbie next morning. 'I'll go to Pickling, gentlemen, to speak with Mr Wight,' he said to Madge and Bobby. They knew why but said nothing. Their respect and admiration for the young station master continued to grow.

The train stopped at Pickling and its only passenger alighted. A local farmer and her dog stood waiting. The woman waved to the footplate crew as the loco chugged away. She addressed the SM.

'I don't know what to suggest, George,' said Freda. 'If he's gone doolally, he's a danger to himself and to anyone who comes to Pickling. All your hard work to save the branch could be for nothing.'

'Are you sure he's not angry thinking these passengers are trespassing on his land?' She shook her head. 'I didn't tell you, a while back when investigating the vandalism, he took a shot at me.'

Freda gasped. She cared for people, even unconventional folk like Danny Wight. It's possible she empathized with people who were not "normal" because she herself slipped easily into such a category.

'Can we bring a doctor out to give him the once over?' she asked.

'Of course but what if it sets him off.'

They stood on the Halt staring at one another wondering how to tackle the tricky problem. Unless Danny changed his behaviour, the few tourists at Pickling would disappear and more than likely along with the branch line.

George knew he should lead. 'Let's find him and hope he doesn't do anything crazy.'

Freda nodded and the three visitors headed to the rundown farm run by the rundown farmer.

They arrived at the collection of buildings and called. No reply. 'He's always here,' said Freda and set off calling. George followed, his anxiety growing. They were between a hay shed and a piggery, although which was which they couldn't say, when a shotgun exploded. George cringed. The man who survived constant bombardment on the Western Front endured more fear in times of peace from a single-bore shotgun than from half the German army. Freda ran, turned a corner and screamed. George flew after her.

She knelt on the ground beside her faithful dog. Danny held his smoking shotgun and spoke angrily with spittle a part of his language. 'It tried to kill me sheep.' The sheep were a hundred yards away.

George joined Freda beside the dog. Blood oozed from its back.

'I'll take him,' said George elbowing Freda aside. He picked up the dog, glared at Danny and set off for the Halt and Freda's farm. She followed with a breaking heart.

At the farm, they "operated" on Freda's kitchen table. Rufus lost his rugby-tackling, face-licking demeanour. His eyes spoke volumes as he stared at his two favourite people.

George "wore" a fair amount of blood. He thought of Mrs Monty and her ability to extract stains from anything including engine oil from human hair.

Using his fingers, George searched for any tiny pieces of metal, found a few and dropped them in one of Freda's mismatched saucers. 'Sponge there,' he'd say and Nurse Freda set to work. If he missed a piece of shot, he and Rufus would become shrapnel brothers.

They used sticking plasters and managed to stop the flow of blood. 'Have you any ham?' asked George.

'I'll make you lunch once the boy is settled,' said Freda not best pleased George started thinking of himself.

'Not for me, woman, for Rufus.'

She changed instantly and fed her dog who attacked it with vigour. 'Is that a good sign, George?'

He nodded. 'Where's his bed?' She fetched it. 'Put it by the fire.'

As Rufus reclined and slipped into his period of rest and recuperation, Freda made George a doorstop sandwich and a mug of tea you could stand a spoon up in. Over lunch he told her the true tale of the lost puppy from his first day at Whittleton. Rufus listened with interest before falling asleep, his breathing becoming relaxed.

The humans discussed Danny, the Pickling attraction and the fate of the Crabbie. They agreed to close the Halt until the authorities paid Danny a visit and did something about his dangerous behaviour.

As George prepared to leave, he knelt and gently patted Rufus. The dog licked the station master's hand. Freda kissed George on his cheek but hugged him for a good wee while.

He waited for the Up Crabbie pondering his future.

Could Jack Rogers be right? Is it time for me to make a move?

Chapter 3

Christmas at Whittleton saw Connie cooking for her children, her son-in-law, Bert and her intended, John Beckwith. Everyone except the station master would dine elsewhere on Christmas night.

Emily beamed. She found married life to be everything and more she hoped it would be. Bert too seemed a new man. Mr Beckwith behaved in his usual polite and restrained manner asking proper questions and making helpful and respectful comments. Everyone could see he and Connie would make an ideal couple.

George became the odd man out, his true love being absent. He'd managed a phone call to Tudor House soon after little Annie was born and the conversation with Louisa included pauses and silent crying. She explained her obligation to stay and care for young George until life returned to normal. Lover George reluctantly accepted her situation and the conversation reached its conclusion. As they said their goodbyes, George suffered another of his blurting responses and spoke without hesitation, 'I love you, Miss McClaren,' before hanging up and finding a tear appear in each eye.

Being the sole LNER employee on Christmas night at Whittleton station, he tried to keep busy. He didn't starve.

Earlier, with Christmas Day lunch over, the two couples prepared to leave. 'There's plenty of ham and cold turkey for your supper, George,' said his mother.

'Thank you, Ma, I'll be fine.'

Emily kissed her brother and whispered, 'Say hello to Louisa for me and tell her marriage is a seriously good idea.'

John and Connie walked the short distance to John's cottage before taking the pony trap to his sister's house in the next village. Emily hopped up behind her husband on one of their farm's horses and trotted off down the High Street heading to the Culpepper farm.

Alone in the kitchen, George thought about Louisa before remembering his shift resumed at 4:30pm. Luckily his journey could be measured in seconds.

John Beckwith's family consisted of his widowed sister and her two children, nephew Clive and niece Phoebe. These young adults were not related to Sophronia and Enoch Hamilton-Weir of Belgravia, the half-siblings of Louisa McClaren, but they did share the odd similar thought with the twins.

Years ago, John's nephew and niece were told by their mother they were the main beneficiaries of Uncle John's will. He wanted to leave money to the church in which he'd worshipped all his life but the bulk of his estate would be left to his sister's children.

They'd known their uncle all their lives and been to his home in Whittleton on countless occasions. The siblings discussed their possible inheritance, not constantly but more so as the years rolled by as dear Uncle John's hair turned from grey to white.

How long before he pops his clogs?

But a thunderbolt hit when one night their mother dropped her bombshell; Uncle John is to marry. It didn't take long to figure out the consequence. John told his sister his will would remain unchanged other than Connie would have exclusive use of the family home until she died.

The siblings did a much less spiteful imitation of their Belgravia "cousins", being forced to share their inheritance with an interloper meaning they couldn't receive their inheritance until their new aunt fell off the twig. C'est la vie.

'I heard she's ten to twenty years younger than Uncle John so she could live another thirty years or more,' said Phoebe when she and her brother were alone.

'Them's the breaks, sis,' said Clive as they prepared for Christmas and the chance to meet their new soon-to-be step-aunt.

George worked alone at night on Christmas Day. Train services at Whittleton were reduced and the Crabbie only ran two trains; mid-morning and mid-afternoon. Darkness arrived in the late afternoon and light snow fell.

George heard a gentle tap and Stephen Fitzsimons appeared bearing a gift.

'Compliments of the season, sir,' he said as they shook hands with Stephen's being bitterly cold. He handed George a well-wrapped gift, a tin of the finest Scottish shortbreads.

'Thank you, how kind,' said George, embarrassed his gift to the local Lord didn't exist. 'Come to the fire, sir, your hands are frozen.'

They chatted about the past year and the one fast approaching. Inevitably the subject of the Carruthers' and Louisa's situation arose and George didn't know what to say.

Stephen helped him out. 'Once little Annie finds her feet, you and Louisa can make plans and wed and you'll have your girl living next door to your place of work.'

George thought about speaking his mind and, true to form, did.

'True,' he said, 'but not necessarily at Whittleton.'

Stephen's ears pricked. 'Hey ho and what does that mean?'

'I'm thinking aloud,' said the SM. 'There's nothing definite yet.'

A week after Christmas, George's phone rang. 'Happy New Year, George,' said Jack Rogers.

'The same to you, Jack, and how is life in the big city?'

'Cold and busy but listen, I've heard the Wolverton SM is retiring after 40 years in the job.

'Wolferton?'

'Now don't tell me you haven't heard of it.'

'No, I have. It's on the King's Lynn to Hunstanton line.'

'It's the so-called Royal Station, George, with impressive buildings and an even more impressive list of passengers.'

'Jack, Wolferton will attract a huge number of applicants many or most of whom will have years more experience than me.'

'I can't believe the nephew of the great Fred Carmody would ever express such negativity. You have to be in it to win it, George. Keep an eye on the vacancies and if you don't apply, I'll jolly well apply for you.'

They laughed and ended the call. A few seconds later, the phone rang again.

'George, it's Oscar Wilding. Happy New Year to you and yours.'

'And to you, Oscar. It's lovely to hear your voice.'

George recently told Oscar about the success of the Pickling tourists and the wine tasting in the manor house next door, largely due to the expert marketing skills provided freely by Daisy's son.

Oscar explained the reason for his call. 'Listen, George, we have a new house guest by the name of Miss Woods …'

'Daisy,' cried George remembering with great fondness his former housekeeper in Norwich.

'Can you drag yourself away for a few hours and have a meal with us? We'd all love to see you and especially my beautiful mother.'

George didn't hesitate. They settled on a date and the SM took steps to have all the porters on duty.

He told his mother. She showed interest but George could see her distraction; she wanted to marry the man with whom she'd fallen deeply in love. With Louisa feeling obliged to keep working for the Carruthers, George's wedding plans were well and truly on hold, and worse, nobody knew for how long.

On January 3, 1924 he arrived at Cricklewood and he and Daisy hugged with feeling. The delicious meal played second fiddle to the happiness and conversation. Laughter roamed free.

It took George an age to realize Daisy's status in her son's home was not so much a guest but a permanent resident. She spoke plainly.

'When Mr Ramsbottom retired, his horrible replacement gave me little choice but to leave. I could never keep house for such a man.'

'Mum, visitors and children are present,' mildly rebuked Oscar.

'My sister in Cornwall has always wanted me to live with her but her husband is a bit like the new station master in Norwich. My dear son, Oscar insisted I come here but I know I've pushed my favourite grandson out of his room.'

'No Grannie, I'm fine,' protested 14 year-old Michael Wilding. He lied in his polite reply because sharing with his two younger siblings he now discovered could only be described as beyond horrible.

'Liar,' replied Daisy smiling as she spoke squeezing the boy's hand. So station master Miracle, I'm after a housekeeper's position, if you please.'

'Done,' said George and the room fell silent.

'I beg your pardon?' whispered a stunned Daisy.

'How soon can you pack?'

The silence grew louder. George explained. Again he lost control of his mouth and brain. His uncle often warned him about saying little if anything until he worked through the possible consequences.

'Here's a prayer for you, George,' said Uncle Fred. 'Dear God, please help me to engage my brain before I open my mouth.'

18

He told everyone at the Wilding table, people who knew nothing about his love life, how he planned to wed but his bride-to-be couldn't leave her present position. He panicked not yet having asked Louisa to marry him and worried he'd announced what may never happen. *What if they meet Louisa and congratulate her? Cricklewood and Hampstead are only a few miles apart.*

On and on he went. His mother wanted to marry but refused to leave her "poor, helpless little boy" alone. To find a housekeeper, and one he loved dearly, would be the perfect solution.

'Daisy, you are the answer to our prayers.'

People bubbled and grandson Michael discovered the word *hallelujah.*

I'm going to have my room back!

'But what will your mother say?' asked Daisy, yet to be convinced.

'She'll be thrilled because now she can wed.'

'But you can't mean today?' again queried Daisy.

'Your room is ready, the larder is well stocked, and I'm not sure my shirts have been ironed this week. Time to make a move, Miss Woods and if we're quick, we'll arrive on the 4:16pm Down.'

The Wilding household erupted. Grannie could leave. They all helped her pack. She caught the excitement. The whole family accompanied George and his new housekeeper to the nearby station. There were hugs aplenty.

They did catch the aforementioned Down train from Liverpool Street and duly arrived at Whittleton. George carried Daisy's luggage. His porters were there to greet their SM and nodded politely when George introduced his new housekeeper. The arrivals headed to the station house and to the reaction of his mother.

'It's me, Ma,' he called at the door, 'and with a special visitor.'

Connie juggled a spot of ironing with preparing the evening meal.

The two women smiled at one another. 'Hello Mrs Miracle,' said Daisy. 'George has told me so much about you.'

'This is Daisy, Ma, you know my housekeeper from Norwich.'

'Hello,' said Connie wondering why Daisy stood in her kitchen wearing a hat and why George stood beside a large suitcase.

'Daisy's come to stay, Ma. She's going to take your place meaning you and Mr Beckwith can wed.' Connie went to speak but didn't know what to say. 'Now let's have no argument. Daisy can have Em's room and yours when you move out.'

'I hope this meets with your approval, Mrs Miracle,' said Daisy seeing the surprise and shock on the mother's face.

Connie struggled. 'It does but it's a bit of a shock.'

'Why don't you show Daisy her room, give her a tour of the cottage then pop round to Mr Beckwith's and make a date for your wedding. But right now, I must return to work. I'll see you soon, ladies.'

He smiled at both women and left and as he walked to the station, instinctively crossed his fingers.

George wrote to the police inspector he met after the attempted robbery explaining as best he could the situation with Danny Wight and his dangerous behaviour.

I don't wish to deprive a man from working his own land, but I've seen two incidents now where he's put lives in danger.

George posted the letter, told the Crabbie crew they were not to stop at Pickling unless there were people other than Mr Wight waiting to board or alight, and at Whittleton he put up a notice stating the Druid tourist trips were cancelled until further notice due to maintenance. Mind you the Pickling Halt needed minimal care.

'What happens if tourists turn up for Pickling, boss?' asked Madge.

'I'll be here,' said George. 'I'll offer them a free ride all the way to Crabbtree where Owen can give them a guided tour of the engine shed and his office.'

'Haven't you heard, boss?' asked Bobby.

'Heard what?' asked George starting to worry.

'Owen's leaving.'

'What? Why wasn't I told?'

'He's only just told us. He came in this afternoon on the 2.10 Up and you weren't here. He said his father's died and he needs to go back to Wales to sort out the family estate.'

George lost what anger he produced. 'I'm sorry. Oh dear, we'll need a porter to move to Crabbtree until we can find a replacement.'

'I think you need to talk to your platform staff, boss,' said Bobby, 'unless you want us to double as footplate crew, guards *and* porters.'

George saw the comedy or irony or whatever in their reply and waved them away.

His great efforts to save the branch line were being derailed. With an armed and mentally unstable man at Pickling and the company not rushing to appoint a porter at the terminus, now might be the time to move from Whittleton.

But wait. I've just hired a housekeeper.

Scratching his head became an automatic reaction.

The police arrived at Danny's farm and saw firsthand what George described in his letter. The farmer threatened the two unarmed officers with his trusty shotgun causing them to beat a hasty retreat. When they returned with reinforcements and a plan, Danny found himself arrested and before a magistrate.

The poor fellow was sectioned with orders to have his animals placed in the temporary care of a willing neighbour. All this took time and with the Druid site visits on a temporary ban, public interest waned.

George informed the LNER about his departed porter at Crabbtree. Their question became, 'Does the amount of passenger and freight traffic justify the station being manned?'

What could George say? He told them the truth and Head Office stated they would attend to the matter as soon as possible. Inertia took over and Crabbtree became an unmanned station like the other stations and halts on the branch. Talk about the last rites, the writing being well and truly on the wall.

Chapter 4

Connie and John Beckwith's wedding went as planned; quiet, no fuss, with a few guests. Naturally the bride's children were there as were the groom's sister and her children. Throw in worshippers from the Whittleton congregation and Daisy Woods.

The wedding breakfast at *The Crown* in the village featured George proposing the toast to the happy couple. The station master kept learning. He discovered the right time for levity even cheeky comments. This occasion called for neither and he spoke well.

His latest letter to Louisa gave her all the news about the wedding, the new housekeeper and how he missed her and hoped little Annie would soon be well enough to leave hospital and go home.

The branch line situation went from grim to on-death-row. George saw the Wolferton vacancy notice and applied. He held little hope of success, and said nothing about his application to anyone except Jack Rogers asking him to tell no-one.

After the wedding breakfast, he kissed his mother and shook hands with his new stepfather, wished them well on their honeymoon in Yorkshire, farewelled his sister, brother-in-law and the other guests and walked back to work. At home, Daisy prepared his favourite meal from their days in Norwich. When he arrived home, he wasn't hungry.

'You're spoiling me, Miss Woods,' he said and she smiled. The smile on her face matched the one in her heart.

'So tell me, young man, with your sister and mother both married, when are you going to do the right thing by your girl up in London?'

She spoke her mind did Daisy and with force. She knew all about George and Louisa and the baby Carruthers still in hospital.

George enjoyed the best steak and kidney pie he'd ever tasted. 'Well, Miss Woods, why would I be in a rush to marry when I have the best housekeeper in England serving suppers like this?'

'Your problem, George Miracle, is you're always joking. I hope to God you're not worried about me once you wed.'

He stopped chewing. 'As a matter of fact, Daisy, I *am* concerned. I brought you here to Whittleton and I feel responsible for your future.'

'Stuff and nonsense,' she fired back. 'Your only task right now is to find a way to ask Louisa to marry you. I'm a big girl, George, and can take care of m'self.' She paused and pointed a fork at him. 'Do you hear me?'

He nodded and whispered. 'Yes ... and thank you.'

'Why don't you propose and give her a ring, and then worry about the station and the branch line and anything else? Start the ball rolling, George. Pop the damn question.'

Her eyes told him about the seriousness of the matter and he loved her for what she said and tried to get him to do.

In 1884, a young railwayman, Harry Saward, from a pool of more than 100 applicants, found himself appointed station master in Norfolk at Wolferton, two stops from King's Lynn on the line to Hunstanton. What a remarkable station, the arrival and departure point for Queen Victoria, her son Edward VII and grandson George V, and other Royals together with their friends and families. A cabinet of prime ministers made their way to and from Wolferton to be greeted by the courteous and efficient Mr Saward.

In the first 25 years of Harry's time as SM at Wolferton, 645 Royal trains arrived at his station; six hundred and forty-five. Harry's wife, Sarah, worked with her husband and even ran the Wolferton post office and it would be fair to say their life was never dull. Greeting Royals from home and abroad became part and parcel of the job. It's not known if Harry ever challenged a Royal for travelling without a ticket but there exists an interesting story involving Edward VII who once went hunting with his Russian cousin, the future Tsar.

They chose to travel back to Sandringham, at least part of the way by train. They were dressed in riding outfits, sans crowns or ermine robes, and boarded a train heading to Wolferton.

The ticket inspector, presumably oblivious to the high status of his passengers, approached the new arrivals requesting their tickets.

The Monarch attempted to brush the minion aside. 'My good man, I'm the King of England and my companion is the future Tsar of Russia.'

Surely such a claim would have most, if not all railwaymen backing off bowing profusely en route.

Not so in this case. The ticket inspector fixed a beady eye on the Monarch and retorted. 'And I'm the Archbishop of Canterbury, now may I see your tickets please.'

True or not it sits well with the four decades SM Saward served at the Royal station. Admired by all classes, his pending retirement in 1924 stimulated George Miracle, 75 miles away in Whittleton, to apply to become Harry's replacement.

The phone rang in the Whittleton SM's office. George responded.

'George 2, this is George 1.'

Such friendly banter between Carruthers and Miracle happened often. Being older, George Carruthers labelled himself George 1.

'George,' cried the SM. 'It's lovely to hear your voice. How are you, your wife and children?'

'We're fit and well, my friend and I'm ringing for two reasons; apart from asking how you are.'

'I'm well, my Lord, thank you.'

'The first reason is to tell you little Annie, your godson's baby sister, has improved so much she's coming home.'

'Wonderful, marvellous,' nearly shouted the SM with a tear forming in both his eyes.

'And the second reason is to invite you to Tudor House to give us all a chance to see you and have you meet our newest addition.'

'I'd love to come. When do you suggest?'

'Well the sooner the better, old man. We're all keen to have you visit and when I say all, I include your godson's nanny, Miss ... Damn, I've forgotten her name but I think you know who I mean.'

They laughed and George Miracle stood and walked around his office with phone in hand delighting in the conversation.

They agreed a date and George 2 hung up wearing a massive grin. Pip appeared wondering why his boss appeared so happy.

'Good news, sir?' he asked.

'Splendid,' replied his boss. 'Now whatever it is you want, young man, the answer is yes.'

Pip wished he'd changed his order.

Over supper, George waited until Daisy's pudding appeared—lemon and raspberry bread and butter pudding—before he announced his planned visit to Tudor House.

'Hallelujah,' cried Daisy slapping her hands on the kitchen table. 'Now it's not for me to tell you what to do but ...'

'Go on,' said George, 'you've come this far; don't stop now.'

They settled and Daisy became serious. 'I'm thrilled for you, George, you must know that, but have you bought the ring?'

'Ah,' said George through gritted teeth. 'I don't know where to go, how much to pay or even what to buy.'

Daisy gave him the sort of talk a parent might give their child. George posed questions which the housekeeper answered or batted away as "not important". He retired rehearsing his marriage proposal and imagining all manner of replies from his girl.

Two days before his visit to Tudor House in Hampstead, he made a secret trip to London to examine the contents of jewellery shop windows in Bond Street. He remembered his only visit to a fashionable shop in this fashionable street many years ago, and now, peering in shop windows, the range of engagement rings seemed overwhelming and the prices terrifying. He searched in vain.

In a side street he stopped outside a smaller shop. The prices looked less intimidating. A young couple came out of the shop, arm in arm and beaming. He continued to procrastinate.

'There stands a young man wanting to marry,' said a woman behind him. George turned and her smile helped him relax.

'Do you tell fortunes as well?' asked George returning her smile.

'My father's the expert. Come inside. There's no obligation.'

And so young station master Miracle met a kindly jeweller and his daughter and left with what he hoped might be regarded as the perfect engagement ring for his perfect young lady. An opportunity to propose and her acceptance would complete the ideal scenario.

His trip to Tudor House in Hampstead was on a Sunday, a time when Whittleton handled the fewest services of any day, and when the fading-fast branch line stumbled along with a handful of passengers even though the Druid site was back on the agenda.

Being in the dead of winter, George sported coat, scarf and gloves when he farewelled his porters and caught the 10:19am Up.

His walk to Tudor House came with a host of memories. In this property he encountered the late Lord Carruthers and his murderous wife. Here he first met the beautiful Louisa McClaren and here, today, he planned to propose marriage to her.

With a small packaged item safely tucked in his coat pocket, he gave his scarf a final tighten and attacked the burly pedestrian gate. Through the magnificent garden he went, switched to the driveway and approached the imposing entrance.

He pictured the front door to the Whittleton station house then the door to Ripley Hall and now faced the one to Tudor House. Size may not matter but it certainly creates an impression.

The manservant appeared. 'Welcome Mr Miracle, please come in.'

What a start. George's emotions kept dancing. He handed over his scarf, gloves, cap and coat before panicking. He asked the man to wait as he rescued a small package from his coat pocket.

'The family's in the front sitting-room, sir, if you'll follow me.'

George's heartbeat started racing as he walked through the mansion. The door opened and George entered, nervous.

Lord Carruthers, now seriously mobile on his prosthetic leg, and sporting a huge grin, moved to George. 'Ah, 'tis the station master himself.' The men embraced. 'Come and meet the extended family.'

Valerie sat on the nearer settee with her baby daughter wrapped in quality garments in the mother's arms.

'George, it's lovely to see you.'

He kissed the young mother before admiring the new addition.

'She's beautiful,' said the SM while pondering her tiny size.

'And these two I think you know,' said the father leading George to another settee on which sat his godson beside the SM's beloved.

'Good day, Mr Miracle,' said Louisa whose smile gave George's heart a jolt.

'Miss McClaren,' he said, bent and kissed her cheek than sat on the settee with his godson in the middle. George took hold of the toddler's hand. 'And how is my favourite godson?'

Well trained, the child knew Uncle George, the station master and "your godfather" would arrive, and the lad responded in a kind and surprisingly mature way.

'Hello, godfather,' he said taking and squeezing George's hand. The others were moved although the SM positively glowed.

Despite the warm even lighthearted conversation, an undercurrent of nervous tension permeated the room. Lord and Lady Carruthers wanted their visitor and their employee to have a moment alone.

Well, actually more than a moment and so the rehearsed and much discussed plan to create the moment-alone situation began. Valerie instructed her husband on the plan, her plan.

She could well be described as the perfect matchmaker. 'Please forgive me, George, I must feed Annie and see she has her daytime siesta. George stood as the mother and her baby left the room.

The father remembered his cue and lines. 'And you, young George, need to help me tidy your toy box.' The toddler and his father departed leaving the station master resuming his seat beside Miss McClaren. She spoke first.

'Do you think that looked rehearsed?'

He smiled fighting hard not to make a gushing statement of love. 'Just a little,' he said giving a nervous smile. Wow, this was serious.

'It's lovely to see you, George. I've missed you.'

He scoffed in a friendly way. 'I bet I've missed you even more.'

'Oh yes?' teased Louisa. 'And how do you measure that?'

George blurted his response. 'Must we stay here?'

'Here, in this room?'

'I mean, could we go for a walk? There's so much I have to tell you and being outside might help.' He looked and sounded on edge.

'Of course but I'll need to find warmer clothes. Will you wait? I won't be long.' She kissed his cheek and left. He watched her go as he fondled the small box in his pocket.

When she returned, he caught his breath. She wore a long woollen bright red coat with a black fur trim, a black woollen hat pulled tight over her hair, and black leather gloves with a fur trim to match her coat. Her shoes were replaced by sturdy black boots.

'Ready when you are, Mr Miracle,' she smiled and he wanted to skip the walk and kiss her like he did on the Whittleton Down platform before Christmas.'

'I'll fetch my coat,' he said leading her to the front of the house.

'You'll need it. I think it's going to snow.'

His nerves tingled as his heart rate raced. He put on his coat, scarf, cap and gloves and opened the front door and down the drive they went. Valerie watched from upstairs and wished her friend well.

'Would you like to walk on the Heath?' he asked.

'I'd like to walk anywhere with you, George Miracle.'

He offered his arm which she took and they headed towards the huge park on the outskirts of London. The trees were bare, the wind biting and their cheeks blue. Hampstead Heath was theirs alone.

Is this such a good idea? thought George.

'So your sister and mother are married,' she said. 'How are you managing on your own? Oh I forgot you have a new housekeeper.'

'Daisy is over-feeding me, ironing my shirts with razor-sharp creases, and giving me all sorts of advice.'

'Advice?' George wanted to bite his tongue. 'I'm intrigued. What sort of advice do you receive from your housekeeper?'

He floundered. 'Oh, general advice.' He thought of the night his now brother-in-law asked about making a marriage proposal and sex.

She gazed at him and he knew it and struggled to return her gaze.

He indicated a bench. 'Would you care to sit over there?'

'No, I wouldn't care to sit anywhere. It's freezing George and walking will stop us turning into statues.'

He took direction and they continued strolling. He decided to bite the bullet. 'There's something I want to ask you, Louisa.' He stopped as did she and they faced one another. He hesitated as his heart raced faster than a piston on a locomotive running downhill with a full head of steam. He froze—in two ways. She wanted so much to help him.

'Can I help?'

Her offer threw him. 'No, thank you. I need to do this on my own.'

She waited and still he paused. She thought of a prompt.

'You do know what year it is, George?' He did. Of course he did.

'Yes, it's 1924.'

'But did you know it's a Leap Year.' His mind raced, she persisted. 'And you do know what that means?'

Confusion troubled him. 'Yes, there's an extra day in February.

'And?'

'I'm sorry; I don't know what you're talking about?'

'An ancient Scottish law states in a Leap Year women may propose marriage and if the man refuses he has to pay a fine.'

He saw a twinkle in her eyes, her stunning, sparkling eyes, and lost his fear. He produced the small box, opened it, she gasped, he dropped onto one knee which squelched in the snow, and on a windswept Hampstead Heath, as snow silently decorated everything, George held out the box displaying the ring and stared into Louisa's eyes which went from the ring to him. Cue the much rehearsed script.

'I love you with all my heart, Louisa McClaren. Please will you honour me by becoming my wife?'

Her tears began to flow but struggled in the bitter cold. She helped him to stand, stood on her tip toes, moved closer and spoke with a clear voice. 'I would love to marry you, George Miracle.'

They kissed but he broke clear. 'You haven't tried on the ring.'

This became comical. It took time as a glove needed to be removed. It wasn't easy and so off came a second glove. It became seriously funny as he took her gloves, shoved them in his coat pocket, and struggled to remove the ring from its box forcing him to remove *his* gloves. Eventually he held the precious item and Louisa offered her finger. The tight fit caused concerns until it settled and she fell in love with the ring and again with the man in front of her.

They embraced and kissed and were interrupted by a barking dog.

'Sorry, folks,' said an elderly man. 'She's normally friendly.'

George forgot the dog because he wanted to announce his news. 'We're engaged to be married,' he celebrated.

The elderly woman with the man smiled, clapped her gloved hands and congratulated the couple. 'I hope you'll both be very happy.'

'Thank you,' replied the couple overflowing with happiness.

In a teasing voice, the man added, 'Are you sure, young man? I mean it's not too late you know.'

He smiled, the woman gave her husband a friendly slap and they departed with their dog adding its congratulations.

Alone, nothing or no-one interrupted their passion.

'Can we go back?' asked Louisa. 'Valerie and George will want to know what's happened and besides, I'm freezing.'

With his arm around his bride-to-be, George Miracle did an about-turn and walked his fiancée back to Tudor House.

Chapter 5

Belgravia is about five miles from Hampstead Heath. As George and Louisa were making their love for each other official, Louisa's father, Sir Jerome Hamilton-Weir struggled out of his bath to collapse on the marble floor. The pain in his chest terrified him. He sensed air being squeezed from his body. Dying alone, naked, on his bathroom floor, produced a scream of anguish. He yelled for his life.

Being hugely rich and owning a home built with the best materials by the best craftsmen meant the rooms offered privacy. No paper-thin walls in this "ten-up ten-down".

The servants were all below stairs, as good as a mile from Sir Jerome's palatial bathroom. Gasping, he sprawled on the floor. A valuable vase with flowers rested on a stand in one corner. He slid, trying to swim towards it. Reaching to grab it increased his pain. It was too high above the floor. He pushed the stand; the vase teetered, toppled and fell. Smash! He grasped the largest piece of ceramic and flicked it towards the door. This created another unusual sound.

In the kitchen, a second feeble smashing sound grabbed the domestics' attention. Sir Jerome's man stopped drinking tea. The housekeeper told him to investigate. Halfway up the stairs he called. 'Sir Jerome, are you all right?'

No reply. At the top of the stairs, a third crashing sound was loud and clear. A glass bottle of male perfume smashed on the floor.

The servant ran, opened the bathroom door and discovered the philanthropist. Avoiding fragments of glass and ceramics proved a challenge but an hour later after a trip in an ambulance, Sir Jerome rested in a private hospital suite where London's leading cardiologist supervised proceedings. It helps to make generous donations.

Two of his children, the twins Sophronia and Enoch, relaxing at the family's country estate in Cambridgeshire, were telephoned and told of their pater's serious health problem. A possible life-threatening situation meant they should return to London post-haste and prepare for the worst.

Both twins uttered a variety of oaths complaining more because of their interrupted relaxation as opposed to the possible demise of the old man. Distress at their pater's likely death didn't exist.

They were driven to Cambridge and travelled up to London by train. The failure of their associate, the Earl of Fakenham, to remove their half-sibling, the newly-engaged Louisa McClaren, stuck in their respective craws.

Valerie and George were thrilled with the engagement news. Whilst not surprised, it became a time of great joy to see their dear friends agree to marry.

George Miracle was already a family member as Lord Carruthers' best man and as godfather to his first born. Louisa and Valerie's mothers were friends from childhood and their daughters followed suit. Their mothers would be over the moon and George's sister would be thrilled.

'Right you two,' said the George with one and a half legs, 'when and where is this big event to take place? We can offer you the grounds of Tudor House for the best reception in London. We can turn this place into a Buck House garden party.'

The engaged couple were nonplussed. They'd not discussed the date or venue or in fact anything about the business of getting married, and the offer from Lord Carruthers stunned them.

'We've not made any plans,' said Louisa and her fiancé agreed.

'I've not even met Louisa's mother,' he confessed.

'Well it's far too cold to marry right now,' said Valerie. 'May or any time in summer will be best. It'll give you time to find the most beautiful wedding dress in London.'

'I won't be wearing a dress,' retorted George M and the laughter continued. There were more hugs and kisses with champagne being summoned. Teetotaler George Miracle selectively sipped.

'Would you allow me to place your engagement notice in *The Times*?' asked George Carruthers.

'It's usually the prerogative of the bride's family,' said his wife.

Of course Carruthers knew Louisa's family situation—certainly not the identity of her real father—and only offered to help so as to assist Mrs McClaren with the cost and procedure.

'I'm sure Mummy will be most grateful,' said Louisa.

'Good, I shall send her a draft of the notice, and with her approval, have *The Times* tell the world the good news.

'It might be better if Mrs McClaren hears the news first from her daughter before meeting her future son-in-law,' added Valerie.

'Right again, my dear,' said the Lord, 'as always.' Smiles were wide and plans were made.

Louisa sent a telegram to her mother with the news and suggested the couple travel to her cottage near Cambridge next Sunday.

George became a new man as he alighted at Liverpool Street on his way home to Whittleton. His pride skyrocketed at having captured the heart of such a beautiful, kind and clever girl. He wanted to tell the world his good news and particularly his mother and sister. The one worrying thought concerned his housekeeper.

He'd more or less shanghaied Daisy into moving to Whittleton replacing his now newly-married mother, but once *he* married, it wouldn't make sense to have Daisy stay on, but it would be cruel to send her away.

At Whittleton he found the station running without a hitch and even the Crabbie made it to and from Crabbwell with a few passengers despite now being an unmanned station.

In the station house, Daisy guessed his news with George's face confirming same. She gave her favourite SM a huge hug and meant every word of her good wishes. 'Congratulations, my boy, I am so happy for you and your sweetheart.'

George never thought of Louisa as his sweetheart but now savoured the word intending to use it and often.

Being only a few minutes from the station, George paid a quick visit to the Beckwith house where his mother and stepfather were delighted to hear the news.

'Will you please tell Em, Ma?' he asked before leaving for work.

Lily Bliss possessed two qualities; rare beauty and brilliant acting skills. She excelled on the stage. She didn't *want* to be an actress, she *had* to be one. Men were attracted to her in numbers.

The Earl of Fakenham saw her as a plaything. But Mr Insincerity was skint. Having been used by the Earl, Lily now considered revenge.

Since her excursion to Whittleton, Lily reflected on the whole disaster. She had agreed to become part of a conspiracy to murder a fellow female. Talk about sister solidarity. Lily helped the money-grubbing Earl in his futile attempt to kill an innocent young woman.

If Carrington had succeeded, this Louisa McClaren person would be dead and she, Lily, the beneficiary of a promise to marry an Earl.

In her heart, Lily knew the ungallant Earl would weasel his way out of any promise. She held no bitterness but did feel the urge to punish the instigators of the murder plot. Her conscience came alive.

In a striking costume borrowed from the wardrobe of her latest show at the Vaudeville Theatre in the Strand, Lily found the Eaton Square home of Sir Jerome Hamilton-Weir in fashionable, exclusive Belgravia. The actress was on a mission.

The man deserves to know the truth.

A week after George proposed to his "sweetheart", he collected her from Hampstead and they travelled to the village of Foxton to visit Louisa's mother. His nerves jangled. *Will she like me? Is she like her daughter? What happened to Louisa's father?*

Thank goodness for the railways. They travelled from King's Cross, not from George's alma mater at Liverpool Street, and alighted at Foxton in Cambridgeshire. During the short walk to Mrs McClaren's cottage, the cold weather helped the lovers stay close.

Louisa tapped on the front door of the white cottage with its thatched roof. The small, enchanting home, inside and out, was as bright as a new pin.

Mrs McClaren opened the door and Louisa stayed outside in the cold wanting her first words to be, 'Mummy, this is George.'

'Hello, George,' she said smiling and offering her hand. 'I'm delighted to meet you. Please come in.' Louisa embraced her mother. They entered her crammed but charming sitting-room in which a fire crackled a welcome. A cat opened one eye but remained glued to its spot on the windowsill.

The visitors removed their coats, scarves and gloves and Louisa took them away. 'Please sit, George,' said Mrs McClaren indicating with George waiting until she sat and after Louisa joined them.

'How are you, Mummy? Are you keeping warm?'

'I'm well thank you my dear and haven't been able to stop smiling since I received your telegram.' The others glowed. 'People in the village always ask about my daughter and now I have wonderful news.' She spoke directly to the station master. 'Louisa has told me a little about you George and I feel as if I know you already.'

He thought. *Is that true? What did my girl say?*

'You're most kind, Mrs McClaren and thank you for bringing up such a kind and beautiful daughter.'

George panicked thinking he'd slipped into his gushing routine again. He certainly gushed the first time he met Miss McClaren.

'And when Louisa told me you are a station master I thought you would be middle-aged.' The others smiled. 'You must be extremely efficient to be promoted so young.'

'If I'm honest, I've enjoyed a good slice of luck,' said George not knowing what to call his future mother-in-law.

Louisa wanted to tackle unfinished business. 'Did you receive a letter from Lord Carruthers, Mummy?'

'I did and have replied already.'

'I'm still not sure about my father's details,' said Louisa and her mother handled the matter with ease.

'It's all as His Lordship wrote, I assume from your information. I'm so looking forward to the notice in *The Times*. That will definitely impress the ladies in the church.'

'And another thing; we haven't decided *where* we'll marry.'

A silent pause seem to last too long. George hopped in. 'Where would you like your daughter to be married, Mrs McClaren?'

This took her by surprise. 'I haven't thought about it. I brought Louisa up in our local St Laurence's but she left here years ago. Do you have a preference, George?'

He smiled. 'I have always thought the wedding to be the bride's day. I would be happy for the McClaren family to choose the date and the venue.'

Louisa, already in love with the station master, sensed her mother now headed in a similar direction and at a rapid rate of knots. It became a grand meeting for all and especially for the would-be groom and mother-in-law. The light luncheon proved ideal.

Lily Bliss, dressed to the nines with a hat having its own postal district, rang the impressive bell beside the impressive front door of the impressive Hamilton-Weir home in Eaton Square. It seemed like an age before the door opened. Lily, hardly a tramp or beggar, received a civil welcome.

'Yes, madam, how may I help?' asked the manservant.

'Good day. I wish to meet with Sir Jerome on a matter of great urgency.' Lily rehearsed her speech planning to tell all.

'I regret, madam, Sir Jerome is ill and has been taken to hospital.'

Lily reacted with genuine shock. The thought flashed in her mind. *He might die not knowing his children tried to murder his daughter.*

'I'm so sorry. Is he all right?'

'We're hoping he'll recover,' said the servant giving away nothing.

'I should like to send flowers to his room. May I know the name of the hospital?'

Lily oozed acting class. Sincerity poured from her lips, making it easy to believe her performance was genuine. She dressed stylishly, appeared magnificent and carried the air of an aristocrat. The servant fell for her charms and revealed the hospital details.

Her mission became more difficult but her determination grew and soon she entered the reception area of one of London's most expensive private hospitals. The receptionist couldn't help but be impressed. The woman standing before her could easily be taken for a relative of one of the many wealthy patients in this hospital.

'I am Sophronia Hamilton-Weir, Sir Jerome's daughter and wish to see my father.'

'Certainly, madam; please take a seat and I'll call a nurse for you.'

Lily took her time in selecting a chair and sat using her umbrella as an item of fashion. A nurse arrived moving straight to Lily.

'Miss Hamilton-Weir?'

Lily rose. 'How is my father?'

'I regret he is unable to see any visitors at this time.'

Lily kept calm but laid it on the line. 'If he is recovering, I will see him. If he is dying, I *must* see him.'

The nurse couldn't fight such logic and led the way through the hospital. Outside Louisa's father's room she spoke.

'Please understand your father has suffered a serious heart condition. He must not be disturbed in any way.'

'Do you think I would do anything to harm my beloved father?'

The rhetorical question received no answer with Lily being led into the suite. The patient lay motionless appearing lifeless with another nurse by his bedside attending to various matters.

'This is Sir Jerome's daughter,' whispered the first nurse and the second nodded and smiled.

Lily moved close to the patient. His eyes were closed and his breathing laboured. 'Papa,' she spoke using her vast histrionic skills. 'It's Sophronia. I am here to help you recover.'

The first nurse seemed satisfied and left making eye contact with her colleague. The patient showed no reaction.

'I love you, Papa,' said the actress using a stage whisper and moving in close. The nurse heard nothing as Lily, on the other side, whispered in Sir Jerome's ear.

'Your twins have tried but failed to murder your daughter, Louisa.'

Hearing movement outside, Lily reckoned a speedy exit stage left became essential. She leant in and gently kissed the forehead of the man in the bed. Did he hear what Lily told him? Did he understand and believe the message?

Lily departed leaving through a back entrance as the real Sophronia and her brother Enoch arrived in Reception; every stage performer craves perfect timing and Lily cracked it.

The train trip home from Foxton saw the lovers on a new level of excitement. Both their mothers, having met their child's choice, could not be happier.

'My mother thinks you're wonderful, George,' said Louisa as their train headed back to London.

'She told you that?' he queried. 'When?'

'She didn't have to say anything. Mothers and daughters have an understanding.'

George sparked up but struggled for words this being his first experience with a mother-in-law, albeit in waiting. Louisa continued.

'And she will be happy wherever and whenever we wed. It could be in Foxton, Whittleton or Hampstead in May, June or July. Let's take our time and decide in the next few weeks.'

'I'd rather we married tomorrow.'

She considered his expression, and with only an elderly couple who appeared to be deaf or drowsy or both sharing their compartment, she kissed his cheek. He faced her and they kissed as young lovers have been known to do.

Their train made a regular stop but took an age to start moving. Typical station master Miracle opened a door and peered out. A porter stood nearby and George called.

'Is there a delay, sir?'

The porter approached. 'Good afternoon, sir. An elderly passenger has taken ill and we're helping her from the carriage.'

George nodded his thanks, closed the door and smiled at his fiancée.

'Are you responsible for the *entire* railway, Mr Miracle?'

He looked into her eyes with a mixture of excitement and delight.

From central London they travelled out to Hampstead where they enjoyed a "proper" kiss before the door of Tudor House opened. Lord and Lady Carruthers were desperate for news and, while delighted with the Foxton meeting, hid their disappointment as both a wedding date and venue remained undecided. Opening their home for the wedding of their dear friends was their big hope.

Please pick Tudor House.

Chapter 6

When the terrible twins, Sophronia and Enoch, arrived in Reception to see their father, they were unaware Lily Bliss had been there a few minutes earlier having told their father of the twins' murder plot to kill Louisa. The twins' demeanour of "We're superior and important and expect to be treated as such" permeated the room.

Sophronia led the charge. 'I am Sophronia Hamilton-Weir and this is my brother, Enoch. We are here to see our father.'

The receptionist gulped feeling sick. There are *two* Sophronias! Her employers stressed the fact that people treated in this hospital pay a great deal of money and expect the best service at all times. Treat the patients and their families with the utmost respect and go out of your way to keep the "clients" happy.

The receptionist thought she might vomit. Members of this family set her pulse racing especially as two sported the same name.

Do I tell these two their sibling is with their father as we speak?

Talk about tricky. The receptionist needed help. 'Please take a seat, madam, sir, and I'll have a nurse attend to you.'

'Don't keep us waiting,' called Sophronia as the receptionist fled.

'Relax,' said Enoch hating the way his sister bullied anyone and everyone. He preferred to pick and choose his victims.

He sat, she paced the room.

'The bloody incompetent fool, Carrington,' fumed Sophronia.

'Keep your voice down,' hissed Enoch.

She whispered with venom. 'If he'd done the business in the first place we'd be quids in now the old boy's about to cark it.'

Enoch's dander erupted. 'Will you stop this? He's our father for God's sake. Show a little respect. We don't even know how he is.'

She knew he spoke the truth but allowed a huge serving of hate towards Louisa McClaren to infect her mind and body.

Down the corridor, the receptionist shook as she explained the latest arrivals to the first nurse who struggled to believe the tale.

'So who's the woman we allowed into Sir Jerome's room? Did she have any needles or tablets with her?'

'How on Earth would *I* know?' replied the sweating receptionist.

'My God, did she touch any of the equipment?' The wretched nurse could hear dismissal and possible criminal charges striding down the corridor. 'I'll tell Doctor Fletcher-Evans. You stall them.'

The nurse left in a flap with the receptionist having her own nervous breakdown.

George proved true to his word and alighted at Whittleton. The staff knew to expect him. Pip took himself to the carriage and closed the door after his boss stepped out.

'Good evening, sir,' said the lad porter busting to win approval. Pip's thinking included a vision.

If my SM can reach such lofty heights at a young age, I can become a porter while still in the early years of my career.

'How was your trip, sir?'

'Enjoyable,' said the SM not keen to discuss his love life with a lad porter. 'What's happened at the station?'

'All clear, sir. The Crabbie carried eleven passengers today and all trains here at Whitty were on time on both the Up and the Down.'

They walked to the end of the platform where Pip became brave. 'And may I ask about the health of your lady friend, sir? Is she well?'

George liked the boy. He wondered if he, George, would have ever spoken those words to any SM when he worked as a lad porter at Liverpool Street. He smiled. 'Thank you, Pip, she is well.'

After checking with the other porters, he went home where his housekeeper prepared a smashing supper and wanted to know every little detail about his future mother-in-law.

What a day.

The senior doctor entered Reception with a plan. The experienced man didn't reckon on the personality of Sir Jerome's legitimate daughter. The nurse followed and tried to hide behind a potted plant.

'I'm terribly sorry to keep you waiting. I'm Doctor Fletcher-Evans and in charge of your father's care.'

'Is he going to die?' asked Sophronia without a trace of concern or compassion making even evil Enoch cringe.

'Your father has suffered a serious heart attack but is receiving the best of care.'

'That's not what I asked,' she snapped and Enoch thought about restraining her. He knew better than to try.

'We are hopeful, Miss Hamilton-Weir.'

'We need to see him *now*,' she replied with a clear threat implied in her tone of voice.

'I'm not sure it would be in Sir Jerome's interests,' said the doctor hoping to send the twins on their way. He failed so fell back on another tactic.

'Sir Jerome didn't respond when visited by your sister.'

The silence was shattered by the gasp from both the twins. Unbelievably Sophronia was struck dumb.

'I'm sorry. What did you say?' squeaked Enoch.

One could have been excused for thinking a bomb had exploded in the reception area. The twins recovered although Sophronia's reaction put her in danger of needing a bed and treatment similar to that currently being provided for her father.

'Did you say my sister was here in this hospital?' she hissed.

'A few minutes ago?' asked Enoch. 'Where is she now?'

The medical man struggled to stay on an even keel. His eyes pleaded with the receptionist and the nurse who both shrugged.

'We believe she's left,' said the nurse now praying for Sir Jerome.

Sophronia stared at her brother and jerked her head. He left knowing his mission. Find the bitch. He knew Louisa. She sat a few feet from him at a recent fancy luncheon in the Hamilton-Weir London home. But as for Lily Bliss, he didn't know her from Eve.

Sophronia attacked. 'You allowed my sister to see my father?'

'We did,' replied a now concerned doctor. 'And your father has been and still is being carefully monitored the whole time.'

Not exactly true.

'I demand to see my father immediately.' A pregnant and scary pause began. A new threat exploded. 'I shall pay a visit to your hospital's next board meeting unless you take me to see my father now!'

Enoch arrived, puffing, and shook his head.

'Both of us,' snapped Sophronia and the twins were taken to their father's room.

In its early years, the LNER needed to appoint station masters due to the usual reasons of death, resignation and retirement. A small sub-committee worked their way through the applications. Wolferton, the so-called Royal Station, drew a record field of runners. When its current station master applied in 1884, he was one of more than a hundred applicants.

The men on the sub-committee from the former Great Eastern, Great Northern and Great Central Railway companies were old hands at selecting men for vacancies, and fell back on the oft-used routine of seniority. They quickly dismissed applicants with less than ten years' experience as an SM. The form completed by George Miracle found itself being moved without delay to the pile listed as *Rejected*.

The committee members argued to and fro and were at the tea-break stage when a member of the LNER Board arrived to enquire about their recommendations.

Sir Laurence Pennington perused the applications. Nothing seemed out of place. He handed back the short-list screed when his eye fell upon a form in the *Rejected* pile.

'What's this?' he cried retrieving the page. 'Why is this man not being considered?'

The secretary checked the application and advised Sir Laurence of the set criteria regarding seniority with a minimum of at least ten years' service as a station master.

Sir Laurence launched himself. 'How many of the men you've put on the short list have served their country with distinction in time of war?' Nobody replied. 'How many SMs have engaged with the community and turned their station into a veritable botanical garden?' That last claim was a bit of a stretch. Committee members remained silent. 'And how many on your short list have developed tourist venues boosting passenger numbers so much as to save an entire branch line?' The silence continued. The men were nervous.

One brave chap decided to speak. 'You would appear to have us at a disadvantage, Sir Laurence.'

He did and his rave review of Mr Miracle continued. 'You do read the papers I presume, gentlemen?' What could they say? 'This is the man, who at risk of life and limb, foiled an armed robbery at his station, saved the LNER a considerable sum, and kept the trains running despite a potentially catastrophic incident.'

Sir Laurence tossed George's application on the table, stared into the eyes of each committee member and their secretary and departed thinking of the pleasure his wife received in the form of two jars of chutney and one autographed novel from her favourite author.

The clock on the wall announced the end of the working day and the selection panel wanted their glass of beer or supper or both. They needed to choose from their short lists. Blow this for a joke. When it came to Wolferton, they settled on a chap called Miracle for the vacancy at the station a couple of miles from the Sandringham Estate and within easy reach of many glorious, sandy beaches along the Norfolk coast.

With a station to run and his wedding to plan, that same young SM faced decisions. Being appointed to the Royal Station barely crossed his mind. In fact he only applied for the vacancy due to the pressure from his colleague, SM Jack Rogers at Liverpool Street.

Sophronia and Enoch were led to their father's suite. The doctor and nurse stopped outside the room. The twins were in no mood for any delay. Before the doctor could speak, Sophronia jumped in.

'Who entered my father's room with my sister present?'

The doctor didn't know and turned to the nurse. She looked inside and saw the same nurse present when Lily Bliss pulled off her fake daughter routine. 'It was Nurse Hardwicke,' she whispered.

'I can assure you, Miss Hamilton-Weir; your father received the utmost professional care whenever your sister remained in the room.'

Sophronia glared at the medical staff. The door was opened and Nurse Hardwicke immediately worried as the new group entered. The doctor reassured the nurse. Without hesitation, Sophronia moved to stand beside her father and spoke, at last in a soft voice.

'It's me, Daddy. Enoch and I are here to take care of you.'

What a preposterous and wicked statement.

She glared at the doctor. 'We will speak to our father in private.'

The medical man remained at the foot of the bed. 'I'm afraid that won't be possible, Miss.'

Sophronia flared. 'This is a matter of great intimacy for us.'

'This is a matter of life and death for my patient,' he replied. 'I'm sure you want your father to have the best of care.'

Sophronia lost the battle but knew the war would continue. She indicated with her head and Enoch moved to the other side of the bed forcing the nurse on duty to step back. The siblings bent and whispered in their father's ears.

'We're here, Daddy; the children who love you.'

'Yes, Pater,' added Enoch, 'it's me and Soffy.'

She hated her nickname.

The medical staff watched the behaviour of the patient's adult children and heard snippets of dialogue from the visitors.

Sophronia continued. 'Take no notice of the wicked woman who is only interested in your money.'

'It's all true, Pater. She's a money-grubbing bitch.'

Strangely, Sophronia recoiled at her brother's choice of words. Her language would make a sailor blush but she knew foul language would upset the old man and might cost her a fortune.

Dr Fletcher-Evans called a halt. The patient, if not comatose, appeared darn close to such a condition. 'I think that's enough, Miss and Mr Hamilton-Weir. Your father must be allowed to rest.'

The twins were in limbo. Was the old boy about to die? What did the bitch McClaren tell him? They made no impression on their barely alive father. Continuing to talk to him could be equated to taking a whip to a deceased equine. They backed off and were escorted out. The doctor followed.

'We will contact you the moment there is any change in your father's condition,' he said and the terrible twins departed in the highest of high dudgeon.

Of course the classic irony in this situation was the ignorance of the twins having no idea the interloper was an actress acting on her conscience, a word neither twin could even spell, and the woman they detested and tried to murder happened to be nowhere near the hospital and, most ironic of all, Louisa McClaren believed her father died years ago and therefore possessed not even an inkling the man in a London hospital recently made her a beneficiary of his will; a wealthy man currently at death's door.

Chapter 7

Queen Victoria bought 20,000 acres in the parish of Sandringham, Norfolk in 1862. About that time, her son, Edward, turned 21. The question arises, would Her Majesty have purchased the vast property if her boy turned out a well-behaved young man, a model of restraint and gentlemanly behaviour? Arguably not and, if so, the Christmas message broadcast by the British monarch, a tradition which still continues today, may well have been delivered from elsewhere.

Not to put too fine a point on it, Edward became a naughty boy, and his behaviour didn't improve when his father died and in mourning, Queen Victoria faded from view. There seemed to be no restraining hand as the young Prince kept busy sowing his wild oats.

Of course Dirty Bertie wasn't the first member of the British Royal Family to misbehave and he certainly wasn't the last. But when you hail from the House of Windsor, as it became in 1917, your every move falls under the public gaze. And when members of that august family travel to the Sandringham Estate, the station master at the nearby Wolferton station finds himself in a unique position.

But in 1891 when the Prince of Wales became a witness in a slander trial at the Royal Courts of Justice, George Miracle was not even a twinkle in his old man's eye.

Having become engaged, and being unaware of his new appointment, George returned to his regular SM duties at Whittleton with the Branch to Crabbtree continuing to struggle. In his office on the Wednesday after his engagement, the SM encountered an enthusiastic female.

His sister, Emily, recently married and now living on a farm outside the village, heard from her mother about her brother's engagement. Emily set off for the Whittleton station driving a pony trap, cars still being uncommon in many villages of Eastern England.

'Knock, knock,' she said and George's joy erupted having not seen his baby sister for ages and missed her. They embraced and she kissed and teased him about finally being engaged. They exchanged news. Of course Emily wanted all the fine details of her brother's proposal, and about Louisa's response as well as their wedding plans.

'It's in June, I think,' said George.

'You think?' exclaimed Emily. 'The man who can recite every railway timetable from here to London via Llandudno doesn't know the date of his own wedding!'

'It's a woman's thing,' he replied. 'But how are you? How's Bert? How's married life?'

'Well I'm pleased Ma has done the right thing after I asked her.'

George studied her. *What does she mean?* 'Meaning?'

'Do you remember, George, in this office you once told me you were about to become a father?'

'Yeeees,' he replied, still not knowing where this was going.

'Of course I knew you were joking because you meant *god*father.' She paused and he couldn't wait for the punch line. 'My news isn't a joke and you, brother dear, are soon to become an uncle.'

His happiness overflowed. He hugged her but with extra care. *Good on you, Bert*, he thought, remembering the budding groom's request in this office for an education in matters sexual.

'That's fantastic news, Em. But how does Ma feel about being a grandmother?'

'I think it's an understatement to say she's thrilled but there could be a battle royal about which grannie is crowned chief babysitter.'

They laughed and chatted until Emily left to see her mother.

'Give my best to Bert and his family,' called George.

An Up train arrived as the Crabbie pulled in and George became busy. No sooner did the London bound train depart. George heard a familiar sound.

Freda, guarded by Rufus, yelled from the island platform and George girded his loins. Being a rural area and in these parts, news travelled faster than a hungry peregrine falcon. The station master was engaged to be married and Freda, and particularly Rufus, wanted to offer their most enthusiastic congratulations.

This routine of love and affection sprang from George's effort to investigate a missing Freda by walking through driving rain to find her lodged in her outdoor lavatory—there was no such thing as an indoor lavatory—and unable to free herself. George saved the day and ever since, Freda and Rufus became his biggest fans.

Today was extra special though because the SM planned to marry.

Greetings from these passengers often became fulsome but today Freda and Rufus gave their congratulations' routine using the entire ship's company. Once George broke free from these unwelcome amorous activities, he and Freda were up for their usual chat where they switched to the future of the branch line.

'Mr Wight has been placed in a secure hospital,' said George.

'I know and his neighbour is taking care of his farm and animals. But what I want to know, George, is what you're doing right now to save the Crabbie.'

'Well the Druid site routine is back for anyone who wants to visit Pickling but it'll only work if you're willing and able to play your tourist guide role.'

'George, I've made enough jam and chutney to feed half of East Anglia. Please help me sell it. Besides, for me no Crabbie means no Whitty. I can't visit my sister here in town and give you a special hug.'

'Thank you again, Freda for all you've done for the branch line.'

She smiled and she and Rufus wanted to kiss the SM again.

'Your sister will be wondering what's happened to you,' he said guiding his fans off the platform.

Arguably, the next Down was the most important train to ever arrive at Whittleton. Having collected the mail, Pip the lad porter entered the SM's office.

'Mail, sir,' said the boy handing the envelopes to George.

'Thanks, Pip,' said George who hesitated because the lad remained. 'Something I can do for you?'

'I wondered if I might slip away before 5, sir. I need to take Whitty to the vet and he closes pretty much on the dot.'

'What's wrong?' In recent times, George witnessed a mass exodus of animals from the station house. Trixie the cat went with his mother to Mr Beckwith's cottage. George's stepfather didn't approve of canines and Spike the dog, the pup George was given on his first day at Whittleton, now joined the other hounds on the Culpepper farm with Emily. The new dog loved the open spaces and agreed to allow Bert to sleep on what had always been Spike's bed.

'Whitty's been limping and I'd like to have her seen to.'

'Go now,' said George remembering how the lad porter found the pathetic looking kitten and gave it a home as the station cat.

'*Now* sir?'

'Yes, I'll cover for you.'

Pip reckoned Mr Miracle to be the best SM he'd ever worked for; not necessarily high praise with George being Pip's only SM. The lad porter offered his sincere thanks as he took off.

George sorted the mail and the envelope with the LNER details in the top left corner caught his eye. Alone in the office with the station quiet and without traffic of any kind, he removed the contents.

It became one of those moments when the eye sees something which the brain fails to fully comprehend.

April 4, 1924

Mr George Miracle
Station master
Whittleton Station

Dear Sir,

I am pleased to advise that your application to become station master at Wolferton Station has been accepted.

The position becomes available on July 1, 1924.

You are entitled to be reimbursed for removal costs.

Please advise your intention regarding this matter at your earliest convenience.

Yours faithfully,
Peter Graveney
Peter Graveney
Secretary

George began to breathe faster. He saw the words; he knew their meaning and yet, he still struggled to accept them.

Being alone made the situation surreal. He couldn't tell a soul. The news shocked him for several reasons.

He'd been thinking about love and marriage for the last few weeks. He'd been travelling distances with his fiancée to visit her and her friends and family. He'd given himself zero chance of being successful in his job application and only applied after pressure from SM Jack Rogers. The failing branch line continued to occupy his thinking and yet in his hand, he held the news of his new appointment, in writing on LNER letterhead.

Flippin' 'eck!

Immediately he wanted to tell Louisa. Once he told her how marrying him would mean living in a small railway cottage. 'Sounds wonderful,' she replied. *What will be her reaction to living in the so-called Royal Station with Royalty among the passengers?*

Porter Drum popped into the office and without thinking George folded the page as if it was a secret love letter.

'Can't seem to find young Pip, sir,' said Fletcher.

George hopped up and pocketed the letter. 'Yes, I've sent him off to the vet with Whitty. I regard the health of all my staff, human and otherwise to be vitally important.'

Satisfied, the porter, like the lad porter earlier, hung around.

'Is there something on your mind?' asked George.

Fletcher hesitated. 'Tell me it's a crazy idea, sir, if it's what you think.' George's curiosity came alive.

'What's a crazy idea?'

'I'm not too happy boarding with Mrs Rough.' He instantly explained his meaning. 'Oh don't misunderstand, sir, she's a lovely lady but I've always liked my freedom. My last two appointments saw me living on a local farm and riding to work on my bicycle. Here I'm practically living on the tracks and in a cramped cottage.'

George saw a simple solution. 'Well I'm sure you can find a farm in the district.'

'I have already, sir.' George liked the attitude of his porter, impressed with his getting-on-with-life attitude. 'It's the Wight farm behind the Pickling Halt.'

George's jaw dropped. 'But ...'

'I've spoken to the farmer on the next property, the chap who's taken over the place, and he's delighted with the idea. He reckons the sheep pretty much look after themselves but he has to walk a fair way to feed the pigs and hens every day.' George loved the suggestion but Fletcher kept going.

'I've timed the bicycle ride and I can reach Whittleton in 15 minutes. If my bike breaks down, I'll hop on the Crabbie. I can keep an eye on the station at Crabbwell now it's unmanned, and even help with the tourists at Pickling.'

George finally managed to speak. 'Freda's going to love you.'

'Freda?' asked Fletcher with a hint of concern.

'She has a farm on the other side of Pickling. She's the tourist guide for the site with the Druid rocks.'

'Oh you mean the lady with the Irish wolfhound?'

'That's her.'

Fletcher paused. 'Will you back me, sir?'

'So long as you're on time and don't make the others work extra shifts, I'm all for it. Mrs Rough won't be too pleased but if you give her a few eggs once a week, I'm sure she'll be happy.'

They shook hands and Fletcher departed to greet the next Down.

What a day!

George telephoned Liverpool Street station in London.

'Station Master Jack Rogers speaking.'

'Jack, it's George Miracle.'

A huge roar raced down the line. 'Not *the* George Miracle, the new SM at a certain station favoured by kings and queens?'

George reacted with alarm. 'You know? How do you know? Did you have anything to do with this?'

Rogers laughed. 'Me? You must be kidding. No, young man, I know a chap in the office of the appointments committee and this little bird told me a week or so ago. I'm sworn to secrecy but yesterday they told me the letter's been sent which I'm guessing you've received. Many congratulations, George, your uncle will be dancing around Heaven tonight.'

'I still can't believe it. I mean how in blue blazes did I reach the top of what must have been an extremely big pile?'

'I've told you before, George, it's not what you know but who.'

George paused wanting more details. 'And?' he asked.

'I heard Sir Laurence Pennington stuck his oar in.' George twigged. 'You must have impressed him and he clearly believes in reciprocity.'

George didn't know the word *reciprocity*. But escorting Sir Laurence around the station, travelling with him on the Crabbie to Pickling where the LNER boss bought a jar or two of Freda's goodies, and introducing Sir Laurence to the man's wife's favourite author, one Septimus Oldmeadow, George did all that as part of his job. Now those simple tasks seemed to have turned the humble SM on a rural backwater into becoming the SM in what many say is the prettiest station in England.

'I'm still in shock, Jack.'

'You'll make an eligible bachelor, George. A thornback of spinsters would love to live at your new station. Have you seen the station master's house?'

'Haven't you heard?' asked George.

'Heard what?'

He told the London SM about his recent engagement.

Jack roared with laughter. 'Well you have the perfect wedding present for your young lady and jolly good luck to both of you. Come and see me when you're next in town.'

George sat in his office. He wanted to tell Louisa his news. He walked onto the Up platform and looked at the flowers and plants decorating both sides of the station. He and his family moved to Whittleton when World War 1 still raged. His uncle, the SM at Whittleton, tragically died on his retirement day. George became the youngest station master in England and now he would soon marry and leave for a new station on another line.

He desperately wanted to share his latest news.

Chapter 8

The vet discovered Whitty the station cat suffered a cut pad on her front left foot. Patched up and given an extra sardine for her tea, she took a nap before resuming her night rodent-hunting patrols.

Once the last Up departed, George locked up and walked the 20 yards to the station cottage. Daisy dozed in the kitchen, with one of the novels written by P. J. Beaufoy a.k.a. Septimus Oldmeadow resting on her lap. George saw her once he stepped inside so backed up, quietly closed before re-opening the front door and called.

'Stand clear, train departing on Platform 1.'

Daisy woke and collected the supper being kept warm in the oven.

'Good evening, Miss Woods. Was your day interesting?' he asked hanging his coat and cap on the hooks.

'Indeed it was. My grandson, Michael, writes to tell me he has been chosen to trial for Tottenham Hotspur.'

George gave her a suspicious look. 'Isn't he a bit too young to play for Spurs?'

'It's their youth team. And his father's been given a new account writing advertising for the Rolls Royce Motor Company.'

'Goodness, now that *is* impressive.'

'And what about you, Mr Stationmaster; tell me about *your* day.'

A warm plate housing a magnificent cottage pie resplendent with mince and mash landed before him and the sight and smell became a massive distraction. But George hesitated. He desperately wanted to tell Daisy, to tell the world about his appointment but what would it mean for his housekeeper?

I marry Louisa and we move to Wolverton. Does my wife want a woman to cook and clean the station house? What would Louisa do? And if Daisy doesn't come with us, where will she go?

'Daisy, when Louisa and I marry, would you be happy continuing to live here in the station house?'

She ate her supper with about half the amount of food on her plate than on his. 'Of course I'd be happy but the question is would you?'

George went to speak but Daisy raised a hand containing a fork. 'Newlyweds want to be on their own. There's no way I'll be living here with you two love birds chasing each other around the kitchen table.'

They studied one another and she winked. He couldn't stop a grin.

'Well you do have a choice because I won't be here much longer.'

She twigged and froze. 'You've been appointed to another station.'

George nodded and couldn't wait. His news kicked and shouted to break free. He went to his coat, produced the letter handing it to his beloved housekeeper. She read and whipped her hand to her face.

'That's the Royal Station,' she whispered.

George nodded. She hurried to him then hugged him with tears rolling down her cheeks. She broke free, changed tack and demanded.

'What do you mean, I have a choice?'

George returned to his cottage pie. 'My replacement could be a single man, a kind gentleman who would be thrilled to have the best housekeeper in England take care of him.'

'Or he could be like the bloke who arrived at Norwich and caused me to flee to my boy in Cricklewood.'

George thought about it. 'Let's wait and see.'

Daisy thought about it. 'Have you told Louisa and your mother?'

'The only person in the world I've told, Miss Woods, is you.'

She became all warm inside. They were a great team.

'There's sticky-date pudding for afters,' she said.

He became all warm inside.

The Hamilton-Weir twins were enraged. They belted the front-door of the Earl of Fakenham's flat and were ignored. Finally he spoke.

'Go away, there's no-one here,' cried a feeble but angry voice using emphasis on every word. 'And I have no money!'

Sophronia spat through the letter opening. 'Open the bloody door, Dickie, or we'll break it down.'

After a pause, the door opened. The twins gasped. Their occasional friend/lover/co-conspirator might have been dead. His fall from the balcony at Ripley Hall left him with a scratched and seriously bruised body. Walking hurt, even lying down set his nerves afire. His stubble groaned. There were dark rings under his eyes and the usually dapper dresser sported an outfit of unwashed pyjama bottoms and a food-stained vest. His fall at Ripley Hall was both symbolic and literal.

'I'm broke, skint. I'm dying and there's nothing you can do to me to make me change my mind so piss off and leave me to die in peace.'

Normally both twins would attack him demanding the 25 quid they gave him as a down payment for his role in murdering Louisa McClaren. They said nothing. The wretched man deserved sympathy.

Shockingly the siblings actually turned domestic, removed dirty plates and empty gin bottles and sat. Sophronia led the discussion.

'There's been a development, Dickie.'

'I told you, I'm dying.'

'Shut up and listen,' snapped Enoch.

'The bitch you failed to fix has launched a raid on the old man.'

'Good and I don't care.'

'She's gone to the hospital to tell him about your murder attempt.'

'What hospital? Who's in hospital? *I* should be in hospital.'

Enoch explained. 'The pater's copped a heart attack and is dying.'

'So am I.'

Sophronia wanted details. 'Tell us about your partner on your failed expedition to Ripley Hall?'

'Go away.'

The twins each grabbed an arm of the Earl. He screamed in pain.

'Tell us everything,' hissed Lucrezia Borgia. 'Who was with you?'

Dickie was a soft touch when fit and well. Now in agony, he folded and told them about Lily Bliss, her Russian princess routine, the lot.

'What did our sibling tell your actress?'

'How would I know? I wasn't there,' he moaned. He screamed when they twisted his bruised arms. 'I was waiting outside.'

'So this Lily Bliss knows our bastard sibling?'

'Yes, yes, she spoke to her,' he whined.

The twins wanted the truth about Lily. 'Where does she live? What does she do? What have you told her about us?'

Dickie blabbed with only half of it being true. The desperate twins believed anything. This woman was the only lead to Louisa McClaren. Did Lily tell Louisa the plan set by the twins? Find Lily. She could give them a line on their thief of a relative, the one who fought dirty like them. The one they believed crept into their father's hospital bedroom. Find Lily and persuade her to eliminate the bitch McClaren. She tried it once. Why not again?

After supper, George wrote two letters. The first to the LNER thanking them for their offer and accepting the position at Wolferton.

The second to his sweetheart, a word he kept pondering. He liked using flowery words and addressed Louisa as, "My darling girl".

He told her about Wolferton suggesting they take a trip to inspect their new home. The letter finished with a question.

'As my appointment begins in July, could we wed and have our honeymoon in time for me to start at Wolferton on July 1?'

He smiled as he placed the letter in an envelope. It would be posted tomorrow in the Whittleton High Street. What a day indeed.

Lily engaged in a typical theatrical pastime; resting. Her latest gig at the Vaudeville Theatre finished last week with the actress between shows. The twins reached the building in which Lily rented a room. Her landlady knew all the tricks of the trade; tenants doing a moonlight flit, sneaking lovers and clients in without paying, leaving the lavatory in a disgusting state, and more. She heard the front door and flew out of her ground floor room in a flash.

She struggled to believe the appearance of the two visitors because they dressed far too well to be seeking rooms in her bare-bones of an establishment, and they looked spookily alike.

'We're full,' she said before they spoke.

'Lily Bliss room number,' said Sophronia.

The landlady saw the money being offered, took it, gave the room number and directions and landed back in her room before the twins even began climbing the stairs.

Lily heard the door knock and wondered who it could be. She pulled a robe around her undressed body and opened the door. She knew who they were. The Earl pointed them out when he took her to a recent debauched event for aristocrats.

'Hello Lily, we're friends of the Earl of Fakenham and we know you know who we are,' said Sophronia. 'May we come in?'

They moved in without waiting for a reply.

'Nice place,' said Enoch ignoring the room and mentally undressing the occupant.

Lily played it cool feigning ignorance. 'What do you want?'

'Information,' said Sophronia, 'and for which we are prepared to pay.' Lily's heart rate crept higher.

Enoch explained the background. 'We know you know about our family dispute. We know you've met our distant relative, the bitch who is trying to defraud us of our rightful inheritance.'

'Who are you talking about?' asked Lily playing Miss Ignorant.

Wrong move as Sophronia let fly. 'Don't piss me around, Lily. You and your boyfriend blew your chance and you saw what happened to him. This is your chance to *not* fall out of a window and also to make a few quid.' Sophronia spoke slowly. 'Do you understand?'

Lily nodded. 'Yes, now I do.'

'Good girl,' said Sophronia who could smarm for England.

Enoch took over. 'Our evil half-sister has been to see our dying father in hospital trying to make him change his will in her favour.'

Lily enjoyed years of displaying emotion on stage. Now it helped her remain calm despite her heart rate being right off the scale. Her mind raced. *They don't know it was me playing Louisa McClaren.*

'You were in her room at Ripley Hall,' continued Sophronia. 'Tell us what she said about our father.'

'You were a Russian Princess,' said Enoch. 'We want you to become the Princess again, go to our sister, and ...'

'*Half*-sister,' growled Sophronia.

'*Half*-sister,' he said, 'and find out what she said to our father.'

Lily played the weak character. 'I'm not sure I can.'

'You're a bloody actress,' threatened Sophronia. 'You pretend for a living. You did it before, and will do it again.'

'And this time you will be paid,' added Enoch.

'Fifty pounds,' said Sophronia and her brother blanched. They'd agreed twenty-five. Sophronia removed a small silver pill box and handed it to Lily. 'And if finding out what the bitch said to our father doesn't work, or even if it does, slip the contents of this pill box in her drink and you will be paid your money ... with a bonus.'

Lily became the young woman in the flickering black and white film tied to the railway tracks. 'You want me to kill her?' she gasped in melodramatic guise.

'No, no, no, of course not,' replied Sophronia trying to appear calm. 'It'll make her vomit for a day or two, which is the least the conniving cow deserves.'

Massive relief overtook Enoch. 'Yes,' he said with a pathetic laugh, 'it'll make her sick for a few days.'

The twins studied Lily whose mind worked overtime. She prepared a plan of her own as Sophronia moved in for the kill.

'You know where she lives. She knows you so will be happy to explain how she tried to con our dear Papa.'

Lily threw in her dramatic skills. "And you say she went to the hospital where your father is recovering from a heart attack?'

The ignorant twins were hooked by the actress.

'The nurse saw her talking intimately with the pater,' said Enoch. 'Find out what she said and slip her a Mickey Finn.'

'Sure,' she said taking the pill box and speaking a la Princess Razumoffski from Leningrad. 'I sink ve can do zat.'

The twins rejoiced. Finally they had a new lead on the woman they called the Bitch. Finally they could remove her from the will.

In the library at Tudor House, Louisa received George's letter and the news gave her palpitations. She would live anywhere with him as her husband but this appointment knocked her sideways. A station near the King's country estate sounded exciting, no, unbelievable.

'Good news, I hope?' asked Valerie. Little George played with a toy train given to him by his godfather, another George. Baby Annie accepted her mother's milk. The infant put on weight counted in ounces, even parts of an ounce.

'I can't believe it,' said Louisa and the adults paid attention.

'What's that station master done now?' asked His Lordship.

Louisa announced. 'Mr Miracle has been appointed station master at the Wolferton Station.'

The parents gasped. 'The Royal Station in Norfolk?' asked Valerie.

Louisa nodded, her heart pounding with excitement.

'Dark horse Miracle,' said George. 'That fellow is making his mark in the world. Please give him our heartiest congratulations.'

'Don't reply by letter. Give him a telephone call,' said Valerie. 'Use the telephone in George's study.'

Carruthers led Louisa from the room. Valerie called. 'Give him our love and don't let my husband listen in. Lovers require privacy.'

George winked at his wife and, in his study, found the Whittleton Station number, made the call and handed the receiver to Louisa. He squeezed her arm and left.

'Whittleton Station, George Miracle speaking.'

The SM's heart endured a minor hiccup when the caller spoke.

'Hello, Mr Miracle. This is your fiancée speaking.'

She sounded joyful inspiring his reply.

'My darling girl, how lovely to hear your voice. How are you?'

'I'm well, dear George, and ringing from Tudor House to congratulate you on your latest appointment.'

'Thank you but are you happy with the move?'

'I told you I'll be happy to live anywhere so long as we're together. Oh and George and Valerie send their love and congratulations.'

'Thank you. Now how are the plans for the wedding going?'

'*The* wedding? Do you mean *our* wedding?'

He laughed and she loved the sound but continued.

'How would you feel about being married in Whittleton?'

She surprised him. He'd been told couples usually married in the bride's church.

'But what about your mother? Isn't she expecting her daughter to marry in the McClaren family church?'

'I think she's happy her daughter has found a wonderful man and where she marries is not important.'

'Do you say that to all the boys?'

She laughed and he loved the sound. 'If we can't decide, George, we could always run away to Gretna Green.'

That knocked him for six. *Is she serious? She can't be serious.*

Two trains arrived close to one another and George needed to go. 'I'll come to Hampstead next Sunday, and we'll take a trip to Wolferton,' he said, made a kissing sound and hung up.

Lily pondered her next move. She could go to Louisa and tell her what her siblings have asked her to do. She wondered if Louisa knew the identity of her real father. Lily pondered going back to Sir Jerome and telling him what further evil two of his children were up to. Or, and last and definitely least, she could do as the twins asked and, for her trouble, pocket £50, knowing she had no work and little money.

What's in the tablet I'm to pop in Miss McClaren's drink?

She could ask the Earl of Fakenham for advice. Ha, fat chance of that happening. Finally, she thought of one more option.

Chapter 9

When George Miracle first arrived at Whittleton towards the end of the Great War, another George, a slightly more important gent and known as His Majesty, George V was the reigning British monarch having succeeded his playboy father, Edward VII. In 1924, when George Miracle moved to Wolferton, George V's mother, Queen Alexandra, was a widow in poor health and living up the road from the station in the main house at Sandringham.

Her father, Christian IX of Denmark, once hoped to marry Queen Victoria. The Dane missed that union but won second prize by having his daughter marry Victoria's son and heir, Edward VII. It was akin to George Miracle's appointment—it's not what you know but who.

When in Norfolk, her son and his wife, George V and Queen Mary, lived in a smaller residence on the estate with the King wanting his mother to be as comfortable as possible in her twilight years.

During her reign as Queen and Empress, Alexandra became a victim of what people would later refer to as male chauvinism. As a child she read and heard stories from the lips of a fellow Dane, Hans Christian Anderson, and grew up with opinions on various subjects including matters political. As a Dane, she became particularly concerned about German advances in the years leading to the Great War. In 1917, she took pleasure in her son's decision to change the family name from the German, Saxe-Coburg-Gotha to the decidedly English, Windsor.

When he heard that piece of news, and while still recovering from his war wounds, George Miracle applauded the move.

When Queen Alexandra made comments on political matters, the Establishment murmured and overreacted by stopping her being able to read certain government documents. They even prevented her from accompanying her husband on certain trips. A woman's place is in the home even if you are married to the Monarch.

Visiting hospitals and opening charitable events were seen as her ideal occupation. Those in power were happy for Her Majesty to be a leader in fashion, a role which she fulfilled with many of her subjects copying her outfits.

To her credit, Alexandra put up with this unsubtle sexism and proved a popular member of the Royal Family. When George Miracle moved to Norfolk, the Queen Mother had been a widow for 13 years.

Having told his housekeeper, mother and fiancée of his appointment to Wolferton, George knew not telling his Whittleton colleagues would be seen as discourteous even stupid. He called them to his office once the Crabbie arrived after its first run. It would be 12 minutes before the next mainline train.

The railwaymen were anxious. Their SM rarely called such a meeting and when he did, he invariably made an important announcement.

'Gentlemen, thank you for your attendance. This won't take long.'

'You're leavin',' said Monty and a silence settled in the SM's office.

George paused. 'Monty, are you an expert on the football pools?' The man from the signal box bared his multi-gaped teeth. 'Gentlemen, I've been appointed to the Wolferton Station on the line between King's Lynn and Hunstanton.'

'Isn't that the Royal Station?' remarked Gordon thinking about his jealous cousin, the porter who once tried to ruin George. This latest posting would make Gordon's cousin furious.

'It is. Now I don't start till July and there is the little matter of my wedding to sort out first.' The others were amused. 'Let's continue as usual and no doubt in time my replacement will be appointed.'

'I hope he likes cats, sir,' said Pip.

'I hope he likes rabbits,' added Madge. George smiled and ended the meeting. Everyone wanted to shake his hand.

'Congratulations, sir,' said Fletcher Drum and the others joined in.

As George promised Louisa, on the following Sunday, he travelled up to London escorting his housekeeper, Daisy. He requested she come with him on the trip he'd arranged with the retiring SM at Wolferton, Mr George Saward.

'I'll only be in the way,' protested Daisy.

'You'll not be in the way, you'll have a chance to get to know my fiancée, you can give both of us advice on the domestic situation in the new station house and, most important of all, you will be our chaperone and thus the protector of my future wife's impeccable reputation.'

She eyed him up and down. 'What a mouthful, George Miracle. Don't tell me you're now putting on airs and graces?'

He laughed aloud. On the Up platform he spoke briefly with all his porters. Even Monty and Desmond came from their hideaways to wish him well on the first visit to his new station.

'We'll return on the penultimate Down and remember, I'll still be the SM here till early summer, so don't go getting ideas I'll be turning all soft beforehand.'

Pip opened a carriage door for Daisy and his SM. The cheeky yet respectful lad saluted as his boss boarded the train.

The Hamilton-Weir twins returned to their "shack" in Belgravia still discussing their predicament. Enoch feared his sister's rage.

'That pill you gave the actress, what did it contain?'

'What does it matter?' She despaired. 'Oh for Christ's sake, Enoch, wake up! That bitch McClaren is trying to persuade the old man to give us nothing. She's more devious and greedy than both of us put together. It doesn't matter what she said to Daddykins. What matters is her disappearing—permanently.'

Enoch worried. 'Do you trust that actress?'

'For fifty quid I do. She's skint and we all know actresses are prostitutes in disguise.'

'How come she knew the pater suffered a heart attack?'

Sophronia stopped dead. 'What are you talking about?'

'She said, "And you say she went to the hospital where your father is recovering from a heart attack"?'

'So?'

'We didn't tell her that.'

'Yes we did.'

Enoch confronted his sister. 'No we didn't. We said, "Our evil half-sister has been to see our dying father in hospital," and nothing else. We didn't tell her anything about why he was there.'

Sophronia's blood pressure sought an escape artery. She whispered. 'So how did she know about the heart attack?'

'She could have guessed or unless McClaren told her.'

60

Sophronia swallowed hard. 'Or unless *she* was McClaren.'

The twins were struck dumb, a rare occasion.

'Jesus,' whispered Enoch. 'Have we been swindled?'

George avoided former colleagues at Liverpool Street and with SM Rogers not on duty, escaped unseen. He and Daisy took the Tube to Hampstead and walked to Tudor House in weather cool but sunny.

In the mansion, George and Louisa found it tricky to behave in a normal fashion. They were keen to do more than embrace and kiss politely. Daisy proved a big hit being genuinely interested in the Carruthers' children.

The others wanted to talk about Wolferton with George keen to move, so they arranged a repeat visit. Lord Carruthers insisted on having his manservant drive the group into London and soon they were on a train travelling north.

Daisy became uncomfortable, as in two's company three's a crowd but soon discovered why George fell for Louisa who treated the housekeeper like a grandmother. In fact the women chatted so easily, it was George who became the odd one out.

The train was on time. They reached King's Lynn and headed north towards Hunstanton to reach their destination, Wolferton. George stepped out and offered a hand to his two companions. A voice sounded behind them.

'Mr Miracle, I presume.'

The trio was met by the retiring SM, a mustachioed older gent, Mr Harry Saward. He treated them the way he treated all visitors to his station be they royalty, heads of state, stars of the stage, scientists or socialites, villagers, even newly-appointed station masters. Harry led his visitors on a tour.

George took an interest in the mechanics of the place—tickets, storage, office, equipment and the like. The ladies wanted to be elsewhere. But all three visitors were stunned when they entered one of the Royal retirement-room suites. Stunned is an accurate description. No expense was spared in the design, building and decoration of the rooms in which Her Majesty, Queen Victoria, her heirs and successors would use on their travels to and from Sandringham. There was another Royal suite on the other platform.

The Whittleton station master struggled to speak. This station with its many outstanding features would soon be his to command. He observed the station lamps were topped with a small crown. He glanced at Louisa who too appeared to have her heart in her mouth.

'Now I don't suppose the ladies will have much interest inspecting the signal box,' said Harry with a wink. The trio smiled.

George replied. 'I will certainly enjoy a visit, sir, but I would like to accompany the ladies to see the station house if possible.'

'Of course,' said Harry and led the way.

The short walk from the station to the SM's stately and striking accommodation took little time. In Whittleton, the humble cottage paled into insignificance alongside this "palace" at Wolferton.

The large two-storey brick building with a conical tower-like room, massive chimneys, patterned quality brickwork, windows and more windows, two gates with one for vehicles, an impressive verandah and a surrounding garden would make a perfect dwelling for a successful businessman or local politician. The visitors gazed in awe.

They knew the Royal estate lay two miles away but even so, what other station provided an SM with such prestige, space and size? The front gate boasted brick posts with each supporting a stunning lamp with a blooming garden surrounding the house.

'Come and see the inside,' said Harry and led them along the garden path. The trio of new people entered the house where the interior left them struggling for superlatives.

'My dear,' called Harry, 'come and meet our visitors. Sarah Saward, Harry's wife and mother of their three daughters was introduced with smiles all round.

In Norwich, Daisy, and for a time George, lived in a large old Victorian house but the Wolferton residence was bigger, brighter and gloriously more beautiful. Breathtaking well described this residence.

George spoke his mind. 'I'd heard stories about the Royal Station but never imagined it or even the SM's house to be so magnificent.'

Harry grinned. 'Most people say that on their first visit. We've been here forty years and I still pinch myself working at Wolferton.

'The kitchen is wonderful,' said Daisy.

Despite George telling Louisa there would only be the two of them in the "cottage" at Wolferton, Louisa now worried wondering if the size and beauty of the place would bring about a change of mind from George or Daisy or both. All three could become lost in this home.

'Why don't we leave the ladies to chat with my wife while we continue exploring and inspect the signal box?' suggested Harry.

They agreed and the two SMs set off to meet the signalman and discuss levers, timetables, tokens and other details of the trains travelling from London to King's Lynn and on to Hunstanton.

George met the signalman and struck up an immediate rapport. Brendan "Cluffie" Clough began pulling levers at Wolferton only a few years after Harry became its SM.

From the signal box, George was taken back to the station to meet the porters. All were impressed with their boss-in-waiting and much admired his youthful appearance. George worried they might not take to such a young SM. When he and Harry were alone in the SM's office, Harry said something George found reassuring.

'I became SM here in 1884 as a young man. There were over a hundred applicants. It's good to see you're maintaining the tradition.'

A train approached so the two SMs wandered onto the platform. People alighted or boarded the train. George stood back and observed. He liked the efficiency and courtesy shown by the station staff. The train departed and Louisa and Daisy arrived.

To George, they continued singing the praises of the station house.

Harry chatted to a man and brought him to the visitors. 'May I introduce you to our local rector? The Reverend Kenneth Attwood, this is Mr George Miracle the newly-appointed station master, his fiancée Miss McClaren and his housekeeper Miss Woods.'

The greetings were friendly and the rector showed a genuine interest in those he hoped would be three new members of his flock.

'So may one ask when and where your wedding is to be?'

George hesitated. 'At this stage, sir, we're not entirely sure. There's my family's church in Whittleton, Louisa's family's church in Foxton, and the parents of my godson, Lord and Lady Carruthers, have offered the grounds of their magnificent home in Hampstead.'

'Spoilt for choice,' said the rector. 'Well not wishing to confuse you, there's always St Peter's here in Wolferton.' He pointed and across the fields they could see the tower of the local church.

George and Louisa exchanged glances. They thought alike. An independent venue would avoid leaving one family disappointed. And if the church is as pretty as the station and surrounding buildings, well let's at least consider it.

'Would you care to inspect the church?' asked the rector.

Daisy declined on the grounds of being tired and accepted the offer of reclining in what was once Queen Victoria's retirement-room. Daisy dared to use the throne room, excited to think her posterior settled where once or thrice Her Majesty did the same.

George and Louisa instantly fell in love with the Wolferton church. They said little during the inspection but knew in their hearts this setting would be perfect. The rector waxed lyrical.

'Our organ has nearly 500 pipes with two manuals, was built according to Sir John Stainer's specifications, and King Edward VII, when Prince of Wales, donated generously to its building.'

The engaged couple smiled, were most impressed, but knew nothing of stops, pedals and pipes. *And who is Sir John Stainer?*

'There's a club nearby for your wedding breakfast but depending on the number of guests, you might wish to celebrate at the station.' The couple stared at one another, thinking. *Is that possible?*

'Over the years, many shooting parties visiting Sandringham have enjoyed luncheon at the station and let's face it,' continued the rector, 'if anyone's entitled to celebrate their nuptials at the Royal Station, it would have to be the station master and his wife. If needed, we have a few small round tables you could borrow.'

The clergyman proved a good salesman and even non-believer George imagined himself as a parishioner at St Peter's. They thanked the rector and asked for time to make a decision on the venue.

The trip home consisted of non-stop chatter interrupted by periods of silence as the impact of the visit to Wolferton slowly seeped into their bones. The station, the station house and the church were individually impressive; together they proved overwhelming.

Chapter 10

Lily Bliss couldn't sleep. Thanks to being a friend, casual lover or the plus one of the Earl of Fakenham, she'd joined a murder conspiracy. Killing someone in a play fired her heart but killing someone in real life; forget it. She wanted out. She wanted separation from the twins, the Earl and any of their cohorts. But how?

Not having someone she could talk to about her predicament proved a stumbling block. Going to the police would expose her to the raid at Ripley Hall. Going to a criminal—she knew a few strange characters—could see her disappear, permanently. Picking the wrong person might put her in serious danger even prison.

She'd met the target, Louisa McClaren, in a bedroom in Ripley Hall, Whittleton and liked her. Meeting the target face to face put Lily right off murder. That meeting played havoc with her conscience.

If she went to the twins and returned the silver pill box, unopened, would they have her killed? They were desperate, and being on their second and possibly last attempt to do away with their half-sibling meant they would kill for a result.

When offered a part in a new musical play at the Hippodrome, Lily's problems eased a tad. Rehearsals gave her something to do.

Across town, the twins wallowed in anger and confusion. What if anything has Lily done? Has she contacted the target? Where is the pill box? Did she once impersonate the target? Was she capable of double-crossing them? Is the old man dead?

They made plans to visit Lily again.

The twins contacted the hospital daily for news about their dear Papa, the key to their financial security. 'No change,' was the reply.

They worried. Does the patient know his twins are desperate to eliminate their half-sibling? At least if the old bugger's still comatose, Sir Jerome is in no position to make any change to his will.

George, Louisa and Daisy arrived back at Liverpool Street and the housekeeper, wise woman that she was, told them she needed to powder her nose when in fact she wanted the lovebirds to enjoy a bit of privacy.

'Be back here before 6,' said George and winked at her. Daisy left and George escorted Louisa along the platform he knew like the back of his hand. He started his railway working life right here in 1910 as a 12 year-old station lad before being conscripted in 1916.

He led Louisa behind a newsstand which offered a semblance of privacy, faced her, squeezed her hands, leant in and kissed her lips.'

'I've been busting to do that all afternoon,' he said.

'Me too,' she smiled becoming serious. 'I still can't believe we're going to live at Wolferton, George, it's such a magical place.'

'You once said you'd be happy to live anywhere with me.'

She loved him even more when he teased her and this time she initiated the osculation. He took the plunge and embraced her and gave her a forceful and lasting smooch until a voice rang out.

'Unhand that woman!' Frightened, the lovers separated. 'You don't know where she's been.' Louisa stared at the fierce-looking man but George relaxed and burst into a broad grin when his friend and former mentor, SM Jack Rogers, approached with hand extended.

The SMs shook hands and Louisa met the London railwayman. Jack congratulated the couple, and heaped praise on his younger colleague finishing with a warning.

'Now Miss McClaren, if ever you want a rundown of young Mr Miracle's seriously bad habits, I know a tale or two.'

He grinned and they all appreciated the situation.

'I now see where my fiancé gets his sense of humour,' said Louisa.

'Blimey,' said George checking his watch. 'We'll miss our train.' Jack offered to help. 'Thanks Jack, if you could escort Louisa outside, there's a car to collect her.'

He kissed his girl and set off to find Daisy. She waited on the correct platform with their train champing at the bit. They boarded and were soon on their way back to Whittleton.

Daisy took out her handkerchief and offered it to the young SM. 'Spot of lipstick right there,' she said indicating. George produced his half frown/half grin, removed his own handkerchief and carried out running repairs.

'So,' said the housekeeper, 'I gather your intended took a shine to Wolferton.'

He laughed and reckoned he'd never been happier. A few issues remained, the thorniest of which involved his housekeeper. *What am I going to do with Daisy?* He procrastinated in raising the topic.

She helped by talking about a different matter. 'So have you decided where you'll marry?'

'We're still not sure,' he replied thinking about other issues.

Can I leave Whittleton and the Branch in tip-top condition? Being appointed to the Royal Station will start tongues wagging but they'll wag far more if I leave Whitty in a mess.

All three porters were waiting for their boss when he arrived as predicted. 'Good evening, Miss Woods,' said the lad porter opening the door and helping Daisy. George followed. 'Good evening, sir.'

'Thank you, Pip,' said Daisy who turned back to George. 'It'll be leftovers, Mr Miracle, so I'll expect you when I see you.'

She toddled off and George wanted any and all news about his station. There were no delays or incidents and George released Pip and Gordon.

Fletcher followed George into the SM's office. 'How are you getting on with the planned move to Pickling?' asked George.

'All set, sir. Mrs Rough seemed jolly decent about it and the offer of a few free eggs went down well but when I told her there are daffodils and hydrangeas coming into bloom, she actually kissed me.'

George laughed. 'Of course, they're for the church. Now, can I ask you to handle the Up?'

Fletcher disappeared as the train arrived and George made notes. *Tasks to complete before leaving Whitty.*

Lily Bliss worried. Back in rehearsals for a new show took her mind off a certain problem but at night she struggled to sleep. Every time she heard the downstairs front door open, her heart got busy.

Could this be the twins returning to check on progress?

She knew doing nothing was as bad as actually doing the deed. *Procrastination never helps,* she thought. Leaving town was an option but as she'd landed a new role, to walk out would blacken her name in the business and be the end of her stage career.

Another thought caused even more concern. She might not be the only assassin. The twins were evil and determined. They would surely have a Plan B, and if their other killer, a professional, succeeded, Lily might cop the blame and worse, the innocent Louisa McClaren would be dead.

Lily's goal changed. *Don't kill the woman, save her. But how?*

Once the actress wrote a marriage agreement asking the Earl of Fakenham to sign and date it. Of course he never honoured it but the writing routine inspired her. She penned an anonymous letter.

The following weekend, a handful of tourists walked between the pot plants dividing the island platform at Whittleton and boarded the Crabbie. Once the Druid inspections were cancelled thanks to the erratic Danny Wight, naturally tourist numbers fell away, but now the difficult farmer resided safely but sadly in an institution, George jumped back on the publicity bandwagon.

With Stephen Fitzsimons, who never closed his wine tastings, together they resumed promoting their respective offerings.

Madge knew the deal. If there were tourist passengers for Pickling, he would "play" a certain two-toot message and Freda would have her bag of jars of homemade jams and chutney and her homemade megaphone ready, and with Rufus leading the way, head to the Halt to greet her customers.

On her farm, Freda heard the Morse code-like message from Madge, started her journey, tripped on the back step meaning her bag of goodies set about proving the theory of gravity to be a law.

'Buggeration!' she yelled and Rufus wanted to know how he could help. It took precious time for her to sort her wares. A couple of jars broke and raspberry jam and pickle chutney spilt and decorated the intact jars. No-one would buy jam smelling of chutney or chutney sticky with jam. What a mess. Clean those jars, Freda.

Finally she left home and hurried as best she could to the Halt. The Crabbie offloaded the tourists and departed and as Freda drew closer, she couldn't see anyone so uttered another Buggeration.

Rufus barked agreeing with his mistress. Why would Madge tell her to move if there were no passengers to chat to and separate from their money?

Dog and owner crossed the track and stepped up onto the miniature platform. Not a soul to be seen or heard. 'I'll kill Madge,' she said and headed to the Druid site.

She arrived and again, saw no-one. The Druid rocks looked lonely. What a waste of a journey and worse, she sold nothing, not a single jar of jam or chutney. Starting to head home, Rufus became agitated.

'What's up, Rufus? Seen a rabbit?'

'No,' he barked. 'There are people coming this way.'

Freda struggled with Barking and froze, confused but she too heard the sound. Voices became louder. 'Well done, old boy,' she said to her dog as eight tourists came walking out of the forest. Actually there were only seven tourists with Freda not spotting the ring-in.

'Hello,' she cried greeting her potential customers. 'Have you come to see where the ancient Druids used to meet?'

The excited tourists answered as one and soon she sat them around the rocks and delivered her spiel. They were fascinated and listened intently before asking a number of relevant questions. Freda was back on song and already mentally counting the cash.

But a problem arose. Because Freda arrived late, the tourists disappeared. By the time they'd been rounded up, lectured to and asked so many questions, the Crabbie came steaming back on her way home. The tourists wanted to return to Whittleton and visit Ripley Hall for a spot of wine tasting. They heard the little loco and were up and off leaving Freda to fume and her products unsold.

This time the Buggeration could be heard loud and clear.

Freda didn't even begin to announce her wares. To rub salt into her wound, nobody tipped her. Grumbling, she traipsed after the group as they returned to the Halt and climbed aboard the single carriage. She gave them a pathetic wave before turning to collect her bag and dog when she spied one of the tourists.

'You've missed your train,' she said. 'There isn't another for ages.'

'It's okay,' said porter Fletcher Drum, 'I'm not a tourist.'

Freda thought she recognized him but wasn't sure. On Wednesdays when she visited her sister in town, Fletcher enjoyed his day off. They'd never been introduced. Rufus stopped wagging his tail standing ready to protect his mistress.

'My name's Fletcher Drum and I'm a porter at Whittleton and at Crabbwell when I can.' His simple sentence raised a number of questions. 'I gather you're Freda, the tourist guide to the Druid site.'

Still Freda didn't speak. Fletcher thought he should continue.

'When those tourists arrived, I popped out to see them and hear your talk. I've been told it's very good. When you didn't arrive, I invited them to see the hens and pigs on the farm back there.'

He pointed into the woods. This explanation wasn't going well.

'Fortunately they were all townies otherwise they probably would have laughed at me.'

Freda copped the double—fascination and anger.

What the hell is he talking about?

'I mean imagine what farming folk would have said if I'd asked them to stare at a few hens?'

Finally Freda found her tongue. 'Has George sent you out here to spy on me?'

'What?' gasped a shocked Fletcher. 'No, of course not; Mr Miracle is a gentleman.'

'Well why is there a porter at Pickling when even Crabbtree is officially unmanned? And how do you know about the hens and pigs on Danny's farm?'

'Because I live there.'

'Live there!' Freda found herself in a tangle. Dropping and breaking her precious products and being late and selling nowt upset her no end. Now, without warning, one of George's porters bobs up and announces he's her neighbour.

Why haven't I been told?

He explained. 'I've always lived on farms and when I heard this one had become vacant, I made enquiries and they granted me permission to be a sort of caretaker tenant. Mr Miracle agreed to me moving in and I ride my bicycle into Whittleton for my shifts.'

'Did he now?'

Fletcher became wary. This meeting flirted with danger. 'I'm sorry if I've upset you. I only invited the tourists to my farm because ...'

'*Your* farm? It belongs to my friend Danny Wight.' Freda slipped into the world of fibs. Danny remained firmly in the enemy camp and anyone who shot her dog would ever more remain so.

'Well yes, of course, as I said I'm only a tenant but I'm also responsible for feeding the animals.'

'Look Mister I have an arrangement with George where I act as tourist guide and in return, can sell my jams and chutneys but when you invite my customers to your heap of run-down buildings to gawp at squabbling hens, you kill my business.' She glared and pointed at him. 'You haven't heard the last of this. Rufus, come on.'

She dropped off the platform, a whole seven inches, stepped onto a sleeper and headed home with the Irish wolfhound obedient as ever. They stopped when Fletcher called.

'Excuse me, Miss, is this yours?'

He held up Freda's homemade megaphone she'd left behind. Everything Freda owned and wore was homemade.

Oh dear, how humiliating. She retraced her steps with Rufus following confused, reached out and snatched the item. She mumbled, 'Thanks,' turned and set off, her steps giving the fields a decent stamping.

Fletcher scratched his head and spoke to himself. 'Okay, so that's the mad woman from Pickling and her Irish wolfhound; and a jolly good morning to you too.'

Lily made a plan. She told her landlady she'd be going away for a couple of weeks.

'I'll need your rent in advance or I'll let the room.'

Lily expected such a response and handed over the cash.

'If anyone asks, I've gone to my sister in Cardiff,' she said.

She didn't even have a sister and moved in with one of the stage-door Johnnies who'd take her for supper before trying to seduce her. His flat in Chelsea with its far more palatial and comfortable bed was way better than her poky little single with a wafer-thin mattress. Sure it meant yielding to his carnal desires but there were benefits—her security and anonymity. The Hamilton-Weir twins were desperate and dangerous. Avoiding them was essential.

Besides, with Godwin the stage-door Johnny getting on a bit, any form of exertion became a tough gig for the old boy. The next day, he'd go home to his wife in the Cotswolds for a week of rest and recuperation. Too much excitement didn't help his dicky ticker.

So hiding from the twins, Lily put her survival plan into action. Sitting at stage-door Johnny's fancy desk, she took out a piece of classy notepaper and wrote an anonymous letter to Scotland Yard marked *Urgent*.

Dear Scotland Yard Officers

My friends, Sophronia and Enoch Hamilton-Weir of Eaton Square, Belgravia, are in grave danger. A dispute over their father's will means they could be murdered by a gang of desperate killers.

My friends are two of the three beneficiaries of their widowed father's will, the well-known philanthropist, Sir Jerome Hamilton-Weir. The gentleman currently lies seriously ill in the London Private Clinic in Weymouth Street.

I know a criminal gang is being paid by the third beneficiary to have her siblings disappear so as to inherit the entire estate. This includes considerable cash and shares, and properties in London and Cambridgeshire.

A dear friend of Mr and Miss Hamilton-Weir, the Earl of Fakenham, of Flat 12, Edward Street, Stepney, attempted to protect the twins and was viciously attacked. He too is in danger of being murdered.

The three intended victims are unaware of the danger they face.

I implore you to immediately protect the lives of these outstanding members of society.

Yours faithfully

A friend of the twins.

Lily posted the letter en route to her rehearsal. She couldn't imagine the outcome but hoped like hell both she and Louisa would survive.

The Earl's flat in Stepney was a gift from a sympathetic uncle who, having seen the dysfunctional and destitute family from which Dickie Carrington emerged, took pity on his nephew. Unsurprisingly, the gratitude from the young Earl was about as sincere and genuine as a public executioner apologizing as he picked up the axe.

Chapter 11

Summer was itching to start and the Horace Gardiner Gardens at Whittleton Station were eager to show their wares. George's reign as SM was drawing to a close and he wanted to leave the place in tip-top condition. By the time he departed he reckoned the garden would be at its summery best.

Louisa showed little interest in Whittleton being madly in love with Wolferton, its Royal connection, station house and particularly its church. The 13th century St Peter's oozed history and solemnity and the rector's kindness won her vote as the venue for her wedding.

'Oh George,' she said during their latest telephone call, 'please can we wed at Wolferton. My mother thinks the idea is perfect and if you can persuade your mother, I'm sure we'll have a marvellous day.'

He didn't care. He only wanted to marry his sweetheart.

'Of course, my darling girl; what would you like me to do?'

'I don't want to upset your mother and if you could convince her that St Peter's is perfect, we can make definite plans.'

Connie agreed and events fell into place. Louisa wrote to the Reverend Attwood and they agreed on the date; Saturday June 14 at 12 noon. The wedding breakfast venue would be chosen later.

George didn't need to write the date, time or venue on any calendar or notebook. The details were locked in his head forever.

'Where shall we go for our honeymoon, Mr Miracle?' asked Louisa.

'We'll have two weeks and two days, Miss McClaren, although I'd like to be settled in the station house a day or two before July 1.'

'You haven't answered my question, George. Where shall we go?'

'King's Lynn would be ideal. It's a short trip from Wolferton, there are several lovely hotels and beaches and we could travel for free.'

She laughed. 'Don't tell me I'm marrying a cheapskate. You only marry once, George, loosen those purse strings and live a little.'

He knew his frugal side came from his mother and reckoned being careful with money brought him no shame. Nevertheless he knew their honeymoon should and would be a time of excitement and great happiness. 'I'll buy you *two* ice-creams every day,' he said and she loved his nonsense remarks.

They both suffered a build-up of butterflies in their stomachs as the days drifted by. Not being able to see one another, and touch and kiss each other made the days seem longer. Both experienced those physical sensations of being in love which grew ever stronger.

With date, church and possibly the honeymoon sorted, the two main issues remaining, oh apart from the wedding dress, were the guest list and the position of the current Whittleton housekeeper.

Would they ask Daisy to live with them in the large station house, and who would they invite to their wedding? The number of guests would determine the venue for their wedding breakfast. Oh, and the cost. Louisa's mother could never afford anything expensive. Louisa's father could have hired the swankiest London hotel but he was unknown to his younger daughter and currently in danger of dying.

Whenever the couple thought the list of tasks to do was being reduced, up would pop another subject.

'Have you chosen your bridesmaid?' asked George.

'Have you chosen your best man?' replied Louisa.

The saga seemed to be on a loop.

The Earl of Fakenham wallowed in misery. His bruises slowly healed over time but staring at his naked body in a mirror brought on nightmares. He re-lived his fall from the balcony at Ripley Hall; knocked off-balance by a maid tossing out dead flowers, the agony he suffered when crashing onto bushes below and worse, the unmitigated humiliation of his failed mission. All his preparation, including a reconnaissance expedition, ended in total failure, which meant no payment for his services and a debt still to be repaid. Ouch.

The Hamilton-Weir twins ignored him, wiping him from their social calendar. The whole *world* wiped him.

Lying on his bed feeling sorry for himself with mainly alcohol for sustenance and medicine, his front door copped a serious knocking. In no mood to see anyone, he chose to remain silent. He waited. The caller tried again. More knocking and this time with a voice.

'My Lord, this is the police. Please come to the door.'

The police, screamed Carrington's mind. *Is there no rest for the wicked? Now I'm to be arrested for conspiracy to murder.*

'We wish to help you, sir,' a manly voice called.

The Earl needed time to comprehend that last remark.

'We are here to protect you, my Lord. Please come to the door.'

This has to be a trick, thought Dickie but a flicker of hope was born. Approaching the door, he called with a croaky voice.

'Who's there?'

'Scotland Yard, sir, we're police detectives.'

The Earl's mind struggled. *Is this a trap?* But surely the twins wouldn't do him over. They were guilty too. Could it be revenge from Lily Bliss? She dumped him when he reneged on his wedding promise. He leaned against the door, his head and heart pounding.

They wish to help me? Surely not.

He opened the door and stared at two middle-aged men in suits.

'May we come in, my Lord?' asked one.

They entered the hovel, the messy, smelly, ideal-home-for-rats flat. He didn't apologize, being too far gone for pretence. In fact if they'd come to arrest him, in a way he would have been pleased.

They explained. 'We've come to take you away, sir, to a safe house.'

This is insane. 'A safe house!'

'We believe your life to be in danger, sir. You and your friends, the Hamilton-Weir twins are being stalked.'

'What?' gasped Carrington.

'All of you will receive protection until the threat is removed.'

'Someone is trying to kill me?'

'We believe so, sir.'

'Who?' He could think of a long list of possibilities.

'Gather up your clothes and personal items, sir,' said the second officer, 'and we'll take you to a safe place.' The Earl froze thinking he'd fallen into a fantastic dream. 'Do hurry, sir, the danger is real.'

Seven miles and an eternity away in land values, in Belgravia, another two Scotland Yard detectives were saying much the same thing to the twins, Sophronia and Enoch. They too struggled to believe the police.

But these men dressed like police officers, carried identification and knew about their ill father and his will. Like the Earl, the twins wandered into this fantastic dream.

Not wanting to move, Sophronia stood her ground. 'We can stay here. We have staff and with security, we'll be safe.'

Enoch agreed. 'I can protect my sister.'

'You can't make us leave,' threatened Sophronia digging in.

The detectives exchanged glances. The wealthy twins did have a point. Unlike the Earl, their home could be described as a fortress. It was one of many in Eaton Square. The multi-storey houses were attached, built to last, had no front garden, sat on the street and would make an intruder's frontal assault tricky.

'As you wish, but we'll have police patrols maintain watch especially during the evenings.'

The Scotland Yarders left and the twins stared at one another. Sophronia fumed with her brother afraid.

'What is happening?' he bleated. 'Who's behind this?'

'It's either Dickie or the bitch.'

They'd dropped the half-sister's name and settled on "The bitch".

'It can't be Lily Bliss. She'd be throwing away 50 quid.'

Sophronia's smarts kicked in. 'Whoever's behind this is clever.'

'Well that rules out Dickie,' said Enoch.

'Stuck in here, we can't fix the bitch. The old man dies, we're left with a reduced amount and she wanders around rich and scot free.'

'What'll we do?' asked the hapless brother.

His sister growled. 'Find a way to rid us of this turbulent priest.'

Enoch, feeling sick, stared seriously confused. 'Who's a priest?'

'If *we* can't kill her, Lily must give her that pill.'

Fletcher Drum said nothing to George about the contretemps he and Freda shared at the Pickling Halt. He put it down to her being an eccentric and hoped their relationship would improve over time. The next day when he arrived for work having cycled into Whittleton, George asked him about Freda.

'She's certainly a character, sir.'

George smiled. 'Her heart's in the right place, Fletcher. I hope you'll be able to help her with the tourists.' The porter slipped away wondering if he should have said more or said anything.

The following Wednesday, Freda and Rufus arrived and sought out George. There were no sloppy kisses from farmer or hound.

No kisses. Wow. She looked angry and sounded rude.

'Why didn't you tell me, George?'

'Good morning, Freda and Rufus.' At least the dog wagged his tail.

'You set one of your porters on Danny's farm to spy on me which is bad enough but you never told me.'

'Well if that ridiculous claim is true, I'd hardly tell you, would I? Look, Wednesday is Fletcher's day off otherwise I would have introduced you last week. Is there a problem?'

Her anger dropped a tad. 'He pinched my tourists. I arrive at Pickling and find he's taken them to *his* farm to show off *his* hens.'

'Come on, Freda, is that what really happened? I spoke to a couple of tourists off the Crabbie, and it seems you were late and Fletcher saved your bacon by entertaining the tourists until you arrived.' He paused. 'By the way, he spoke highly of your talk to the tourists.'

She sniffed. 'Did he now?'

'He's a good man, Freda. With Danny being a dangerous lunatic, the tourist trade died. Now Fletcher's caring for the animals, the tourists can return and the demand for your jam could be sky high.'

'And chutney,' she added moving in for the usual kiss.

Residents of Foxton knew Louisa's mother as the widow, Mrs Rowena McClaren. Her real unknown name was Miss Rowena Hislop with McClaren her mother's maiden name. As a slip of a girl, Rowena became pregnant when seduced by Mr Jerome Hamilton-Weir, a married father of toddler twins. As a guest in a large country house, he encountered Rowena working as a chamber maid. The wealthy businessman did what several so-called powerful "gentlemen" did when away from home. He forced himself on the young woman who became terrified, ashamed and desolate in equal amounts.

The seducer, sober in the morning, discovered a conscience and went to find Rowena. Her eyes were red and secretly, Hamilton-Weir gave her cash and a sort of an apology.

When the confused and desperate chamber maid discovered her pregnancy, she left her post, returned to her parents where Rowena's father struggled with poor health. Together, Miss Hislop and her parents tried to find a way to survive.

Heavily pregnant, brave and determined, Rowena became a sleuth of sorts, discovered the address of Mr Hamilton-Weir and wrote to him. She expected no response or a denial or possibly even a threat.

To her surprise, he replied with an offer which suggested guilt and a conscience but with conditions attached. A rent-free cottage in Foxton became available for Rowena and her parents.

Sadly her father died leaving his wife and pregnant daughter alone. Rowena announced her widowhood status when she arrived at Foxton and discovered she owned a bank account into which Mr Hamilton-Weir made regular payments. He never asked for anything other than his paternity must remain a secret.

Louisa was born, and when she became a young child, her maternal grandmother died. At around that time, Louisa's father accepted a knighthood in recognition of his philanthropy. His generosity towards his illegitimate daughter continued but remained a secret. Sir Jerome hoped, even prayed, it would forever remain so.

He instructed an agent to deliver a subtle but implied threat. If his paternity ever became public, the Foxton cottage would be sold, its occupants made homeless, and the bank account closed. Rowena stuck to her part of the bargain.

Fast forward many years and Rowena's daughter, Louisa McClaren grew up and left home to become a lady companion to her friend Valerie now Lady Carruthers. When Louisa told her mother of her engagement to a railwayman, Rowena's heart began to sing.

Meeting young Mr Miracle only increased Rowena's happiness. After the first visit, once George and Louisa left the Foxton cottage, Rowena set about tackling a major task.

She wrote a letter to the man who seduced her 20 years ago; a simple, business note. She addressed him as Sir Jerome and explained how her daughter—not *his* or *their* daughter—would soon marry and therefore be no longer in need of his generous philanthropy.

She thanked him for his kindness wishing him well for the future and did all this out of a sense of duty knowing her action could mean the Foxton cottage might no longer be available.

But posting the letter didn't feel right. The next day, with letter sealed in an addressed envelope, she set sail for London. Her destination was a magnificent home in Eaton Square, Belgravia.

But would this missive ever reach its intended target and if so, what would be its impact?

Chapter 12

King George V was a spare, an accidental Monarch. His older brother, Albert Victor, heir to the throne of Edward VII, died in the Russian flu pandemic aged 28. George, who grew up in the navy, underwent a major lifestyle change being thrust into the limelight as the heir apparent. He married his deceased brother's former fiancée.

His father died in 1910 and George became Monarch aged 35. A short man, his people loved him unlike several members of his family particularly his children. At least one described his temper as white hot and his fuse short. George clashed with his oldest son Edward, the future King.

"After I'm dead, the boy will ruin himself within 12 months," the King is believed to have said. Many thought the King prescient.

Because Edward began living like his grandfather and namesake, enjoying a hedonistic lifestyle, George V slipped easily into a foul mood clashing with the young Prince. Edward once set up with a scandalous French woman. Their relationship fizzled but the former lover ended up murdering her next boyfriend leaving the King apoplectic with rage. There is such a thing as bad publicity.

Years later, when Edward took up with the American divorcee, Wallis Simpson, the King opposed any relationship between them.

When Edward asked his father if he might bring Mrs Simpson to a social event at Buckingham Palace, the unequivocal answer was "absolutely not—never!", a sort of "over my dead body" reply.

Imagine the father's reaction when Edward arrived with the American on his arm. Again, in private, the Monarch exploded.

And this same King George V reigned as monarch when in 1924, another George, Miracle by name, became the station master at Wolferton, otherwise known as the Royal Station.

George Miracle's appointment was to begin at the beginning of July and he craved as much training in his new location as possible. Being so young when promoted, George copped a barrage of criticism. None delivered to his face but he heard how many in the LNER wondered why an SM so young could be appointed to such a plum position.

The pressure to succeed kept building, and he knew he needed to be on top of his job and to never, well hardly ever, make mistakes.

He needed to keep running Whittleton and the branch, as well as marry so juggling time for a visit to north-west Norfolk proved tricky.

Weekends were best when services on most lines were fewer. He contacted the Wolferton SM, Harry Saward, and made arrangements to travel the following Sunday. George's porters were happy to take control respecting their boss and wanting him to prepare well for his move to Wolferton.

You could describe Harry Saward as an ideal railwayman who, like George, went "on the rail" when young and gave his life to the job.

George arrived and the young and the old SM chatted.

'I began like you, young man,' said Harry. 'When appointed to Wolferton, Queen Victoria was still on the throne.'

'Queen Victoria?' exclaimed a surprised George.

'Aye and I was a young fellah like you when I landed here and have remained nigh on forty year.'

George marvelled at the SM's history. 'I'll be most grateful, sir,' said the younger man, 'for any tips about dealing with important passengers, and especially anything to help me avoid offending members of the Royal Family would be a great help.'

Harry laughed. 'There's a possible problem from the off, lad. I learnt early on how treating all people the same to be the best, the only way to get your job done proper.'

George absorbed the advice his colleague revealed as the older man continued.

'Once you start treating certain folk different, you make a rod for your own back. Of course you don't bow to Mr Jones the butcher or Mrs Wagstaff the baker's wife but they receive the same respect as do members of the Royal Family and the prime ministers and all the other dignitaries who pass through on their way to Sandringham.'

George enjoyed Harry's wisdom believing it ran parallel with his own attitude to people in general and passengers in particular.

'Thank you,' said George, 'you've been most kind to the new boy.'

'As to the Royals, the Queen Mother lives at Sandringham today in the big house. We don't see much of the old lady and we hear she's been poorly these last few years. Her family come to visit and respecting his mother's wishes, King George and Queen Mary stay in York Cottage, one of the smaller houses.'

'I know the King made many visits to his troops during the War.'

'Were you fighting?'

'I was,' said George and left it there.

'His Majesty will be pleased to know the local SM is a returned serviceman.' George grimaced. 'But you won't have seen the notices dealing with members of the Royal family. Come and I'll show you.'

George followed Harry into his office where the senior man produced paperwork. It was headed;

This notice is, and must be kept, strictly private.

Harry continued. 'We receive ample warning of the Royal Train arriving and departing. We aren't told what refreshments are served in each of the saloon coaches but everything else is covered down to the last minute and yard. Read this,' he said pointing.

Wolferton: - *The Royal Train must come to a stand with the cab of the engine opposite a point at which a flagman will be standing on the platform exhibiting a red flag.*

George's heartbeat accelerated. 'I see,' he said worrying.

'And of course you know the rule when meeting a member of the Royal Family.' Harry waited for George to reply. He froze. 'Only speak when spoken to.'

George nodded and whispered, 'Thank you.'

'We're a good team here, lad,' said Harry. He could rightfully call the new SM "lad" because all the others were older, even much older than George. 'The porters are fine chaps. They'll do you proud and you wouldn't have been appointed unless the top brass reckoned you were up to the mark.'

What could George say? They were treating him with respect. There seemed to be no jealousy or bickering amongst the staff. Could this be true? *Surely there must be even a minor conflict.*

Already under petticoat government, George made his way to the local church. The rector expected him thanks to a letter from Louisa.

The newly-appointed SM heard singing as he approached St Peter's. This being a Sunday morning, of course a service could be heard at 11:55. He wandered around the gravestones in the church yard reading the names of the deceased. He remembered hearing of the terrible loss of life of his fellow soldiers, many from the 5th Norfolks who hailed from these parts, when fighting at Gallipoli.

The music stopped to be replaced by chattering voices and footsteps. The path from the church door to the lychgate leant itself to clear-sounding footsteps. George moved to the path as worshippers approached. He removed his cap.

People nodded and he replied with 'Good afternoon'. He chose to wait until all the churchgoers left before he would approach the church and its rector.

A man and a woman stopped. 'Would you be the new station master?' asked the man.

'I am sir, George Miracle.'

They shook hands. 'I'm Bernie Delbridge and this is my wife, Grace.' More hand shaking and greetings ensued. 'The grapevine here in Wolferton can be pretty busy at times,' he said with a grin.

'Well it's nice of you to say hello,' said George keen to carry out his fiancée's wishes.

'You'll be wanting to see the rector about your nuptials,' said Mrs Delbridge smiling. Surprised, George struggled to reply.

The couple laughed and Bernie explained. 'Your young lady told the Reverend Attwood who would have told his housekeeper who would have told the postmistress who happens to be the station master's missus and ... well, you get the picture.'

This time George joined the laughter.

'I come from a small village so I know all about the grapevine.'

The conversation stopped and George wanted them to move on to the lychgate allowing him to head off to the church. The couple didn't move. As it happened, they wanted George to move.

Grace saw the predicament and explained. She pointed to the headstone of the grave near where George stood.

'It's our boy's grave, Mr Miracle.' George nearly died.

He stepped back. 'Oh, I'm so sorry, please do forgive me.'

'No harm done, sir,' said Bernie. 'We always have a chat with the lad after Sunday morning service.'

Feeling terrible, George retreated, walked around the parents and headed for the church. He wanted to say, "Nice to have met you," but didn't because it didn't feel right.

The front door of St Peter's stood open and George entered the empty church. Not being a regular churchgoer, he lacked confidence in moving freely along the aisle and jumped when a voice sounded and the rector appeared from behind a column.

'Mr Miracle, you made it.'

'Reverend Attwood, hello, yes I've been given another tour of the station by Mr Saward.'

'How is your lovely fiancée? I'm sorry she's unable to be here.'

'Thank you, she's well, and as you must surely know, I am here following her clear and concise instructions.'

The men laughed and the rector answered Louisa's questions after which, to George's horror he was led outside to the adjacent vicarage and inside where a place at the dining table was set for the new station master. What could he say?

I can hardly say no. Oh God, oops, oh dear this means I'll miss my train and be late getting back to Whittleton.

After each morning service, the rector invited a few of his flock to partake of a meal. During today's lovely luncheon George met Mr Attwood's housekeeper and four parishioners, two he'd just met.

The new station master was politely grilled with genuine interest being the motivation of all six of his fellow diners.

Fresh from her visit to the graveyard, Mrs Delbridge led the "interrogation". 'You must be excited about your wedding, sir.'

George struggled with the limelight and his non-involvement in the church at Whittleton, and at any church.

'Yes, my fiancée fell in love with the church and the village after her one and only visit, and as we live far apart and our mothers are both widowed, and as we are soon to live in Wolferton, St Peter's would appear to be the perfect place for our wedding.'

There were smiles aplenty. George reckoned one of the parishioners to be a good age—a nonagenarian. Born and bred in Wolferton, Miss Myrtle Forsythe was a rich source of local history.

'You don't see the crowds so much these days, Mr Miracle,' she said with George not understanding.

The rector explained. 'Miss Forsythe is our most senior resident, Mr Miracle. She can remember the early days when the Sandringham estate first became the property of the Royal Family.'

'How wonderful,' replied George.

'Oh yes,' said Miss Forsythe and away she went. 'We all knew when Her Majesty would arrive at Wolferton. The whole village came to the station. We even dressed for the occasion; best hats of course. The gates would be opened well before the train arrived. A few of us waved streamers. In the station yard were two horses pulling a lovely carriage with the drivers wearing top hats and great coats even in summer. Mounted soldiers with helmets and swords rode behind. It was so exciting.'

George wanted to ask a question but noted how the others remained still, listening in respectful silence. George didn't know his fellow diners knew all Miss Forsythe's stories by heart. She continued with several saying her sentences in their head.

'The Royal Trains were my favourite. We couldn't see Her Majesty step from her carriage but we knew once the station gates, not the railway gates, were opened she would soon appear. The horses trotted together as if trained to march in step. Her carriage came out onto the road. We waved and cheered and if we were lucky, Her Majesty would give us a tiny wave.' She paused remembering her childhood experience and raised a hand as she did last century. 'I'm sure she once stared straight into my eyes.'

Silence. Myrtle finished her memorable performance and rested.

'But not today, Miss Forsythe,' said the rector.

She snapped back to the present. ''Oh no, not today,' she said in a solemn voice. 'Members of the Royal Family come and go, occasionally on ordinary trains, and most of the villagers don't even know they're here let alone come out to wave.' She considered George. 'But as the station master, Mr Miracle, you will be told about Royal visits. You could tell us when to expect the King.'

George died. He needed to be friendly and win over the locals but the thought of becoming a snitch when Royalty dropped in, filled him with horror. It was a few moments before he saw the twinkle in Miss Forsythe's eyes and relaxed. The elderly lady enjoyed gentle teasing.

'You gave me a start there, Miss Forsythe,' said George and the others smiled even politely laughed.

Chapter 13

Rowena arrived in London. With her letter addressed to the father of her, *their* daughter, she set off for Eaton Square. She rarely came to London and never ventured into Belgravia so needed help with bus routes, not that all residents of SW1 used buses. A friendly porter at King's Cross put her straight and when she alighted her walk brought her to the Hamilton-Weir property.

She stood on the footpath outside the row of magnificent homes. Giant pillars held up the verandah if that's what you'd call it. The gleaming black door with its golden knocker oozed class and wealth. Upstairs on the first of five storeys, Enoch smoked and stared out at the shrubs, trees and lawn in the lush garden in the middle of the square. No riff raff allowed. Rowena gazed up not noticing her daughter's half-brother. If Enoch, let alone his sister, knew the contents of the letter the visitor carried, bombs would explode.

Breathing erratically, Louisa's mother used the door-knocker. It took an eternity for a servant to respond. He didn't speak. The caller's responsibility meant they spoke first and particularly so when the visitor obviously carried neither rank nor status.

'Good morning,' said Rowena indicating the envelope. 'I have an important letter for Sir Jerome Hamilton-Weir.'

The servant went to take it but recoiled when the caller at the last second withheld the item.

'Can I be sure the gentleman will receive it?'

'Do you wish to deliver the letter?' asked the servant giving away nothing and piling the pressure back on the caller.

'Yes, yes I do.'

The servant said nothing and waited. Rowena hesitated and the servant stepped back and closed the door.

'Wait, please wait,' called Rowena in a mild panic.

The door opened again and Rowena hand delivered the envelope. The door closed and the mother of George Miracle's bride-to-be turned and walked away.

The servant entered Sir Jerome's study and placed the envelope on his desk on top of several other items of mail yet to be opened. The servant closed the study door but stopped when a voice was heard.

'Chivers, have you seen my copy of *Debrett's*?'

'No, Miss Sophronia.' She headed for the study and the servant opened the door allowing Miss Evil to enter. She called.

'Knowing Daddy, he will have filed it in a never-to-be-found place. I'll close the door when I've finished.'

What could the servant say or do? The boss's daughter oozed power. Sophronia used the in-your-face method of skullduggery. Rather than sneak around trying to avoid being seen, she flaunted her presence hoping to give off the appearance of butter wouldn't melt.

She even hummed a trite ditty as if to tell the household her location and how she could never be considered a risk. But refusing to trust her, the servants saw through her act.

She swooped on the mail and Rowena's envelope intrigued her. Most of the items of mail were official begging letters from societies hoping the generous philanthropist would make a donation, or circulars from clubs and associations to which her father belonged. This envelope didn't fit those categories.

She pocketed the envelope and, if it offered nothing of interest to her, would be returned later or more likely dumped. More out-of-tune singing before she made her exit and headed upstairs.

Enoch passed the kitchenette and spotted her steaming open the envelope.

'Hey ho,' he said and investigated.

Extracting the missive and reading, she spoke with a voice trembling with emotion. 'Letter for the dying benefactor,' she replied.

'What's it say?' he asked.

Sophronia's breathing accelerated. 'It's from the bitch's mother.'

'Show me.' He took the letter and read. 'So, the bitch is getting married.' He looked aghast. 'Don't tell me you want an invitation?'

'This is gold, brother dear. This letter gives us the perfect way to have the lovely Louisa struck from the will.'

George arrived late when returning to Whittleton. All three porters were on duty wondering why their "He's never late" SM didn't arrive as stated.

'My apologies, gentlemen,' he said with all three keen to know his news.

'Breakdown with a loco, sir?' asked an inquisitive Gordon.

'Nothing so exciting,' said George heading for his office. 'More like friendly Wolferton locals insisting I stay for lunch. Any problems?'

'No problems, sir and all trains on time.'

'Did you meet the King, sir?' asked the lad porter holding the station cat, Whitty.

'If by the King you mean the station master, yes I did. And I also met the rector who has kindly agreed to marry me and my fiancée.'

Porter Drum, the tenant farmer of Pickling, expressed the mood of the others. 'Do you mean, sir, you'll not be wed here in Whittleton?'

'It does, Mr Drum and I hope it'll not offend those locals who've been my customers and in some cases friends for many years.'

'How will this letter help us?' demanded Enoch frustrated as yet again he demonstrated his sandwich-short-of-a-picnic intelligence.

'We simply tell dearest Papa he needs to scrub the bitch from his current will or else the world will learn about his bastard daughter.'

Enoch turned white. 'You're going to blackmail the old man?'

'We both are.' She scowled at her sibling and despised his lack of ruthlessness. 'Of course our major problem is him dying. He needs to be alive and compos mentis so he comprehends what he's facing.'

'Which is?'

'Having his secret daughter publicly identified. This letter proves he's been handing over cash for decades, *our* cash, to the bitch and her mother all to keep his love child hidden. Unless he changes his will leaving us the lot, his philandering days will be exposed with his glorious titled name and reputation left wallowing in the mud.'

'He'd hate that,' said a head-shaking Enoch who would never have thought of such a plan and never dared to carry it out.

'Prayer could be the key here, brother dear.'

'Prayer!' scoffed Enoch. 'You're the world's greatest atheist.'

She smiled and sniffed the letter. 'Yes but I'll try anything to keep dear Papa alive until we pull off the bloodless coup. He'll fold in a heartbeat to save his reputation and that of the daughter he's grown to love, pathetic man that he is.' She paused and asked a sincere question. 'How *do* you pray?'

George answered the phone in his office. He suffered from feelings of guilt when using the company phone for personal reasons and such guilt surfaced when he heard the caller. It was his sweetheart Louisa in Tudor House, Hampstead.

'I tried telephoning earlier, George but they told me you were late.'

'Are you checking up on me?' he asked with faux outrage.

'Of course,' she returned fire. 'It's called petticoat government and there's plenty more where that came from.'

He laughed. 'I was invited to lunch and it went on forever.'

Louisa smiled inside and out. 'Lucky you, so what happened?'

George set off on a rambling description of the graveyard, the church, the luncheon and more. He even started on one of the tales told by Miss Forsythe.

Louisa tried not to be angry. 'George, are you deliberately trying to annoy me?'

'Of course not, my dear girl, but I do love teasing my sweetheart.' She melted and he answered all her questions.

'So we can have the wedding breakfast in one of the station's Royal retiring rooms if we have no more than 16 guests and there are no official objections?'

'You have it in a nutshell, Miss McClaren. Now I have a question for you.'

'Oh yes?'

'How's your wedding dress coming along?'

'That is none of your business, Mr Miracle. And it's bad luck to see the bride in her dress before the wedding.'

'I promise not to peek,' he said and paused. 'But may I look *after* we're married?'

This suggestion with overtones of undressing and intimacy coincided with a fault on the line; it crackled. George wondered if anyone could overhear them.

'As much as you like,' whispered Louisa and George wished their wedding could happen tomorrow.

'And I've another idea about our honeymoon,' he said. 'I need to investigate a bit more but I think you'll like it.'

'Will you be there?' she asked with a straight face. Obviously he couldn't see that but he loved the fact she teased *him* for a change.

'There's no show without Punch,' he said. A train about to arrive forced him to say goodbye with, 'I love you, darling girl,' thrown in.

Sophronia finished her paperwork. 'We'll go together,' she said to her brother. 'If our father's anywhere near awake, seeing both his children will add weight to our cause.'

'I don't like this. What if he sees the letter, hears our threat, panics and dies? What'll we do?'

'So what's your suggestion? Stay here, sit on your backside and hope a miraculous solution falls from the sky?' He said nothing. 'This way we control the situation and make sure the bitch is kicked out without us having to slit her throat. Now come on, we're going.'

The siblings ignored the Scotland Yard recommendation to stay at home, and set off for the hospital. They entered the reception area where the woman behind the desk recognized the twins and prepared to defend the battlements.

'We're here to see our father, Sir Jerome,' said Sophronia.

'I'm so glad you're here,' said the receptionist. 'A nurse told me your father has made a little progress.'

You would expect the stunned twins to be relieved, excited even but Sophronia flew into a rage.

'He's better! Why weren't we told?'

Enoch tried to control his sister and failed. Off she went.

'You agreed to keep us informed of any change. Why haven't you done so? Would you have said anything if we hadn't arrived to check on our beloved pater? You are a disgrace.'

Her world class standard of hypocrisy caused a kerfuffle which attracted two nurses and a doctor.

'Can I help?' asked the medical man.

Sophronia settled a tad, and Lily Bliss would have been proud of her rival's acting skills. Maintaining her rage while being delighted with her father's progress took a fair amount of histrionic expertise.

'I'm sure you don't wish to upset your father, Miss Hamilton-Weir,' explained the doctor. 'Once you've composed yourself, I'll be pleased to take you to him.'

Sophronia's dramatic performance continued as she slipped into a contrite and remorseful person role. 'I'm so sorry. Of course we are both delighted to hear our dear Papa has made a recovery.'

A sort of calm settled. The twins were led to their father's suite and asked to wait outside. The doctor entered before returning. 'Your father is awake and you're welcome to visit him but please remain calm and speak using soft voices.'

'Thank you,' said Enoch studying his sister who celebrated internally with her plan on track to succeed. She found it difficult or rather impossible to say the words, "Thank you".

The doctor led them inside. A nurse hovered in the background under strict instructions to prevent any misbehaviour. The doctor addressed the patient. 'Sir Jerome, you have visitors. Your children are here.'

Seemingly serene, the patient moved his head slowly to see the twins approach from the same side. 'Darling Papa,' oozed his daughter. 'Thank God you are so much better.'

He gave a weak smile and whispered, 'Sophronia.'

Enoch joined in on the charade. 'You look wonderful, Pater.'

Sir Jerome whispered again, 'Enoch.'

The doctor monitored proceedings and noted how the twins displayed their best behaviour. They chatted telling their father mundane news from home. Sir Jerome listened but gave little in response.

Sophronia addressed a nurse. 'Might we have a chair, please?'

The doctor wanted them gone. 'Your father might be less tired tomorrow.'

The daughter knocked that on the head. 'We wish to sit here and hold our dear father's hand. We don't have to speak because our presence alone shows him how much we love and care for him.'

Enoch thought her bizarre behaviour must be seen as a sham. The doctor nodded to the nurse who collected a chair with Enoch helping. Sophronia sat and held her father's hand creating another "doting and dutiful daughter" moment. Unbelievable!

The doctor whispered to the nurse. 'Five minutes,' he said and left.

Enoch stood behind his seated sister. No-one spoke. After a long period of silence, Sophronia turned to the nurse. 'We wish to discuss delicate and personal matters with our father. Would you mind waiting outside please?'

Sophronia used the word *please* more times on this day in this hospital than at any time in the last decade.

'I should stay here,' said the nurse. 'I'll wait quietly in the corner.'

She came under pressure to move when Enoch joined the pantomime and blubbed. 'Oh Pater, please get better.' His act even impressed his sister. On he went. 'We want you to know how much we love you but it's not easy with strangers around.'

The nurse decided. 'I'll be outside in the corridor. Call me if Sir Jerome needs anything.' She left.

Sophronia hissed at Enoch. 'Good act brother but you can stop your bloody nonsense now.'

He did but scrutinizing him, she wondered if in fact he was acting.

She pulled out Rowena's letter, leant in close to her father, fixed her gaze on him and read aloud in a threatening whisper. Her father's face went from expressionless to fear to horror. He lay there, helpless.

Having read the letter, she attacked. 'We know the whole story, Daddy, have known for years.' His worst fears were realized. 'Now a little bird tells us you have recently changed your will to include your bastard daughter as an equal beneficiary to those of your *legitimate* children.'

Enoch joined in. 'You've been a naughty boy, Pater, and we're sure you don't want the world to know about a certain young woman.'

Sir Jerome's brain continued to work well but he found it impossible to think badly of his twins. His opinion of them as evil, selfish, money-grubbing brats couldn't fall any further. He whispered a croaky question. 'What do you want?'

'A return to the status quo,' said Sophronia. 'You change your will again, remove the bastard completely, and we all forget her. It'll be as if she never existed and your pristine reputation will forever remain unsullied.'

After a long pause, the patient spoke. 'I'll need a little time.'

'No you don't,' spat his daughter. 'Summon your solicitor today.'

'Tomorrow,' added Enoch, 'or the day after. A solicitor arriving straight after our visit may give rise to suspicion.'

For once, Sophronia took advice from her brother. 'Good move, Enoch.' She switched back to their father. 'This week, you give your solicitor the appropriate instructions, and once you do and then sign the final will, this letter and any mention of your past will disappear forever.'

'And no tricks, Pater,' said his son. 'We have contacts inside your solicitor's chambers.' Enoch was doing his sister proud.

Again the patient paused. 'All right,' he whispered. 'I agree. But you must keep your word.'

'Of course we will,' said Enoch who couldn't lie straight in bed.

'I change the will so Louisa receives nothing and, in return, you will say nothing.'

Sophronia leant in and kissed his forehead. 'We knew you'd see sense.'

She headed out with Enoch wanting to shake his father's hand but failing to do so as his sister hissed at him. The nervous nurse in the corridor relaxed a tad when Sophronia appeared and smiled.

'Thank you so much, Sister. Our father appreciated having his loved ones tell him how much they care. Goodbye.'

The nurse breathed a massive sigh of relief and hurried to the patient's bedside. 'How are you feeling, Sir Jerome? You are lucky to have such caring children who obviously love you so much.'

He studied her face unable to believe she or anyone could be so hopelessly wrong.

Chapter 14

Life at Whittleton bubbled along. Knowing their SM was leaving, the station staff wondered about his replacement. Would he be a tyrant, a slob, a nitpicker or worse? He might be kind and efficient but surely couldn't be better than the current occupant.

The LNER filled the hole at Wolferton but in so doing created another at Whittleton. The porters and others watched for news.

A trickle of weekend tourists kept the Crabbie afloat mainly through word of mouth. People who enjoyed the Pickling site or fine wine at Ripley Hall told friends and work colleagues and a small but steady stream of passengers kept coming. The weather played a part and a wet and windy day meant the branch travelled on empty.

The following Monday, George asked Fletcher Drum about his new neighbour Freda and her faithful hound, Rufus.

'Oh there are no problems, sir. She is doing a grand job with the tourists whether she has a handful or a dozen.'

'And how is life on the farm?'

'Everything's fine, thank you.'

George worried. He found his new porter to be straightforward and honest but now his behaviour changed becoming strange.

The SM didn't push the matter and again thanked Fletcher for his additional help with the Pickling project.

The Hamilton-Weir twins couldn't stop celebrating their triumph. They'd found a way to remove the interloper without incriminating themselves. Where the Earl of Fakenham failed spectacularly, in a quiet way they did the business sans bloodshed.

And probably best of all, if the pater did survive, he could never reverse the reversal as he knew his darling twins would carry out their threat to denounce him as the knight who sired a child out of wedlock; the man who fathered a bastard.

They dismissed Lily Bliss as a non-starter. If she got involved, they'd give her up to the police or pay her off.

Sir Jerome survived and was eventually discharged returning not to Eaton Square but to his country estate in Cambridgeshire. A live-in nurse joined the philanthropist and his health prospects improved.

Scotland Yard decided any threat to the twins and the Earl no longer appeared relevant and concentrated on other crimes.

Enoch took himself off to the races where again the solicitor's clerk tried it on in the betting ring.

'Not you again,' said Enoch as the obsequious underling greeted or rather groveled to the wealthy young man.

'I faught you'd like to know, guvna, dere's bin anuvver change to your pater's will.'

'Thanks old man, but we're way ahead of you this time.'

Enoch grinned and the clerk saw his chance of another fiver disappear. He touched his cap and vanished. Enoch glowed and couldn't wait to tell his sister the good news. The pater had kept his side of the bargain.

'I'm not sure,' said Sophronia when Enoch returned to London. 'I want to see the changes in print and to be safe I'm guarding the bitch's mother's letter like the Crown jewels.'

Next Wednesday, Freda and Rufus were both in dazzling form. George couldn't believe the change in their behaviour. She bit his head off a fortnight ago having met porter Drum believing him to be a spy sent by the sneaky Whittleton SM. Today she wore a huge smile and, unfortunately for George, came bearing kisses.

'I must thank you, George,' she sparkled. 'Sending Mr Drum to Danny's farm is a stroke of genius.'

'Oh?' replied an intrigued station master. 'But I didn't send him.'

'Rufus loves him too, don't you boy?'

Rufus barked with enthusiasm. George's brain got busy.

Loves him too? What does too mean?

'Keep sending tourists and me, Fletch and Rufus will do the rest.'

Fletch? She's calling him Fletch? Last month he was an evil spy.

George expected an additional kiss and avoided the sloppy smooch being saved by the next London Up sounding its whistle.

'I'm on duty,' he said scampering away and calling. 'Say hello to your sister from me.'

'Good boy, Rufus,' grinned Freda, 'let's go.'

Louisa didn't need to think when choosing her bridesmaid; matron of honour actually. Of course Valerie hoped to be chosen and the women hugged and both shed a tear when Louisa popped the question.

Lord Carruthers came in on the end of their embrace. 'Oh yes and what scheme are you two planning this time?'

They gave him the news and he expressed his delight. The identity of George Miracle's best man danced around the minds of all three Londoners without anyone mentioning the subject.

Louisa broke the silence. 'Oh, and I've something to give you,' she said producing an envelope and handing it to George.

'Oh no, it's not your resignation notice,' he said with false sadness. He opened the envelope and produced a small white card, a wedding invitation. He showed it to his wife. 'I'll need to check my diary,' he said and Valerie gave him a friendly slap.

'I've already asked my parents to come and stay to mind the children although little George will be mortified to learn his darling nanny, Lou-Lou, will not be coming back,' said Valerie.

Sadness filled the house. Wee George's parents accepted Louisa as a member of their family as did their children. Now she would soon be gone forever.

'You're going to be a tough act to follow, Miss McClaren,' said George. 'You haven't a sister I suppose?' Goodness, what a sick joke.

George Miracle decided to ask his namesake in Hampstead to be his best man. Their strange meeting on Liverpool Street station ten years ago in 1914 marked the beginning of a remarkable friendship with a murder, war wounds and an amputation thrown in for good measure. The fact George and Valerie asked the station master to be their son's godfather demonstrated their love and respect for the man.

Lord Carruthers expressed his delight in being asked and matters fell into place. The future bride and groom settled on the list of invitees without argument. The only doubtful guest, the groom's sister, Emily Culpepper nee Miracle, was with child and due to give birth a month before the big day. Emily was adamant.

'I'm not going to miss your wedding, George even if I have to feed the little mite in the church as you say "I do".' George believed her.

All that remained undecided was the honeymoon location, the transfer of goods to Wolferton, the purchase of furniture and confirmation of the venue of the wedding breakfast.

Daisy put her foot down. 'If there are only 14 guests, I'll do the catering and there's an end to it. I've seen the station house and I'll go there on the Friday before and start baking. It'll be my wedding gift to you both.'

What could George say? Louisa purred with happiness.

With a wedding set for 12 noon on, hopefully, a beautiful summer's day, guests could arrive in plenty of time with most travelling by train. Harry Saward and his wife would leave the station house a few days before the wedding allowing Daisy and Louisa and her mother, and the Carruthers to settle in on the Friday beforehand. As for the groom, George was told to stay well out of the way.

The major unresolved issue was who would give away the bride. Louisa's father died decades ago, or so she thought. Her real father rested, recovering in Cambridgeshire at his country estate. Louisa knew who she wanted but struggled because of her fiancé's choice of best man.

She raised the subject with Valerie. 'Is it silly? Is it against church policy? Lord Carruthers has been so kind to me, you both have, and I would love to have him walk me down the aisle.'

'Ask the rector. If he's happy, George can accompany you to the altar before sliding sideways to hold the hand of the nervous groom.'

They hugged, and after a phone call to St Peter's in Wolferton, George Carruthers happily agreed and George Miracle reckoned it to be the grandest of grand plans.

The appointment of the new Whittleton station master set tongues wagging. Oswald Laughter was a man who, once met was never forgotten. His name matched his personality. Smiling, immaculately attired, he spent his days as a relief SM on the Great Northern Railway which, like George's GER, became part of the LNER.

But after years of constantly moving to relieve or replace ill or deceased SMs, Oswald's wife put her foot down, desiring a place to call their own for the rest of her husband's career. They reckoned the village of Whittleton sounded perfect. It was. In his mid-fifties,

Oswald suited the village and the village suited him. Mrs Laughter loved it. Once appointed, Oswald rang and arranged a visit.

George told his colleagues about their new boss's arrival and expected them to treat him like they treated every visitor. They did.

Should Oswald be told about Freda and her amorous greetings, and about one of Oswald's porters the part-time farmer, and the elderly local, the Capability Brown of the platform's gardens?

George decided to let the new boy discover people himself.

Oswald arrived with Mrs Laughter and both expressed delight with the station and the station house.

For George, it was time to move on.

His mother, Connie, danced with happiness. Her marriage to the loving John Beckwith warmed her heart. To follow her wedding with the arrival of her first grandchild, a boy, John named after Emily's late father, meant Connie shed even more tears of happiness.

She decided to tell George in person. Her husband drove her home from the hospital leaving Emily and the newborn to be fussed over by her husband and his family.

Connie remembered a recent time when she walked along the ramp to the Up platform at Whittleton to be accosted and kidnapped by dangerous armed criminals. That nightmare faded as she revelled in the delight of her daughter's baby.

From the Down platform, George spotted his mother, called and headed across the tracks. He feared there might be sad, even terrible news but drawing closer, his mother's face beamed.

'It's a boy, George, and named after your Da.'

They embraced and staff, who knew of the impending birth, quietly celebrated. Gordon, Madge and Bobby all added their best wishes and Monty bounded down the steps of the signal-box holding a bottle of wine from the cellar of the adjacent manor house.

'Let's be wetting the baby's head, boss,' he called crossing the tracks.' Connie took her leave with George hoping to maintain his good service record by encouraging his members of staff to abstain from consuming alcohol, not only while on duty, but on railway premises to boot. He managed to succeed, just.

The family Miracle enjoyed a time of much happiness. The matriarch re-married, the daughter married and delivered of a child, and the son, the young SM about to marry and take up a new position at a highly desirable station which served members of the Royal Family. This chapter of the Miracle Family story was a book in itself.

The next day, George received a letter in answer to questions he asked regarding his planned honeymoon. The details made his heart beat faster. He wondered what his "sweetheart" would think of the destination and how and when he should tell her.

The rector at St Peter's invited them to a rehearsal of sorts in the Wolferton church on the Saturday before their big day.

George and Daisy set off from Whittleton and collected Louisa in London. Daisy tagged along because she wanted to double-check the kitchen facilities at Wolferton in preparation for her role as wedding breakfast caterer. The trio arrived at Wolferton where Harry Saward greeted them in his usual cheerful manner.

'This time next week, will you be so relaxed?' he teased them.

Their banter overflowed with fun before all three visitors set off; Daisy to Mrs Saward in the station house kitchen, and the bridal couple to the church for their rehearsal.

During the rehearsal but without irreverence, Mr Attwood joked and play acted and the couple loved the experience.

'I see your best man is giving away the bride,' said the rector. 'I think that'll keep everyone on their toes including the jolly priest.'

The rehearsal ended with all in good spirits. 'I'll see you in church,' smiled the rector and the couple headed back to the station.

Louisa joined Daisy in what would soon be the Miracles' new home while George returned to the station. He chatted with a porter until Harry emerged from his office wearing a serious expression.

'Confirmation message: His Majesty is on the next train.'

George panicked but the other staff took the news in their stride.

'The King is coming to Wolferton?' he asked, stunned.

Harry explained. 'There are times when a visit is not for public consumption. We believe the Queen Mother is poorly and her son comes to see her without any fanfare.'

George observed the station staff remaining calm. To them it would be another train and its passengers and any goods would be attended to as per the usual routine.

Of course that wasn't true in every detail because members of the Royal Family were given exclusive use of the Royal retiring-rooms and preparations were in place to have the Royal motor car and its driver allowed access to the side of the station.

'Can I help?' asked George, 'or should I take my leave?'

Harry encouraged George to stay. 'Please remain and observe, sir. This could be excellent training for what you'll encounter many times at Wolferton.'

Excitement gripped the young SM. He heard the train long before he saw it. The car from Sandringham arrived. The train pulled in and the King and Queen were the only Royals but an equerry, a lady-in-waiting and military personnel were the first to alight. Harry waited till their Majesties stepped from the train. He moved forward and bowed his head with a simple movement. The King spoke to the SM.

'Good day, Harry. I'm sorry we've arrived with such short notice.'

'Not at all, sir,' said Harry in a respectful but relaxed way.

'So when is it you're off to enjoy your retirement?'

'Three weeks, Your Majesty.'

'Any word on the new station master?'

'Yes, he's here today, sir.' He turned and saw George turning white. Harry beckoned with a subtle movement and the non-royal George, quietly petrified, stepped forward with his hip giving him gyp. 'Your Majesty, Stationmaster Mr George Miracle.'

The non-royal George stood to attention and bowed his head.

'Trouble with your hip, Mr Miracle?' asked the King.

'No, Your Majesty; a minor war wound.'

'You served?'

'I did, sir.'

'Where and with whom?'

'In France, sir, with the London Regiment.'

'Good show. Well best of luck to you both, gentlemen.'

The SMs nodded as the King turned and followed his wife into the retiring-room and from there into the yard and to their car. It soon swept out heading along the two and a bit miles to Sandringham.

George glanced at Harry who smiled. 'Now young man,' said the retiring SM, 'how did you find your first Royal arrival?'

George thought it went well before discovering he was shaking.

Chapter 15

Louisa purred. On her first Wolferton visit she found the station house overwhelming; now even more so. This trip she explored upstairs and all the rooms, cupboards and quirky spaces filled her head with ideas. The views from the ground floor windows were interesting but those from upstairs were breathtaking. She saw the station, signal-box and tracks and reckoned George would be thrilled to live here. From another window she saw the church.

In the kitchen, Daisy chatted with Mrs Saward and knew she could produce a wedding breakfast to make her favourite station master and his bride more than happy. Louisa joined in and the three women were rabbiting away over tea and cake when George appeared.

'Oh George, it's the best station house in the world and Mrs Saward is so kind and helpful,' said Louisa beaming.

'Wonderful kitchen, George,' added Daisy. 'We've enjoyed a cracking time. What have you been up to?'

'Not much but I did manage a brief chat with the King.'

Silence crashed on the kitchen floor. Mrs Saward took no notice being used to Royalty in the decades she'd lived at Wolferton.

Louisa knew her fiancé often teased her so politely but firmly reprimanded him. 'You shouldn't make jokes about Royalty, George.'

'Hear, hear,' said Daisy.

'I agree,' he said and Louisa and Daisy's jaws dropped as one.

'You met the King?' gasped Daisy.

'I did,' replied George. 'It was not an official visit but as the Queen Mother is unwell, their Majesties have come to visit the dear lady at Sandringham.'

More deep breathing followed from Daisy and Louisa with the housekeeper muttering, 'What a day.'

George checked his watch. 'Our train is due in twelve minutes, ladies.' He held out a hand to the SM's wife. 'Thank you for all your help, Mrs Saward. Your kindness is very much appreciated.'

His female visitors agreed. 'You're most welcome Mr Miracle and I'll be here to help Miss Woods with her baking on your big day.'

The happy departure left all three visitors buzzing. When you add love to the mix, life veered ever closer towards being blissful.

Travelling back to London, the women were desperate for any detail about George's meeting with the King. Their voices were low due to the other passengers. Gossiping about the King would never do.

In London, with a few minutes before the next Whittleton train, George wanted to be alone with his sweetheart. This was the last time they would see each other before their big day. Daisy kissed Louisa and left the couple alone.

'You still haven't told me about our honeymoon, Mr Miracle and what's happening with Daisy? Is she coming with us to Wolferton?'

'I'm sorry, darling girl. Thank goodness you're in charge of the wedding. I've found a delightful cottage in a village down the line from Wolferton.' She smiled. 'We can dine in the pub and go for walks in the countryside and to the beach.'

'Sounds wonderful.'

'You won't need much in the way of outfits.'

She wondered. *Is he teasing, being practical or possibly being saucy?* 'Does your mother know you make those suggestions?'

He smiled at her response and hugged her. She pulled back.

'But what are we doing about your favourite housekeeper? We need to make a decision, George. I know you feel an obligation to take care of her but what am I going to do if she's there to cook, clean, shop and perform all those tasks you expect your wife to do?'

Shame dogged him having let the matter drag on unresolved.

'I promise I will sort this and you will be happy with the result.'

They smiled at one another. A locomotive whistle sounded, George checked his watch and kissed his girl.

'I can't wait till we're married, my darling.' She reckoned her heart would burst. He escorted her off the platform and to the car driven by the Tudor Court driver/gardener. George waved before rushing back with a worried Daisy thinking they'd miss their train.

The trip to Whittleton saw both passengers have difficulty speaking; George plunging into deep despair. To upset his new wife would be terrible. But to give Daisy her notice seemed equally so, even worse.

Daisy broke the ice. 'George, I need to tell you something.' He worried, dreading her next sentence. 'I won't be coming with you and Louisa to live in Wolferton.'

He squirmed with a mixture of pain and relief. He went to speak.

'Please let me finish,' she said. 'We've talked about this and you know my feelings. Young newly-weds need a housekeeper like a railway needs a derailment.' Her comment impressed him. She pointed at him her finger close to his face. 'You don't owe me anything and anyway, I have somewhere else to live.'

George felt his pulse accelerate. 'How marvellous, Daisy.' He paused wanting to know the details.

'I've accepted an offer from a gentleman to become a live-in housekeeper. It's someone local, a person you know.'

She teased him dragging out the identity of the mystery man. George's mind ran through a laundry list of Whittleton residents.

It couldn't be ...

She put him out of his misery. 'It's Mr Gardiner.' She saw George's smile erupt. 'When I heard how he struggled after his wife died, my heart ached for him. When you announced you were leaving, I asked him if he would like to have a housekeeper and he started to cry.' George wanted to do the same.

'That's the most wonderful news, Daisy. I couldn't be happier for you and Horace.'

'And Melville. Apparently the dog's given me his seal of approval.'

George smiled again and kissed her cheek. The rest of the trip home contained non-stop banter of wedding breakfast suggestions and Daisy possibly becoming a bit of a gardener.

Connie became the travelling grandmother visiting both her son and grandson. She mothered the little one to bits. She mothered the big one too.

George worried about his suit for the big day. His late father and uncle were smaller than George and there was no such thing as a demob suit after the Great War. He possessed his SM uniform and a dinner suit courtesy of the Whittleton scribe, Septimus Oldmeadow.

What to do? Well speak of the devil, who should appear but the novelist himself. Septimus called at the station house with what he called his suit for weddings and funerals.

'I know you don't own a decent suit, young man, and my dinner suit proved such a hit, I thought you'd like another redundant outfit.'

George stood there gobsmacked. 'This is too much, sir,' he protested in vain and the garment quickly moved to his mother's new abode where she worked her magic.

Daisy moved her few belongings to Horace Gardiner's cottage, and Oswald Laughter and his wife moved their belongings to the Whittleton station house. Time didn't stand still, it fairly raced towards the big day.

Wednesday morning dawned, George's last in Whittleton. He feared Freda's farewell. He started work here as a mere porter when they first met and together, they'd enjoyed a few adventures over the years. Would this be one heck of an emotional farewell?

The Crabbie pulled in with Freda and Rufus. Surprisingly, she didn't wave or call and Rufus took a vow of barking silence.

There's a problem, thought George and worried.

'The top of the morning to you, George,' she said greeting him on the Up platform. Her usual full-on kiss transformed into a polite peck on the cheek and even Rufus didn't jump but nudged the SM.

Something is definitely up, thought George saying good morning to both the farmer and her hound.

'So you'll be wed on the weekend, George.'

'You're right, Freda; I'm on my final week of freedom.'

She didn't laugh or respond but instead became serious. Now George switched from worry to anxiety.

'I admit I made a mistake, George, about your porter the spy.'

Now the penny dropped. *She's discovered Fletcher's a decent chap and helpful.* But no, George got it wrong and hopelessly so.

'So he's able to help you even from Danny Wight's farm.'

'Oh he's a help all right but not from Danny's place. He's moved in with me, George, and we're in love.' George appeared flabbergasted only because he *was* flabbergasted. 'Even Rufus likes him, don't you boy?' The wolfhound barked with delight.

Rufus thought this new bloke was a bit of all right; not as good as George but okay. It did mean the dog needed a new position on the bed at night but hey, what's a new part of the bed between friends?

'He's up early to feed the animals on Danny's farm to make sure he's on time for his shifts at Whittleton.'

When the grinning dog and mistress left, George shook his head. Daisy has a new home and Horace and Melville a new housekeeper, and Fletch too has a new home, and Freda and Rufus have a new man about the house. *I should move stations more often.*

Oswald agreed to start work on the Thursday giving George the day to visit people in and around the village to say his goodbyes. Calling on Horace thrilled the departing SM.

'I hope you don't mind me pinching your wonderful housekeeper, Mr Miracle,' he said with a twinkle in his eye.

'I couldn't be happier, sir,' replied George, 'and not having to prepare your own meals means you'll have more time to spend with your gardens at the station.' Their farewell handshake was firm.

George's visit to the home of Septimus Oldmeadow, he of suit-giving fame, went as would be expected. The novelist and limerick-writer produced a jug of his famous home brew and George broke his non-imbibing routine as a final gesture of their friendship.

'I'll be sure to send you a photo of your suit, sir,' said George, 'and I'll change for my honeymoon so my mother can deliver your goods the next day.'

No, no, no,' he said. 'It's a gift, sir. I've been having a clean out and I'll not need the suit any more. You keep it for your next meeting with the King at Sandringham.'

George stared at the man he met on his first day at Whittleton.

'That's awfully kind of you, Mr Oldmeadow. Are you sure?'

'Most definitely and here's a parting gift.' He handed George a novel. 'It's hot off the press, my new novel which I've signed and,' he turned a page, 'is dedicated to my favourite station master.'

Struck dumb, George saw his name printed on the dedication page. Struggling to speak, he studied a grinning Septimus.

'You could read it on your honeymoon,' he said expanding his grin. George joined the smiling finding it hard to describe his feelings.

'I'm deeply honoured and this is extremely generous of you, sir. I shall treasure this book for the rest of my life.'

'Ah, but will you read it?' teased Septimus.

'Most definitely I will but perhaps not on my honeymoon.'

Now their shared laughter became loud and long.

Septimus became serious. 'It took a youthful man to make me see that worrying about what people think of me and my work is a waste of time and energy. You taught me that, Mr Miracle, and how I must be proud of what I've done and should push on with my writing and let others take it or leave it. Life's too short to worry about critics.'

He held out his hand. George moved the book to his left hand and the men shook with feeling and strength.

'Thank you again, sir, for your friendship and if you're ever invited to Sandringham, I'll be delighted to welcome you to Wolferton.'

Septimus stayed by his open door and waved as George set off for his final walk along the Whittleton High Street.

He returned to the station now being run by his replacement. He wanted to say a personal goodbye to all his colleagues, the men and Audrey, the one woman who worked for him for one day, but knew how tricky it could be with the Crabbie crew out and about.

He wandered up the platform ramp knowing there wasn't a train for eleven minutes. He stepped through the gate and saw a group of railwaymen, and one former railwaywoman, gathered obviously in a pre-arranged meeting. As one, they applauded.

A few passengers were gathered waiting for their train and they joined the applause. In the crowd, George saw Stephen Fitzsimons and his mother, and Mrs Monty, stain-remover extraordinaire and wife of the signalman. Horace Gardiner and his housekeeper and dog were there, seated and puffing. Freda and Rufus were there standing beside the new porter. Eric the retired porter smiled for the first time this year. George couldn't speak for the second time that morning.

In a touch of irony, the person appointed as spokesperson turned out to be one Gordon Littleton, the porter who once worked to ruin the youngest station master in England. George reckoned Gordon singing his praises might well be his, George's greatest achievement.

'On behalf of all your colleagues, sir, we want to thank you for putting up with us for all these years and to wish you and your wife ...'

'He's not married till Saturdee,' yelled Monty which prompted a laugh all round. Gordon continued.

'We wish you and your good lady all the best. You've kept the branch line from closing and turned our station into a place of horticultural beauty.'

'Hear, hear,' came from many lips.

'We weren't sure what to choose but we hope this small gift will remind you of your time here at Whittleton.'

Gordon handed over a well-wrapped gift as the resultant applause became loud and lingered. Silence settled as a clearly emotional George knew he needed to reply. He started with a regular refrain.

'I think the next Up is due in five minutes.'

'Four,' said Audrey which made people laugh.

'Thank you, Gordon, for your kind words and everyone for this gift. I'm keen to know what's inside.' He paused. 'I know I've been extremely lucky to be the SM here at Whitty.'

The long-serving members of staff liked his use of their adopted station name, Whitty and the cat in Pip's arms looked at the speaker.

'I've enjoyed every single day working here, with a few rare exceptions.' A murmur of laughter sounded. 'I think my strongest feeling right now is one of sadness. I'm looking forward to my next post but leaving this station with its ... unusual branch line makes me sad. Thank you for your friendship and professional work ethic.' He paused. 'Goodness, that's a big word for me.' More laughter began. 'And I'll always have fond memories of the people I've met and worked with here at Whittleton.'

More applause broke out and only stopped when SM Laughter called. 'Incoming train, stand clear.'

Staff broke away to perform their railway tasks. Visitors moved to George and said their farewells. He found himself shaking hands and hugging folk while juggling his farewell gift. Eventually he broke free and walked the length of a cricket pitch to the station house.

Opening the present gave him great delight. Bobby, a.k.a. John Smith the fireman on the Crabbie, painted a marvellous picture of the Whittleton Station with its gardens in full bloom. Along the bottom of the picture were three postage stamp size drawings of the little 0-6-0 locomotive and the station/halt at Crabbtree and Pickling.

Chapter 16

The weather did the right thing for George and Louisa's wedding. No wind or rain proved a godsend with sunny Norfolk skies smiling. A few clouds hung about wanting to see the bride arrive.

Word had whistled around Wolferton about their much-loved and long-serving station master retiring with his replacement, a young chap called George Miracle, about to marry in their local church.

A few tongues wagged. 'Why marry in Wolverton?' 'His bride is not from around here.' 'He hasn't even started work.'

Such comments created a bit of interest and attracted a crowd of curious onlookers. Of course the bride is the centre of attention but in this case, locals also wanted to take a peek at their new SM.

Louisa, Lord and Lady Carruthers, Rowena and Daisy all arrived the day before the wedding in His Lordship's Rolls Royce Cabriolet. Mrs Saward welcomed them to the station house. She and her husband moved their personal belongings to their holiday cottage, now their new home near Old Hunstanton.

Valerie and Louisa retired upstairs to rehearse a dress-the-bride routine. Daisy, Rowena and Mrs Saward were busy in the kitchen and Lord Carruthers went exploring wandering around the village.

The groom would normally spend the night before the wedding with his best man and possibly male friends. George spent his last night with the Liverpool Street SM, Jack Rogers.

When Jack discovered George's wedding venue and that his best man, the chauffeur, would be in Wolferton on the night before the nuptials leaving George alone, Jack insisted George spend Friday night with the London SM and his wife in their Epping Forest bungalow.

'We'll have a slap-up meal, celebrate your success and make sure you catch the train to Wolferton in plenty of time in the morning.

George quietly rejoiced. He could have found accommodation with his mother or somewhere in Wolferton but with his bride a short walk away, not being in Wolferton appealed. After a grand evening, next morning George with his suit and suitcase stood on the correct Down platform in plenty of time for the rail journey to Wolferton.

He arrived with time to spare. He knew the station was half a mile from the church, and provided the weather agreed, he and his namesake could stroll and be on time for the service.

Mind you his best man was on a sort of double date, and while he could keep the groom on the straight and narrow and ensure his safe arrival at the church, Lord Carruthers would later need to desert his pal in order to walk the bride down the aisle.

Both George Carruthers and SM Saward were there to greet the highly-strung husband-in-waiting. As the train drew ever closer to Wolferton, the groom's pulse and sweat glands moved into overdrive. Having thought and worried about derailments, delays, locomotive breakdowns and accidents, he breathed normally when his carriage finally stopped. He chose the last carriage to be as far from any wandering smoke, soot and cinders even if his suit was in a carry case stretched out on the seat in his compartment.

'See, the Conqu'ring Hero comes!' said Lord Carruthers taking George's case and shaking his hand at the same time.

'May I see your ticket please sir,' said Harry Saward with a grin and a proffered hand.

'Good morning, gentleman,' said George feeling his pulse put on its brakes. 'Train on time I see.'

'Bloody station master,' said the best man. 'Stop thinking railways, George, and concentrate on wedding vows and your honeymoon.'

They crossed the tracks and Harry led them into the Royal retiring-room. 'I'll fetch you a brew, gentlemen,' he said but stopped. 'I think I should advise you the King and Queen will be arriving from Sandringham for a return to London this afternoon. I'd keep the matter under your hat to discourage your guests from wanting to pop outside to observe.' He smiled and left.

'Well Mr Miracle, you certainly don't do things by half, and how are you my friend?' asked the best man.

'I'm not sure,' said the SM. 'I'm between nervous and excited. Is that normal?'

'You're never normal, George,' said Carruthers attending to the groom's wedding suit, checking for any bits of fluff or dirt. 'My dear wife and your dear mother have both given me strict instructions on how to be a valet.'

The groom wandered around the room set up for the wedding breakfast. 'What a marvellous building. I wonder how many station masters have dressed and celebrated their wedding in such a setting.'

'I reckon you're the first,' said the current SM entering with a tray of tea and homemade biscuits courtesy of Mrs Saward.

'Thank you, sir,' said his replacement. 'You and your wife have made my move to your station as smooth and as friendly as could be.'

Harry became mother, and the wedding duo helped themselves to milk, sugar and biscuits.

George reminisced. 'I found it emotional leaving Whittleton after about one decade. How must you feel after *four* decades in the one place?'

Harry nodded. 'Yes it's been a big part of my family's life. We've raised our three girls here and been a huge part of the village.'

'Not to mention handling important visitors,' added Carruthers.

'Of course,' said Harry, 'but it's the people and the produce which most need your attention. I think I'd be teaching your grannie to suck eggs if I tried teaching you that, Mr Miracle.' He stepped forward to shake the groom's hand. 'I have a train to clear and I'll be wishing you well for the service and am keen to welcome you and your bride back here for a slap-up luncheon. Good luck, young man.'

He left and the best man indicated the suit with the name Oldmeadow on the inside jacket pocket.

'It's time for your costume change, my friend. I have the matching flowers for our button holes.'

They donned their outfits, gave each other the once over and set off walking to the church. The weather gods smiled upon Wolferton.

They reached the lychgate at St Peter's. A few locals were there to watch with the women keen to see the bride's dress. 'Which one's the groom?' asked a local within earshot of the Georges times two.

'I think he's limping and called George,' said another local.

The men exchanged a grin. Into the churchyard limped the chums with the SM entertaining a hundred and one thoughts. He whispered. 'Where are the ladies right now?'

'If you mean your bride and the matron of honour, I should say definitely not inside the church. They'll have a spy in the station house who will have seen us head off.'

'They won't walk though will they?'

'Hardly, it'll be a carriage ride for the girls.'

The gents reached the open front door of the church to be greeted by two members of the congregation acting as ushers. One would have been enough. Organ music drifted through the building.

'Good morning, gentlemen,' said the male usher smiling. 'Which one of you is George?'

The men smiled at one another. Lord Carruthers explained. 'You might need to ask a different question; we're both George.'

The ushers hesitated. Marriages in St Peter's Wolferton usually involved a local even two and stewards would know at least one of the bridal party.

'Then may we know which one of you is the groom?'

''Tis I,' said the station master.

'Welcome,' said the female steward. 'If you'd both care to follow me, I'll show you the way.'

The two visitors remained where they stood. 'More problems, I'm afraid,' said Lord Carruthers and explained his dual roles.

The confused volunteers finally understood allowing the groom and female usher to head down the aisle.

The bridegroom turned back and called. 'The rings my Lord?'

The best man tapped his jacket pocket. 'All under control, my friend.'

As George followed the usher along the aisle, his heartrate accelerated. New experiences bring their own challenges but this was unique. Seated at the front on George's right were members of his family who turned to smile at him.

His mother and step-father, his sister and her husband and their baby, currently sleeping, were there, and so too sat Daisy with a hat defying gravity and beside her, Horace Gardiner positively beaming.

Where is Melville? Of course, their friendly neighbour would be taking care of the beloved pooch. Why am I thinking about dogs?

George panicked when he saw Daisy before remembering Mrs Saward would be keeping an eye on all the baking they did yesterday. Daisy wasn't going to miss this wedding for anything.

He turned to his left and saw Rowena McClaren, his future mother-in-law, alone, smiling and unaware her letter had been intercepted. The bride's father rested in his manor house near Cambridge totally unaware today was the wedding. George perked up as a familiar face appeared from a side aisle. Septimus Oldmeadow, dressed as a dandy, slipped into the front pew beside the bride's mother. He saw her sitting alone and chose to keep her company. Septimus grinned at George and introduced himself to Rowena.

The groom tried to forget the guests and concentrate on his role. Before he could continue worrying, the rector appeared, all smiles.

'Ah, the bridegroom himself,' he said offering his hand.

'Good morning, sir,' said George in a croaky voice.

'Thank you, Rachel,' said the rector to the usher who smiled and left. 'This way,' whispered the Reverend Attwood and led George to a small room full of hymn books and choristers' robes.

'I'm yet to meet a groom who didn't suffer from nerves right before the ceremony.' He handed George a small glass of sherry. 'This may help settle your nerves.'

George didn't think about the contents but thanked the clergyman and drank.

'Better?' asked the priest.

'Much,' said George.

Rachel returned and knocked on the door. 'The bride has arrived, Rector.'

'Thank you, Rachel.' She left and George's heart took up drumming. 'Do you remember the piece of advice I gave you and Louisa when last we met?'

The groom's mind was a bit of a jumble but within the fog of various issues he remembered. 'Could it be to enjoy the moment?'

'Exactly,' replied the rector and ushered George into the church.

The organist stopped playing. George moved to his designated place, the rector to his. From a mirror, the organist saw the bride stepping from the porch and went for the all-stops-out performance.

George didn't rehearse this next bit. *Do I stay staring at the altar, or do I turn to greet my sweetheart?* The pressure kept building. He saw the priest smiling but not at him. *He's watching Louisa.* George couldn't help himself not turn, at least a little.

He saw Louisa and George with Valerie following. His excitement meter began firing but so too did the stares and gasps of many people in the church. The bride was a hit; no, a huge hit. George was shocked. When he entered a few minutes ago only a handful of people sat in the pews with two on the bride's side. Now there were dozens.

Where did they come from? The locals turned out in force.

Louisa arrived, turned and handed her flowers to Valerie. The bride's dress and headgear were stunningly beautiful as was she. George could hear his mother's voice from years ago.

'It's rude to stare, George.'

He didn't care. He stared.

'Hello,' he whispered and she smiled.

The first sound George became aware of was silence as the organist stopped playing. The congregation made sounds with dresses rustling and males coughing. Having rushed a fag before entering a church always gave a chap a ticklish throat.

The rector introduced the standard service with, "Dearly beloved, we are gathered here ..." et cetera. He knew the best man doubled as father of the bride so eased into the, "Who gives this woman to this man" bit and George Carruthers metaphorically handed his wife's companion to his best friend before moving behind and thus beside the groom ready to perform his second task.

To say the service went smoothly would be an understatement. George's nephew behaved superbly making his grandmother happy beyond measure. Both her children were married and settled and the future with more grandchildren seemed endlessly promising.

After the, "I now pronounce you man and wife" part, George took his time in lifting Louisa's veil with every eye, except the baby's, transfixed on the couple. Their kiss proved so delicate and touching, without hesitation the congregation applauded.

'It's the nicest wedding I've seen in our church,' said the male usher to Rachel. Obviously she agreed quietly dabbing a tear.

The organist encouraged the instrument to sing as the happy couple signed the register and made their way back along the aisle. George wondered if they were now on an Up or Down train.

He reckoned his current feeling must be better than going to heaven. He wallowed in pride feeling excited, delighted and nervous, and eagerly anticipated the future. Being in charge of an important and well-known station meant a great deal but marrying the woman he loved with all his heart topped the lot, it being simply the best.

Connie and John Beckwith were in charge of the baby enabling Emily to lead those with rice and confetti to start sprinkling. It can be difficult to rehearse events once a couple wed and here was a perfect example. The newlyweds greeted guests as a couple and individually and a traffic policeman, if available, would have been overworked. Eventually with photos and congratulations complete, the bride and groom made it through the lychgate, to the road and their carriage. Cars lined up to transport guests. The villagers walked home.

The biggest buzz for the interested locals was the venue for the wedding breakfast. Older folk knew about luncheons at the station for Royal shooting parties but few remembered it as a wedding venue.

Apart from the glowing newlyweds, the venue became the fascinating drawcard. No-one in this party ever attended a wedding breakfast in a station before let alone the Royal Station and what a celebration it was.

As locomotives snorted and sneezed arriving and departing on both platforms and passengers boarded and detrained, George and Louisa Miracle and their guests enjoyed a wonderful meal, locally prepared and cooked. The speeches from the two men called George were ideal with laughter and tears produced in equal and copious amounts. Only two toasts remained; the loyal toast and the toast to the happy couple.

Lord Carruthers completed his speech and proposed the loyal toast. Guests stood and raised their glass to the Monarch.

Guests sat. The best man prepared for the toast to the bride and groom. Harry Saward slipped inside and whispered in the groom's ear. He turned pale and beckoned to his best man. He too turned pale. The two men whispered and Louisa and Valerie could see but hear only snippets of their hushed conversation.

Louisa couldn't believe terrible news would appear without warning and spoil, even ruin the best day of her life.

The bride and matron of honour stared at their respective husband wanting to know the details of their concern.

Lord Carruthers rose and tapped his glass. The room fell silent. The best man lost his previous cheerful countenance and turned solemn. Why?

'Ladies and gentlemen, may I ask you to be upstanding and raise your glass for the loyal toast.' A buzz erupted. Everyone stood.

He's repeating himself.

With glasses being held by the confused guests, Harry Saward opened the door to the retiring-room whereupon an Equerry entered, noted all were upstanding and announced, 'His Majesty the King.'

George V, King of the United Kingdom and the British Dominions, and Emperor of India strode into the room. The gasps were audible.

His Majesty gave a short nod and spoke. 'Please be seated.'

The company sat and there were now two items you could cut in his grandmother's retiring-room; the wedding cake baked by Miss Daisy Woods formerly of Norwich, Cricklewood and now of Whittleton, and the silence in the Royal retiring-room at Wolferton station in Norfolk.

The King spoke as if with friends. 'Last week I met the new Wolferton station master and have since discovered both he and his best man, Lord Carruthers, are former soldiers who served their country with distinction, both being wounded in battle. I wish to publicly acknowledge their bravery and more importantly to congratulate Mr and Mrs George Miracle and to wish them a long and happy marriage.'

Being a station master and thus always well prepared, Harry handed the King a glass of wine. His Majesty raised the glass and spoke in a louder voice.

'To the bride and groom,' he said and everyone, apart from the newlyweds, repeated the words.

Without further ado, the Monarch handed his glass to the current SM, turned and departed. His train stood waiting being held for possibly the only passenger who could cause such a delay.

Inside the retiring-room, silence and shock vanished to be replaced by the sound of a thousand bees going about their business.

George glanced at Louisa. She spoke first. 'All this grandeur isn't necessary, Mr Miracle. I told you a small cottage would be perfect.'

He grinned, leant in and kissed her while the hubbub continued growing ever louder.

Chapter 17

George and Louisa loved their honeymoon. They were two young, healthy lovers having the best (so far) time of their lives. One night as Louisa snuggled into her husband, he thought of the time his brother-in-law asked for advice on making love. He told his wife the story.

She laughed so much George worried if he'd done the wrong thing. He found her reaction delightful and disturbing in equal amounts. 'Were you speaking from experience?' she asked.

'What experience?' he replied. 'I survived the war and never went anywhere near those French towns where certain ladies offered their services.'

'I'm not sure I believe you, George Miracle.'

He pretended to be mightily shocked. 'On my honeymoon of all occasions, I discover my wife doesn't trust me suggesting I'm a liar.'

'But you seem to know so much about making love, and are so good at it, I find it hard to believe you have no prior experience.'

He saw her laughing eyes and knew she'd joined the teasing club. She squealed as, beneath the blankets, he tickled her and they stopped talking settling instead for making other interesting sounds.

Their rented honeymoon cottage stood only a short walk from Snettisham on the King's Lynn to Hunstanton line two stops from Wolferton. Months ago, George toyed with taking his bride on a trip on an LNER train all the way to Scotland and on to the newly-opened Gleneagles Hotel. Apart from the expense even with free rail travel, he realized they would travel for hours and be changing trains whereas in this close-to-home cottage, they could spend most of their honeymoon discovering one another a bit better; even much better.

They went for walks, caught the train to Hunstanton where George introduced himself to the SM, and strolled along the beach front eating ice-cream and basking in the sunshine.

Louisa wanted to cook at least one proper meal and George worried she might set herself too high a standard and possibly fail. He need not have worried. The superb cook, Rowena McClaren, had taught her daughter well.

'What a fool I am wanting Daisy to be our housekeeper in Wolferton when all along my wife is a brilliant cook.' She kissed him. 'And you're a much better kisser than Daisy.' She proved it.

Louisa confessed. 'I must admit I expected we would have our first disagreement over Miss Woods. I thought, what does he expect me to do while he is away playing trains?'

'Playing trains?' he protested. 'Now *that* is our first disagreement.'

She ignored his pretence. 'I would become a kept woman needing a lady's companion to help me dress and fetch my tea in the front parlour.'

'You'd make a beautiful kept woman,' he said being sincere.

'Don't change the subject and I'm still having trouble believing these new events have actually happened.'

'What new events?'

'Our first home is like a mansion, my husband is in charge of a magnificent station, and how many couples have the King of England propose a toast to them at their wedding? I mean, what else have you hidden up your sleeve, George Miracle?'

'I'm sorry to say, absolutely nothing, my darling girl. Lots of trains of course and the occasional Royal visitor and prime minister but about the only other important arrival will be our first child.'

Talk about a conversation stopper. She held his hand.

'We haven't talked about children,' she said.

'I said child not children. Why, how many are you planning to have?'

She loved the way he teased her while always remaining serious beneath the surface.

'Remember Mrs Saward has told me the station master's wife is unofficially in charge of the Royal retiring rooms.'

'Good for you.'

'So I won't be a kept woman after all.'

He replied in a deadly serious manner. 'I think you should be kept on your toes.'

She gave him a friendly slap which he anticipated, caught her flailing hand and pulled her towards him. She squealed but stopped sharpish as his lips engaged hers.

Having been the Wolferton SM for 40 years, Harry and his wife accumulated plenty of furniture and other bits and bobs. They bought their retirement cottage at Old Hunstanton years ago with no need of the goods at Wolverton. George and Louisa needed furniture and furnishings so the couples agreed a reasonable fee.

With their fortnight of bliss over, the honeymooners arrived at Wolferton where they were greeted by Harry and his four porters. All these men were a decade or three older than the new SM.

George shook hands and introduced his wife.

'Gentlemen, this is my wife Louisa, and these fine men my dear are Mr Thomas, Mr Greene, Mr Carroll and Mr Mason. You know Mr Saward of course.'

Caps were doffed and Louisa made a powerful impression. Her natural beauty dazzled the middle-aged railwaymen and her smile knocked them sideways.

'Your trunk and cases arrived last week,' said Harry, 'and they've been locked in our store awaiting your arrival.'

'Thank you kindly, gentlemen,' said George.

Two of the porters fetched the goods which were placed on station trolleys and the men led the way. Mr and Mrs Miracle followed on the short walk to the station master's house. And what a house; the Miracles' life at Wolferton began in what could never be called a cottage.

Mrs Saward greeted them with a pot of freshly brewed tea and her delicious shortbread. The porters pinched a few of the baked items and left. George wanted to escape but reckoned it rude to do so. He helped his wife to unpack and sort their belongings and eventually excused himself. He changed into his SM's outfit and set off to the station he would run in three days' time.

'All settled in?' asked Harry when George appeared.

'I hope you don't mind me being here before the official handover.'

Harry laughed. 'Not at all; I like enthusiasm,' he said. 'Now here's a task for a keen SM. The chap in charge of the grounds at

Sandringham would like to show you the ropes. His name is Jasper Hird and I told him you might be out there today.'

George found himself shocked but pleased. 'Oh righto, thank you.' He paused. 'Ah, how do I travel?'

'What are those skinny objects with your shoes stuck on the end?'

George reckoned the remark about his legs came straight from the Miracle joke book. Harry's eyes twinkled as he pointed along the platform.

'There's the station bicycle or we might find you a horse.'

George smiled. 'Thanks, I'll try the one with wheels.'

He pushed the bicycle off the platform, watched by a couple of grinning porters, and headed to Sandringham.

George cycled in his youth but not since he collected shrapnel. He pedalled along the road with a gradual but steady incline the closer he came to the Royal estate. A few hide-and-seek rabbits kept him company. It reminded him of the branch line to Crabbwell. Here there were trees and more trees with pheasants still hiding from Royal rifles. In 1913 King George V once shot a thousand pheasants in less than a week. Magnificent rhododendron bushes proudly displayed their blooms.

A journey of two and a bit miles brought him to Sandringham which was impossible to miss. Apart from the sign, the massive gates left George in no doubt he'd arrived.

His shrapnel-lined hip continued to trouble him as he rode as slowly as he could towards the main house dismounting about 50 yards from the front. A stable boy appeared at the end of the house and called. 'Are you the new station master?'

George followed the lad to the back of the main house. 'Mr Hird is in the orchard,' he said pointing. 'I'll take your bike, sir.'

As well as being expected and wearing his uniform including a cap featuring the word STATIONMASTER, the Head Gardener easily identified the approaching gent.

'Jasper Hird,' he said offering his hand. George introduced himself. 'I'm not surprised you're a young fellah. Harry Saward arrived as a whippersnapper when he first took over at Wolferton.'

There wasn't much George could say in reply. For the next hour he took the guided tour of a few parts of the Sandringham estate. You could safely describe it as big. They met a couple of the tenant farmers and a handful of the hundreds of estate workers but didn't venture into the vast and ancient woodlands and wetlands.

The fruit farms boasted trees laden with apples, pears, plums, quince and walnut, and the whopping vegetable garden could have fed an army. There were pastures with sheep and cows and sheds with pigs. He could only guess at the number of chickens. The estate's dogs gave George a right royal inspection.

Jasper spoke plainly. 'As you've no doubt been told, we take a great deal of produce to your station, Mr Miracle. We need your railway to transport our goods safely and quickly. Packed in Sandringham this morning and consumed in London the same day is what we aim to achieve. Your predecessor runs a tight ship. We hope you can maintain the service.'

George wondered if this was a warning or a request delivered albeit in a calm manner but he respected the man and liked a challenge. 'I'll do my best, sir and please contact me should there be any problems. I like to think I'm always on duty.'

This time George offered his hand and they shook with the SM walking off to find his transport.

'Find the place did you?' asked Harry when George returned.

The new SM smiled and suffered a tinge of sadness knowing he wouldn't be working with the retiring Mr Saward who reminded George of his late Uncle Fred. Harry was retiring as a man on top of his game and with his sense of humour still intact, even firing.

'Why don't you go home lad, and help your wife. You'll have plenty of time to run the station when you start on Monday.'

He set off only to see two women walking towards him.

Louisa and Mrs Saward approached. George stopped. 'Are you checking up on me?' he asked pretending to be shocked.

'Mrs Saward is to give me a tour of the Royal retiring-rooms and explain my duties. Oh and George, I didn't peel the potatoes for our supper. When you've finished peeling, pop them in the saucepan of water on the kitchen table.'

She smiled at her husband, the man she loved, and waved a hand without turning back as laughing, she and Sarah Saward headed to the station. George went home amused their roles were reversed.

Louisa learnt the Royal routine duties in parts of the station while at home he tackled the spuds.

At home, he discovered mail aplenty. His mother and sister both wrote with their miniscule amount of news to be followed with their massive amount of questions and comments about the wedding, the fact the KING was present and how, they asked in polite and respectable terms, did the couple enjoy the honeymoon.

An envelope addressed to him in what appeared to be a child's handwriting arrived from Pip the lad porter. George's replacement, Oswald Laughter, didn't want the station cat, Whitty, at the station. Apparently he didn't like cats. Pip despaired. His grandmother, his elderly landlady wasn't keen on the feline, being afraid of tripping over Whitty. Mrs Monty would take the mouser but lived within spitting distance of the station. Let out, Whitty would be back to her old haunts in no time. 'Please, Mr Miracle, what should I do?'

Blimey, thought George. *How would Solomon handle this?* He planned on asking Louisa until he thought of an idea. He suggested Pip should ask important people—Lady Fitzsimons, Horace Gardiner and Miss Woods, even Freda from Pickling—when they next visit the station, to inform the SM they missed the cat and how they so dearly wanted to have a chat with the moggie.

George's potato peeling passed muster and when his wife returned buzzing about her new station responsibilities, he delighted in her happiness.

She not only loves our new home but also our new station!

Over supper, they laughed a lot reading the mail from friends and family.

'What should I say about our honeymoon?' asked George.

'You mean you can't remember?' replied Louisa who now adopted a similar style of teasing and joke telling used by her husband.

He took a genuine interest in Louisa's unofficial role at the station. 'So tell me about the Royal retiring-rooms and your role at the Wolferton station, *Missus* Stationmaster.'

She enthused about her involvement. George already believed marrying this woman to be the best thing he could have ever done but now reckoned life was even better when Louisa discussed her visit.

'The Sawards are wonderful people, George. They're kind and ever so helpful. I asked about the Royals.' She became serious. 'Not as a nosey parker, you know I would never become a gossip.'

'I know that.'

'The Queen Mother lives in the big house on the estate but her health is not good. When younger, apparently she once set an example as a leader of fashion, and high society in London would see women copying the style she set.'

'That'll soon happen here in Wolferton.' Louisa frowned. 'You wait; my wife will soon be the trend setter in the village.'

She forced a smile and moved on. 'Mrs Saward told me the Queen Mother walks with a slight limp and became so influential, several aristocratic ladies mimicked her gait.'

'You're pulling my leg.' His pun died a death.

'You can see for yourself when she next comes to the station.'

George came alive. 'What did you hear? When is she coming?'

Louisa smiled at him. 'Ah, *now* you're interested, and well done with those potatoes.' He grinned. 'In fact you did such a good job; you can peel them again tomorrow.' His grin grew bigger.

After supper, Louisa raised the topic of church attendance. 'I know you're not a great churchgoer, George, but in a small village, not going might give the wrong impression.' He nodded. 'And yes I know the trains run on Sundays but surely you can manage an hour and after all, the Reverend Attwood went out of his way to marry us, two strangers in his parish.'

George swallowed. 'I agree entirely, my dear. Should I wear my wedding suit or my SM's outfit?'

She thought about flicking a pea at him but settled for a grin.

They went to church on the day before George officially became the Wolferton station master, and the rector's smile spoke volumes. He'd enjoyed marrying the couple and took delight in having them as new members of his flock.

The Reverend Attwood, about a decade older than George, was a single man with a passion for physical fitness, and would make a perfect model for a good health advertisement. His teeth sparkled.

There are times when two people meet and an instant bond is formed, not by design but by natural means, because they're suited. Such a bond developed between George Miracle and Kenneth Attwood much as it did between the Georges Miracle and Carruthers.

'Will you join us for supper this evening, Rector?' asked Louisa as they shook hands after the service.

'I would be delighted,' replied the priest.

'Tomorrow my husband officially begins work and heaven knows when he'll next be available.'

'Then I shall be on time enabling your husband to have an early night.'

'Straight after Evensong?' suggested Louisa.

'My sermon has already been cut in half,' he whispered. She laughed and the married couple walked home arm in arm.

'You were kind, my dear,' said George.

'I think being friendly with any polite and well-read person can be beneficial in all sorts of ways and especially in a small village.'

He leant in and kissed her cheek. His wife kept going up in his estimation. *She's also wise,* he thought.

George too became Solomon-like when he received a brief note from young Pip at Whittleton.

Dear Mr Miracle
Thanks for the tip. Whitty's back home.
Hurray!
Pip

Louisa sparkled when serving her first meal with company in the station house. Mr Attwood lived with an excellent housekeeper, Methuselah's great-granddaughter and as deaf as a door post. Louisa's food too was delicious and the company delightful. The recently married woman loved watching the men bounce ideas off one another.

'When I first met you, George, I sensed you would be a perfect fit for Wolferton,' said Kenneth.

'Oh?' asked his wife, 'in what way, sir?'

'Well of course there's the Royal connection but this is a lovely area with a lovely line. There is the freight aspect with Sandringham and other farms producing lots of desirable produce plus the holidaymakers. In summer, the bucket and spade brigade as I call them, pack the trains heading to King's Lynn and other beaches along the coast. Wolferton becomes an important place to many people and you, sir, are the ideal man to not only keep the station ticking over but to bring new ideas to the village and surrounding district.'

'Thank you for your kind words, sir,' replied George, 'but I would prefer you to lower your expectations. I am but a humble railwayman.'

'I can vouch for his ideas,' said Louisa. 'He singlehandedly saved a local branch line at his last station.'

'How marvellous.'

'Yes, well enough about me,' said George. 'We know little of you and your background, Rector. Kindly reveal yourself.'

During pudding and coffee, the Reverend Kenneth George (yes, *another* George) Attwood ran through his life story; his family, education, career choice and life to date. The reason he kept talking was simple; his life was interesting, even fascinating, and he was a damn good storyteller. The Miracles would interrupt occasionally to ask a question but both found the man to be genuinely intriguing.

By the time he stood to leave, Louisa and George discovered so much about the man and both wanted to know more. George walked him to the front gate.

'Now George, I know you chaps have a railway to run even on the Sabbath, so please don't feel any pressure to attend services. I'll be honest, there are times when I'm not so keen on my own sermons and I'd hate you to come along and be bored.'

He offered his hand and George shook it wishing the man of God good night. Inside, he helped his wife with the dishes.

'This is romantic,' she said. 'I wash and you dry.'

Thinking about his visitor, George replied. 'That rector is a most impressive man.'

Chapter 18

When George became the station master at Whittleton, he'd been a porter there for a few years. At Wolferton, he stepped straight into the role as SM and two activities made his first week a success; the mutual respect between him and the other staff members, and the confidence he enjoyed in his own ability. But Whittleton and Wolferton were not the same.

Obviously the VIP passengers were a huge difference, and there was no branch line shooting off from Wolferton.

The line from King's Lynn to Hunstanton opened in 1862 and was originally a single track, as in the branch to Crabbwell. But when the Norfolk line attracted more traffic, it was doubled. Hunstanton became a mecca for golfers and when Wolferton acquired the unofficial title of the Royal Station, this 16 mile line served a special purpose.

Goods from Sandringham such as vegetables and flax arrived and were sent on their way. Coal for the Estate arrived by train. The August Bank Holiday meant excursion trains were packed. VIPs arrived to be ferried to and from Sandringham in horse-drawn carriages and later in motor cars, with George personally greeting dignitaries. He slipped into the routine with everything becoming tickety-boo.

On the home front, he would watch his wife at different times and decided she changed becoming ever lovelier and their marriage appeared rock solid and blissful—only because it was.

Louisa suggested her mother come to stay for a week and Rowena wanted to cry when she arrived and inspected the house and the station in detail and saw the obvious happiness her daughter enjoyed with her husband.

Of course, inviting only one side of the family would never do and soon George's mother, step-father and his sister Emily and her son arrived by train. George's brother-in-law, Bert, was flat out lambing and cried off the visit.

Again the visitors enjoyed a grand time with George showing off the station and Louisa in charge of the retirement-rooms tour.

After the second group of family visitors departed, alone in the seriously large station house, George and Louisa relaxed.

'Well so much for entertaining our families,' said George. 'It was wonderful to have them but it puts a strain on you my darling girl.'

'It does,' she said and left it there.

George went to continue his comments but stopped before asking. 'Are you unwell?'

'Thank you, I am well, Mr Miracle, and also pregnant.'

He froze. He knew she would never say such a thing if it were not true. He moved to sit beside her holding her hand in both of his and squeezed but not too hard. 'Oh Louisa, what fantastic news.' He leant in and kissed her. She was relieved having wanted to tell him a week ago. 'When did you find out?'

She studied him feeling a tad guilty. 'I found out a few days ago.'

He gasped. 'But why didn't you say?'

'When you were showing your family the village, I took the train to King's Lynn to see Dr Jamieson who told me but it seemed wrong to announce the news while the others were here. I wanted to tell you first. I hope you don't mind, George.'

'Mind? My darling girl I am over the moon and now I want to tell the whole world.'

She tried to keep his enthusiasm in check. 'And that's another thing. The doctor said it can be wise to wait a while to make sure everything is okay with the baby.'

George agreed. 'Of course, forgive me and please tell me what I should say and when.' He squeezed her hand again and gently embraced her as they sat listening to their breathing and thinking about the future.

'Do you want a girl or a boy?' asked Louisa.

'I'll be happy with whatever comes along with you and the baby healthy and well.'

George struggled to keep secret the news he would soon be a father. Days went by, then two weeks with Louisa due to see the doctor. 'Let me come with you,' said the SM.

'If we both board the train to King's Lynn, it may start tongues wagging. Why are we both going?'

'I don't mind a few wagging tongues,' he replied but agreed to her request. Louisa travelled alone with George knowing which train would bring her back to Wolferton. He opened the carriage door.

'Well?' he whispered.

She smiled at him knowing how much he wanted to shout their news from the rooftops.

'Dr Jamieson said everything is sound and we can make an announcement whenever we like.'

His smile broke free. He kissed her and walked with her to the exit. 'Been shopping in Lynn, Mrs Miracle?' asked Lennie Greene.

'I have, Mr Greene but now I must go home to prepare the station master's supper.' She glanced back at her husband whose grin continued. Lennie reckoned he missed something.

When George came home, he gently hugged his wife wanting to protect her. He held her shoulders staring deep into her eyes.

'I think we should tell our mothers first,' he said and Louisa's heart grew warmer. Their mothers would be thrilled with the news. 'I can send two telegrams tomorrow.'

'You do realize the postmistress will tell the world and its mother as soon as you've left the post office?'

'But I *want* the village to know. I'm so excited I want the whole world to know.' He stopped. 'I can finish the supper; you need to rest.'

'I'm fine and if I need your help, I'll ask. Now go and write letters to all those folk we need to tell. George and Valerie, Miss Woods, Lord Fitzsimons and anyone else you can think of.'

He kissed her and went to write the letters.

The word spread around the village by lunchtime. Men were hesitant to offer their congratulations; women couldn't wait to express their delight. Station staff offered their hand. Passengers waiting for their train would seek him out to express their best wishes.

In his office, George battled with paperwork when Kenneth Attwood arrived. 'My dear fellow, I've been told your splendid news.'

He held out his hand. 'Heartiest congratulations and please convey my love and best wishes to your wonderful wife.'

'Thank you, Rector,' he replied. 'It's not due till next year so we'll have to wait a while.'

'Well if I say so myself, I do a nice line in christenings and would dearly love to make a diary entry as soon as you're ready.' They heard an approaching train and the priest took his leave.

The letters from friends and family flooded in. Despite having only been the station master at Wolferton for a few months, the locals took a shine to the young couple and the Miracles were stunned to receive fruit and flowers and one family delivered a delicious, wholesome meal ready to pop in the oven.

Their first Christmas at Wolferton saw them set up a tree with all the usual decorations. Station masters don't usually have the option of visiting relatives on Christmas Day, especially those far away. Trains run and need staff to make them run safely with everything being supervised by the chap wearing the SM's cap.

Being a single lady, they invited Louisa's mother to spend Christmas at Wolferton. Rowena couldn't wait to be with her daughter especially with Rowena's first grandchild soon to appear.

In Whittleton, with daughter and grandson nearby, George's mother and her husband spent Christmas with the Culpepper family.

George, Louisa and Rowena went to St Peter's on Christmas Eve. Mr Attwood spoke about the nativity as if speaking to a child. Many thought it a wonderful sermon. George continued to be fascinated by the rector, his sermons and life story.

Winter is not a great time for seaside holidays but Christmas is a popular time for visiting friends and family meaning George was kept busy as passengers came and went. Snow can make life difficult even for powerful locomotives, and studying weather forecasts and talking with colleagues up and down the line became a constant activity for station masters.

They didn't call Wolferton the Royal Station for nothing and at Christmas, members of the House of Windsor came together and nearly always by train from London before using another conveyance for their final leg to Sandringham.

As the King had proposed a toast at George and Louisa's wedding, George became more at ease in dealing with his important passengers. It's not every station master who has the opportunity to offer the King and his family best wishes for the festive season and beyond.

This Christmas, His Majesty arrived and spoke briefly with the station master. The King enquired after Mrs Miracle and George, both nervous and excited, happily announced they were expecting their first child.

'Heartiest congratulations,' said His Majesty, 'and please give my best wishes to your good lady.'

'I will, your Majesty, and thank you for your kind words.'

At a distance, he followed the Royals to their vehicle and watched as an official secured the door. George needed to be careful and stick to his area of responsibility because there were guards, a driver and other staff with the task of caring for the Royals.

At night he told his wife and mother-in-law of his little chat with the King. Louisa relaxed hearing about such Royal interaction whereas Rowena, with pride to burn, found it hard to believe.

They embarked on their first Christmas at Wolferton and their last without a young family.

1925 arrived and Rowena departed. With the baby due in the spring, Louisa invited her mother to return to help with the newborn.

A letter arrived which threw Louisa into a spin. 'Valerie and George have invited me to stay at Tudor House when the baby is due.'

The SM stopped reading a newspaper report about what the Royal Family did over Christmas. 'But we planned to go to a local hospital in Lynn.' George was now using the local dialect.

'They have offered to pay for me to go to a private hospital in London.'

George worried. He liked the idea of his wife receiving the best of care but reckoned local hospitals also offered an excellent service. Would he be treating his community with disdain? Would locals think he didn't respect them? And worse, he hated being in debt to anyone.

'What should I do?' asked Louisa.

'What would you like to do?'

Louisa caught her husband's concern. 'They're our best friends, George. It seems rude to decline such a kind and generous offer.'

They discussed the matter and came to a joint decision. 'Okay,' said George, 'I'll take you up to London a week before the baby is due.'

'Not necessary as Valerie says George will send a car for us.'

'For both of us?' spluttered the SM. 'I don't think I can leave Wolferton until you're ready to have the baby.'

The Miracles were new to the business of starting a family. Like all first-time parents, they worried about a successful birth and a healthy baby, and after more discussion decided to accept the kindness offered by their friends with George travelling up to London by train once Louisa was settled in hospital.

Months slipped by and Louisa grew ever larger. The baby was due in three weeks. George fussed only adding to Louisa's concern.

'I'm fine, my darling; please don't fuss. It might surprise you to know I'm not the first woman to have a baby.'

He realized his approach only added to the stress and so tried to be supportive without the smothering.

At work, in his office, George answered the phone. Lord Carruthers enquired about Louisa and wondered if her husband had given up being a fusspot.

They laughed particularly because the London-based Lord hit the nail on the head regarding the SM's behaviour.

'I'll be out next Saturday, George. If you change your mind and want to come with Louisa, we'll have room for you on the roof.'

They laughed again and George enjoyed the fact he faced a busy schedule of trains to keep his mind off matters domestic.

With the weather warming, more holidaymakers and more produce arrived at or departed from Wolferton station.

Over supper he told Louisa about her car arriving next Saturday. They studied each other's face with a mixture of excitement and fear.

Chapter 19

Two weeks before Louisa was due to give birth, Lord George Carruthers drove to Wolferton in his other vehicle, a Morris Cowley Bullnose Roadster. He stayed for lunch and enjoyed the company of his friends. The SM didn't want to leave his wife but chose to remain at Wolferton with a station to run.

George held his wife's hand as they walked to the car. 'Valerie insisted on bringing far too many cushions,' said the driver. George helped his wife into the vehicle, kissed her and whispered words of comfort and love.

'I'll be on the first train to London as soon as you're admitted to hospital,' he said squeezing her hand before closing the door. He shook hands with his namesake and watched as the car set off slowly and carefully. George Carruthers would drive sensibly anyway but copped a serious speech from his wife before he left Hampstead.

'You have a precious cargo, George. Please take extra care.'

'Yes, my dear,' he replied and did as she asked.

Back at the station, George's excellent relationship with the porters meant they would automatically step in to cover any gaps when their boss left for London to witness the birth of his first child.

'Mrs Miracle set off all right?' asked senior porter, Samuel Mason.

'Yes thank you, Sam and let's hope she'll have a safe delivery.'

'The 11:24 is running a tad late with the same boiler problem but they reckon she'll pick up and be in Hunstanton on time.'

'That's the second time with the same loco. I sent a report but either it wasn't fixed or there's something else amiss.'

''I never thought engine maintenance to be your domain, sir.'

'It's not but Management, Line Supervisors and the like want problems reported whenever and wherever they happen.'

'I'll remember that, oh and the Reverend Attwood popped in asking after you. Nothing important, he said.'

'Thanks Sam. I'll follow him up.'

In his office, George tackled the bane of all station masters, paperwork. There was a knock on his door and the rector appeared.

'Sorry to interrupt, George. How is your good lady?'

'Most kind of you, sir. My friend George Carruthers ...'

'*Lord* Carruthers,' corrected the priest in a gentle jibe.

'That's the one, and the same gentleman, having kindly collected her, is currently en route to his home in Hampstead which is close to the private hospital where she'll give birth.'

'It's nice to have friends and especially ones who are well-to-do.'

George quietly agreed. 'Yes but I admit the issue troubles me. I think I should have sought advice from my local rector.'

'Oh God, don't ask him. A boring bachelor in the wrong profession is the last person you should be asking about babies. Now listen, I want you to take your supper with me while Louisa is away.'

'That's most kind but I'm fine.'

'George, my housekeeper is the best cook in Wolferton, apart from your good lady wife of course. Now what time are you off duty?'

Secretly the SM was delighted. Louisa told her husband she would ask various families in the village to take care of his meals and he politely told her to do no such thing. Now the perfect solution bobbed up although George insisted on sticking to the roster and most nights was the last member of staff to leave the station. Kenneth would wait for him and, once he arrived, they'd heat the meal the housekeeper prepared earlier. On the odd night George enjoyed an early finish and so they ate at a respectable hour. The SM reckoned his girth was expanding. The men enjoyed a coffee after their meal.

George posed a question. 'What did you mean the other day when you said you were in the wrong profession?'

'Oh my,' laughed the rector. 'It's a family joke.'

'It didn't sound like a joke to me.'

'My grandfather was a bishop and my parents are pillars of their local church. But my rotten older brothers went off and found proper jobs leaving me to carry the spiritual can. There are families, including mine, good at applying subtle but effective pressure.'

George considered his question. 'Did you want to be a priest?'

'I can't say I didn't but to be honest, I showed little enthusiasm for the task.' He paused. 'Did you want to be a station master?'

George laughed. 'No choice; I started as a station lad aged 12.'

'Well I started as a chorister aged 8.'

More laughter before Kenneth changed the subject. 'Tell me, George, have you heard of Charles Darwin?'

'I've heard of him but that's about all. Wasn't he the chap who made friends with a monkey?'

'He was and it was a female orangutan called Jenny.'

The rector gave the station master a brief, a very brief synopsis of Darwin's book, *On the Origin of the Species by Means of Natural Selection*. George listened with interest but not overly so. After more silence, the station master posed a big question.

'Did you say you're in the wrong profession because you have doubts about your faith?'

'I think you mean, "Do I believe in God"?'

Their exchange of views travelled at a slow rate of knots, or was that nots? Each man pondered the other's answer, question or comment. The rector continued.

'George, if Mr Darwin's theory is true, it means our planet is very old. Animals need vast amounts of time to adapt, to evolve and not over hundreds or thousands of years but millions even billions. If that's true, what did God do for ages before he made humans?'

'You're asking the wrong man, Rector. Try me on timetables.'

'We've made a few whopping errors, George. Only a few hundred years ago, the Church tried and imprisoned Galileo because he contradicted their scientific belief about the Sun orbiting the Earth. Of course it's the other way round but even today, the Church still hasn't given the astronomer a posthumous pardon although they have removed his famous text from an index of banned books.'

More silence filled the room apart from sounds made by nocturnal creatures in the garden. 'So science has caused you to lose your faith?'

Before Kenneth could respond, the telephone in the rector's study began ringing. 'Sorry old chap,' said Kenneth. 'Duty calls.'

The clergyman picked up the phone, listened then called in a loud voice. 'George, it's for you.'

The station master hurried to take the phone ignoring any pain from his hip. 'Hello,' he gasped, 'George Miracle.' He recognized his friend's voice.

'No need to panic old man,' said Lord Carruthers but Louisa has been taken to hospital. They reckon the little one is on the way.'

George Miracle did panic. 'Thanks,' he gasped. I'll be there as soon as I can.'

He hung up neglecting to say goodbye leaving the caller scratching his head. The SM explained the news to his host and apologized for leaving so abruptly.

'So what's your plan?' asked Kenneth.

Frustration gripped the SM. 'The last train leaves Hunstanton at 4 minutes past 7.' He studied his watch. 'I've got 14 minutes to get home, grab my bag and be at the station.'

'I'll drive you,' said the rector.

'It'll be quicker to run.'

'And more tiring. Come on,' cried Kenneth grabbing his car key.

They piled into the rector's Austin 7 which didn't start. George agonized over the delay. The next train was not for another 12 hours at 07:02am tomorrow morning.

The driver kept trying. George couldn't wait. He opened the door to hop out and run when the engine came alive. He slammed his door shut and the vehicle bounced out onto the road to Wolferton.

It was only half a mile to the station and Kenneth drove as fast as he dared. There were no street lights on the country roads of Norfolk and while the moon helped by giving a little light, shadows were created with what you thought were logs, fallen trees across the road. George in his panic to catch the last train, wanted to grab the driver and call, "Look out" when what he thought was a tree across the road turned out to be a shadow.

They stopped with a skid outside George's home. Being a typical SM who lived for order and preparation, his bag packed for a trip to London sat on the kitchen table. He grabbed it and ran.

The rector stood beside his vehicle as George hurtled past ignoring the discomfort in his hip.

'Good luck to you and Mrs Miracle,' called the priest.

'Thank you,' yelled George who kept on hobbling.

'I'll telephone Lord Carruthers and tell him you're on your way.' He yelled louder. 'Where should he meet you?'

'Where we first met.'

Kenneth didn't understand. 'Where?'

George was about to enter his station. 'On Platform 9 at Liverpool Street. He'll know.' The father-to-be disappeared, re-appeared and yelled. 'You're a saint, your Reverence.'

Of course George knew his timetables and kept checking his watch. Sam Mason was on duty and stood with his boss noting the SM's excitement.

'You'll be fine, sir. Would you like me to tell the footplate lads they have a VIP passenger?'

George was too nervous to appreciate the joke and relaxed a tad when the sound of the last train of the day was heard heading to Wolferton. Sam shook hands with his boss, opened the carriage door and wished him well. George collapsed on a seat, facing the locomotive, and tingled with excitement as the train pulled out heading to King's Lynn and eventually London.

Kenneth drove home, a lot less frantically, and rang George Carruthers. 'He caught the last London train which I think arrives about half past nine.'

'You think and about?' said his Lordship. 'For pity's sake, Rector, when it comes to train timetables, never let George Miracle *ever* hear you say "I think" and "about".' They laughed.

'He's on the last train and said he'd meet you where you first met.'

'That'd be Liverpool Street near the newsagent's stall.'

'Okay and I've never seen him so excited.'

They laughed again. 'I'll drive into town and grab him once he arrives. And Rector, many thanks for all you've done.'

'My pleasure,' replied the priest and the call ended.

George Carruthers checked the train timetable, confirmed his friend's arrival time in London, then made a cup of tea before creeping into the bedroom of each of his sleeping children, kissed them and told his wife the plan before going downstairs to the garages to start his trusty Roadster. He wanted to be early knowing the importance of the father being present at the birth of his child and especially his first.

He found a place to park within easy walk of the station and waited on the platform asking a senior porter if he knew station master George Miracle.

'I think we all know Mr Miracle,' said the porter.

George Carruthers explained the need to not let the SM escape. He didn't. The train pulled in on time and one carriage door opened well before the train stopped.

'Mr Miracle,' cried two voices as one—the porter and the chauffeur—and the two Georges met. The chauffeur explained about his car being close at hand and they hurried out of the station.

'Hop in,' ordered Carruthers and his friend collapsed into the car.

'What news?' gasped George Shrapnel.

'She's gone into labour. Now breathe deeply and try to relax. Louisa will be brilliant and you'll help her by being calm.'

Outside the hospital, Carruthers kept the engine running. 'I'll find somewhere to park then wait in Reception. Now go.' George flew out of the car. Carruthers shouted. 'And stay calm!'

In Reception the SM announced himself. A nurse came forward. 'I'll take you there, sir,' she said and led the way.

'Has anything happened?' asked George thinking about being calm but failing to do so.

'She may still be in labour, sir.'

They reached the room and George could see Louisa surrounded by medical staff. He so wanted to call out.

'You can watch from here, sir.'

'But can't I go inside?'

'You can but you'll need to wear protective clothing.' She saw his desperation. 'This way,' she said leading him to a small room.

'Where shall I leave my bag?' The nurse promised to store it.

Dressed to the medical nines, George prepared to enter. *Stay calm,* sounded in his head. When the door opened, the medical staff turned.

'It's the father, Mr Miracle,' said the nurse and stepped aside allowing George to appear. Helpless described him well.

He muttered, 'Good evening,' and tentatively stepped forward. The midwife assisting the obstetrician spoke quietly to George.

'You'd be better off at the other end, sir. You can chat to your wife and it's a tad less messy up there.'

George took the hint and moved to the head of the bed. He stared at Louisa who tried and wanted to smile but before George could speak she grimaced and screamed.

With frayed nerves and increasing fear, he didn't know what to say or do. A nurse mopping Louisa's brow whispered. 'Won't be long, sir.'

He tried to offer his wife comfort and between straining, Louisa managed to speak. 'You made it then.'

The medical staff encouraged Louisa to push, to make one final effort which made George reluctant to speak.

He wanted to ask if he could help but knew it would be both absurd and insulting. The staff calls grew louder and Louisa responded with an equally loud yell. A baby cried and the obstetrician smiled. George froze as the relief and rejoicing took over.

'Congratulations, it's a boy,' said the medical man and George's eyes filled with tears. He stared at his wife who whispered.

'Another Miracle, Mr Miracle.'

He bent and kissed her forehead when a nurse approached holding a well-wrapped bundle. Louisa took the brand new babe in her arms and she and George stared. The little one didn't stare back keeping his eyes tightly closed. His mouth opened wide and it was abundantly clear his lungs were in fine shape.

George lost track of time when a nurse touched his arm. 'Your wife needs to rest, Mr Miracle.'

He returned to Earth, kissed his wife and son and left with a smile permanently plastered across his face. In Reception another smiling George stood with arms extended. George C politely enquired what won the last and discovered a colt had saluted the judge.

The friends didn't shake hands but hugged. They spoke as they embraced. 'Wonderful news, old man,' said the Lord. 'And Louisa and the wee boy are well?'

The SM nodded finding the emotions surge again. 'Fine, she's fine, they're both fine.'

'Wonderful; now please don't tell me you've called the lad George. Four Georges would be a Royal dynasty.' They laughed.

'I think we agreed on James.'

'James Miracle,' said Carruthers. 'It's impressive, distinctive.'

It did sound impressive and Valerie beamed when the two friends arrived back at Tudor Court with news of the birth. In her dressing gown, Lady Carruthers would never retire until she received the details of the gender, name and wellbeing of both mother and baby.

Chapter 20

A fortnight later, in the Wolferton station master's house, the new parents disagreed, a rare event at any time.

'But why can't I call him Jim?' argued George.

'Because his name is James,' replied Louisa. 'We didn't choose Jim or Jimmy or Jamie. I don't call you Georgy.'

'You wouldn't dare.'

'Georgy Porgie,' she teased and he pretended to be outraged only to embrace and kiss her.

'You're right, Lulu-belle,' he said, she giggled and he kissed her again. She joined in. Both wanted to continue their romantic interlude when a baby's cry came from the nursery.

Louisa headed off to attend to Jimbo.

George called. 'Tell him I don't like being interrupted and especially not when ...'

He froze as his mother-in-law appeared.

'Especially not when what?' she asked and George grinned.

'Mother-in-law, I thought you were in the village.'

'I was but now I'm back and curious about your unfinished sentence.' He grinned by return post. 'But never fear, Mr Miracle. I'm catching the 11:55 on Saturday morning after which you can enjoy your wife and son to your heart's delight.' She winked.

'We'll all miss you.'

'Ho ho. But will you be on duty on Saturday morning?'

'If it means helping you to depart, I will be there with bells on.'

Their repartee reflected the love and respect they shared for one another. Rowena arrived in Wolferton the day before Louisa came home with James. The grandmother did everything and more for her daughter and new grandson. She would be missed.

Of course George's family celebrated being over-the-moon when Connie's second grandson arrived. Secretly she would have loved a girl but a healthy bonny boy thrilled her no end.

'When will James come to Whittleton?' she asked knowing a long trip so early in the child's life was out of the question. George did the right thing sending photos to his mother, sister, the Carruthers and Daisy Woods now caring for the gardener, Gardiner. Back came letters of congratulations with comments about the baby having his father's nose and his mother's eyes. Someone, possibly short-sighted, said he had his father's eyes and his mother's nose.

At the station, the porters, the signalman and even passengers were keen to shake the SM's hand. The news spread and footplate crews and guards would call out to George when their train pulled in. Their good wishes and polite ribbing gave him a warm feeling inside. He adored being a father.

He thought back to his childhood remembering how his father took him fishing and showered him with love. The day his father unexpectedly and tragically died would never be forgotten not least because it happened on George's birthday. Every year, on his birthday, George thought about his caring and helpful father and these childhood memories never faded.

I'm going to do for James what you did for me, Da, he thought as the latest Hunstanton train arrived.

Summer meant longer nights, and visitors to Wolferton came and often stayed. Connie brought her husband, daughter Emily and her little boy John, a cousin for baby James. Being so large, the station master's house easily accommodated visitors.

George's stepfather, John Beckwith, returned to St Peter's where the Reverend Attwood gave him another tour of the church and churchyard. Hearing the organ again gave John goosebumps—again.

For Connie, it was a time to reflect. She raised her deaf daughter and fishing-mad son watching them grow into young adults. Now to see both married and each with a child, gave her enormous pride.

With youngsters in prams, the young mothers and grandmother, walked into the village where Louisa introduced George's family to shopkeepers and shoppers. They all knew Mrs Miracle, the wife of the Wolferton station master.

When the SM took his family on another tour of the station, their admiration for their son and brother reached new heights. Staff and passengers wanted to meet the baby Miracle.

No sooner did George's family return to Whittleton than Lord and Lady Carruthers arrived at Wolferton with their two young children. George Miracle found a new love for his godson and took the youngster to see the trains. He led the lad up the steps into the signal box; his father remained at ground level, where the boy saw the levers being operated and, when picked up, saw the railway gates move allowing powerful locomotives to go steaming past.

With the males away at the station, Louisa and Valerie caught up on one another's news. James slept quietly in his cot and Valerie's daughter, Annie, enjoyed her afternoon nap.

'So,' said Valerie, 'what's it like being a mother?'

Louisa produced a closed-lips grin. 'Horrible and wonderful,' she said. 'I could do without the 2am feeds but to see him gurgle and laugh is the best thing ever.'

'And I bet your George cleans bottoms.'

'He doesn't have a choice,' retorted Louisa. The women laughed then groaned when James began to cry. The wee baby was taken from his cot and stretched out on a small rug on the sitting-room carpet.

Both women tried to help him settle. Valerie put her mouth on his belly button, pursed her lips and blew making a funny sound. The baby stopped crying and smiled. The mothers grinned.

When the baby responded to being tickled, he smiled and made sounds but remained still.

'Does he wave his arms and kick his legs much?' asked Valerie.

'A little,' replied Louisa. 'Should he? Is it important?'

Valerie shrugged. 'Little George did it straight away but Annie took her time although now she's a bundle of movement.'

Louisa studied her son. He appeared happy and content. Before he or the mothers could do anything, George Carruthers Senior and Junior returned without the third George back working at the station.

In their bedroom with the rest of the household asleep, George finally came to bed. 'Busy, busy, busy,' he sighed. 'Freight and passengers I can handle but paperwork is the straw that may one day break my back.'

He gained no sympathy from his wife. She paused and he wondered why. Finally she spoke.

'Have you ever seen James kick his legs?'

Her serious question caused him to change gears. 'What do you mean? All babies kick their legs and wave their arms.'

'Valerie and I were watching James lying on the floor and she asked the same question.'

George pondered. 'I think I have but surely babies are unique. Some start walking sooner than others. It's the same with talking. My godson may develop faster than James.'

He couldn't see her nod. 'You're right, Mr Stationmaster.' She leant in and kissed him. 'Good night, father of James.'

He didn't speak for a few moments before whispering. 'Good night, mother of James.'

Summer faded, the nights drew in and temperatures fell as did the leaves. House guests were few. Wee James continued to thrive; he ate well and slept longer. Louisa kept a close eye on his body movements. Leg kicking didn't appear. She tried activities which might be considered cruel by tickling his ribs, and even gently tickling his feet particularly the soles. He produced little if any movement. She decided not to tell George about these happenings falling back on his comment about all babies being unique, developing at different rates.

George kept busy at work and spoke to the Sandringham Head Gardener when he arrived with a truck load of vegetables grown on the estate and due for delivery to London.

They passed the time of day as the porters unloaded the cargo until Jasper Hird spoke softly. 'There is talk at the estate, Her Majesty, the Queen Mother is poorly.'

'I'm sorry to hear it,' replied George. 'Being a recent arrival, may I ask what happens when a Royal person dies at Sandringham?'

'I believe Queen Alexander's body will lie in state in St Mary Magdalene church on the estate. From there it will be transported to Wolferton and from here will travel by Royal Train to London to the Chapel Royal in St James' Palace. As for your role, I'm sure you'll receive your instructions in triplicate.'

'I'm grateful for your kindness,' said George.

The Sandringham man changed his tune. 'Now these carrots need the shortest way home please,' he said breaking into a grin.

'Perhaps Royal carrots once found their way to my old station, Liverpool Street and if so, I may have helped unload goods from Sandringham when I worked in London as a station lad.'

'From station lad to station master; you've done all right for yourself, Mr Miracle.'

'We do our best,' said George.

'You even talk like a Royal,' he mimicked the SM. '*We* do our best. You and your Royal we,' he laughed. 'Good luck to you!'

As George and his porters dealt with the Royal carrots, his wife entered the local midwife's home pushing a pram with her wee boy.

'Good morning, Mrs Miracle,' said Mrs Blakeney. 'How are you and your baby today?'

'We're both well, thank you, Mrs Blakeney.'

'That's what I like to hear,' she said weighing the young boy and giving him a cursory examination. 'All good,' she said. 'And how is your feeding going?'

'It's going well, thank you and your tips have been very helpful. Most important, so far James has never complained.'

The midwife smiled. 'And does your husband give you a hand with the messy part of raising a baby?'

'He doesn't dare do otherwise.'

'I heard he is the world's busiest station master.'

'So he says.' They smiled before Louisa turned serious. 'Mrs Blakeney, why does James never kick his legs?'

The midwife with all her years of experience had heard every question a mother, and certainly a first-time mother ever asked. She never dismissed any of her clients lightly no matter how trivial the issue, and knew how to humour even the most determined of fusspot mothers of whom there were plenty.

'Babies are unique, Mrs Miracle. They develop at different times. Some are walking and talking early while others do so over a longer period. It's the way babies are.'

'My husband said that.'

They placed James on the bed beside the wall. 'Your husband is right. Now young man, let's have a good look at you.'

The baby behaved well with only a few bleats when the midwife squeezed a little too hard.

141

'I'm sorry to be a nuisance, Mrs Blakeney.'

The midwife smiled. 'You are never a nuisance, Mrs Miracle. A mother's calling in life is to want her child to be happy and healthy.' She handed over James who was popped back in his pram. 'I can't see or feel anything abnormal but only a doctor can conduct a proper examination.'

At her desk she wrote a note. 'Dr Jamieson has sent a few of my patients to a wonderful paediatrician at the West Norfolk and King's Lynn Hospital. If you're still concerned, ask for a referral and help put your mind at ease.'

With great relief, Louisa immediately wanted to tell George her news. When he came home after the last train, James slept peacefully as his parents ate supper. 'I went to see Mrs Blakeney today.'

George quickly responded. 'Oh? Is there a problem?'

'I asked her why James doesn't kick his legs like other babies.'

George stopped eating. 'I thought we talked about that.'

'We did and Mrs Blakeney said exactly what you said about babies developing at different times. She told me about a paediatrician in King's Lynn. I rang Dr Jamieson and he is sending me a referral. James has an appointment for Thursday week.'

George reached across and squeezed her hand. 'I think I'm a genius.' This confused Louisa. 'I picked not only the most beautiful girl but also the smartest.' She wanted to cry. 'You checked the roster and know I have Thursday week free in the afternoon. Now, have you told James or should I?'

This time she did cry knowing she'd picked a wonderful husband.

The trip to King's Lynn was short, a few miles. They took it in turns to nurse their son and from the station made their way to the hospital.

In a small room they waited until the paediatrician, Professor Alastair Reid appeared. 'Mr and Mrs Miracle, please come through.'

They chatted about James and what his movements or lack thereof might mean. The expert's report covered most possibilities from nothing to serious conditions. George found Louisa's grip on his hand to be mildly painful. The professor carried out a hands-on examination, and said he would like to perform further testing. George and Louisa worried even more.

'Why don't you pop downstairs for a cup of tea and come back in half an hour. Don't worry; James will be in the best of care.'

A nurse entered, and after introductions, gathered up the young patient. The parents went to the cafeteria and drank tea. Neither wanted any food.

'It could be nothing, Lou, he could take after me and be a slow developer.' His attempt at humour fell flat.

She produced the weakest of smiles, nodded but didn't speak.

Their conversation struggled with neither wanting to discuss any possible diagnosis. George checked his watch. 'We still have a quarter of an hour. Let's go for a walk.'

Walking beat sitting but it seemed like the longest 15 minutes they'd ever experienced. Back in the waiting-room they sat holding hands. The nurse appeared. 'Professor Reid will see you now.'

The parents entered with their hearts pounding in unison. He gave them a smile. The nurse waited in a corner as the professor spoke.

'I've completed a few tests on James and found making a diagnosis difficult because of his age. Six months is usually too young.

What diagnosis? thought the parents as one.

'His hearing and vision are normal but his movements are restricted. This may improve in time. One possible cause of any problem could be a lack of oxygen to his brain in a difficult birth.'

Louisa froze and George wanted to hold her even tighter.

'I stress diagnosing an infant at such a tender age can be unreliable. Because he is healthy, I would continue caring for him as you are already doing and so well. Monitor his reaction to events around him, the sounds and movements he makes and any words he speaks. Keep a diary and in six months or even a year, come and see me again.'

He stood and the nurse entered with a certain infant. Louisa took James and held him close, dropped her head and kissed his nose. George shook the hand of the Professor and the family left for home.

'You've done the right thing, my darling,' whispered George once the train departed. She smiled at her husband and they both studied their sleeping son. He looked divine.

Chapter 21

Louisa did as suggested and kept a diary, not of the weather, family news or life at Wolferton but rather the actions of her first born.

Oct 12 James slept longer today than is usual.
Oct 17 He seems to want to clap his hands but can't do so.
Oct 30 James good with solid foods and sleeps for long periods.
Nov 9 Always happy but limited limb movement.

The weather grew colder with Christmas approaching and Louisa thought about presents and especially for her son. *What will he like? What will he hold and shake and throw and catch?*

George kept busy at the station. On Friday November 20, 1925, his phone rang at the station. He answered it, listened then spoke.

'Of course, thank you for letting me know. I'll attend to it now.'

At his door he spied his senior porter and called. The two men walked towards one another with the SM's body language telling the porter something was up. They met mid-platform.

'I've been informed the Queen Mother has died,' said George.

He paused out of respect for the late Queen Consort.

'She would have been a good age,' said the porter.

'81 next month. Now Sam, you must have been here when other members of the Royal Family died at Sandringham. Please point out anything I do which is not correct.'

'I think you'll find, sir that between them, the LNER and the Palace will have the entire event planned to the minute and all you need do is comply with their instructions.' George relaxed a tad.

Sure enough, mail arrived listing the train formation which included a car with a locked section for the coffin. The locomotive was named plus the arrival and departure times of the Royal Train. The memo listed dignitaries attending, where they would stand on the platform, procedure with the coffin from Sandringham to Wolferton and once there, from the yard to the platform to the funeral car. Even the bare-headed troops guarding the coffin would have a fellow soldier appointed to hold their headgear.

He contacted Head Office to acknowledge their correspondence.

Queen Alexandra would be interred beside her husband, the late King Edward VII, in the chapel at Windsor Castle.

Alone in his office and with all paperwork complete, George breathed easier with a tinge of pride at his part in the proceedings.

Sam Mason re-appeared giving George a start. 'Mr Miracle, the King is here,' he said in a calm voice.

George checked his tie and cap and went out to the platform. His namesake, George V, stood near the entrance with an equerry slightly behind him.

The SM approached, stopped and bowed his head.

'Good day, Mr Miracle.'

'Your Majesty, please accept the condolences of all the staff here at Wolferton.'

'Thank you and for your work regarding my mother's transfer to Windsor.'

'Everything is in order, sir. Do you wish to see the details?'

'Not necessary as I know you railwaymen are nothing if not well organized. Thank you again for all you've done for my mother.'

He turned to go but stopped with George halfway through a bow.

'How is your good lady?' enquired the Monarch remembering how he "gate-crashed" George and Louisa's wedding breakfast.

'Thank you, sir. She and our son are both well.'

He tried to smile. 'Please give her my best wishes.'

This time he did leave and George the SM completed his bow to the back of George the King.

'He's a man of the people,' said the porter. 'He became popular with the troops in the war and even more popular with the people when he changed his family's name to Windsor.' George frowned looking worried. Sam noticed. 'Are you okay, Mr Miracle?'

'I dodged a bullet when His Majesty declined to see my paperwork. I think I wrote St Pancras when it should have been King's Cross.'

The railwaymen grinned as the 10:11 arrived from King's Lynn.

Over supper, with James asleep, his parents maintained their routine of exchanging news. They discussed the Queen Mother's death after which Louisa would talk about her day with James as George listened in silence and would only comment or ask questions when she finished. With no questions or comments, he began describing his day by making a statement.

'I met someone today who asked to be remembered to you.'

'Oh?' asked an interested Louisa.

'How is your good lady?' he said and George left it there.

Intrigued and annoyed in equal measure, she replied. 'Well come on, George, who was it?'

'Guess,' he said making her even more impatient.

'A clue would help; male, female, local.'

'*He* was at our wedding.'

She pondered the guest list. 'Well that's easy; there were only a handful of men.' She stared at him and he kept a straight face. Her mouth opened and stayed open before she spoke. 'Not the King?'

'Indeed,' he said grinning. 'His Majesty popped in to thank the staff for caring for his mother and then asked after "my good lady".'

'He didn't,' she gasped.

'I told His Majesty my wife and son were in rude health and then he said, "Please give her my best wishes".'

Louisa dropped her guard wondering if her husband, a constant trickster, was playing one of his games. Her expression changed.

'What?' he asked.

'You've tricked me so many times before, George Miracle.'

He indicated the cottage pie. 'You know, this is as good as my Ma or Daisy would make and even, *even* possibly a smidgeon better.'

She knew there were times when he teased her and times when he spoke the truth. Right now his expression shouted, "I'm dead serious about the King *and* the pie."

Events went like clockwork with the body of the late Queen Mother being transported from Wolferton station to London. The locals turned up in droves. Queen Victoria always drew a crowd at the station, coming or going to Sandringham, and on this occasion, her daughter-in-law proved to be as popular.

The Queen Mother lay in state in Westminster Abbey before the state funeral after which she was transported to Windsor Castle and interment beside her husband.

Danish by birth, Alexandra quickly became a favourite of the people and particularly the female sex. She put up with her husband's shenanigans, spoke her mind even on matters political, and gave generously, many said *too* generously, to anyone who asked for help.

December 25, 1925 saw the second Miracle Christmas at Wolferton. Being a single lady with no other family, naturally Rowena was there, and she and Louisa spent time talking about intimate subjects.

'What do you think about James?' asked his mother.

'He seems fine. Your letters did cause me to worry but now I'm here and holding him, I think you're a typical new mother. It's natural to worry. He's grown since I last saw him and his talking and walking will happen naturally. Give it time, my darling. He certainly appears to be a happy baby.'

Louisa drew strength from her mother's comments. 'Do you think I'm a bad mother taking him to see doctors at the drop of a hat?'

'Of course I don't and in fact you're doing a wonderful job raising James while caring for your busy and famous husband.'

'I thought he was teasing me with his tale about the King giving me his best wishes.'

Rowena shifted the tone of their chat in an instant. 'Have you and George thought about having another child?'

Louisa hesitated. 'I think we'll try but wait until James is a little older.' Neither spoke for a moment or more. 'Mother, what should I tell James when he is older if he asks about my father?'

Rowena copped a sudden chest pain. 'The truth is always best.'

'But I know so little; his date of birth, or the names of his parents. I mean are they still alive? They should be told about James.'

Rowena struggled to contain her panic. 'Please my darling, it's Christmas, let's not think about anything sad from so long ago.'

Louisa accepted her mother's reluctance as it was obvious she became sad when Louisa's father and his family were discussed. The women switched to the luncheon planned for Christmas Day.

George's brother-in-law, Bert Culpepper, obtained a leave pass from his father this Christmas, and joined his wife and son and Connie and John Beckwith as they all headed to Wolferton by train.

The dining-room table needed to be extra strong once the food and drink appeared for eight adults and two and a half infants. Now expecting her second child, Emily found herself being feted as the Queen Bee of the hive.

Already pals, the sisters-in-law became even closer. Before the Christmas Day luncheon, the young mothers spent time discussing children. Emily nursed her nephew, James, and found him fascinated with her but still not at the speaking stage. On the contrary, Emily and Bert's son, John, was older and full of beans. His speech and movements were going ahead in leaps and bounds.

George worked until noon on Christmas Day. He discussed rosters at length with his porters and made sure he worked his fair share.

'You have a young family, sir,' said Sam Mason.

'And you'll have visitors,' added Lennie Greene. 'We'll take care of the station so you can go home and tuck into the sausages.'

All the porters laughed and George thanked them.

Of course the SM remained on duty when various members of the Royal Family arrived before Christmas. The King and Queen were still in mourning over the loss of their mother and mother-in-law.

George missed the church service at St Peter's on Christmas morning but all the other residents from the station master's house walked the few hundred yards, even Emily, with infants in prams. Kenneth Attwood starred in the pulpit greeting the worshippers with his electric smile. He would soon join the Miracles for luncheon as his housekeeper spent every Christmas with her son and his family in King's Lynn. The rector became a most welcome guest—the 8th adult.

His evening meal at the home of the church organist and her family proved less boisterous but equally enjoyable. A typical village, Wolferton residents opened their hearts and homes to others.

The Miracle luncheon overflowed with joy as Grandmothers Connie and Rowena thrilled to see their children and grandchildren happy and healthy. Everyone expected George to depart once festivities ended. He did. His station called.

New Year's Eve saw a much quieter Miracle house. All the guests had departed leaving George, Louisa and James to keep warm as 1926 crept into the village.

George saw off the final train, the last at Wolferton in 1925 and kept tackling paperwork. He arrived late to find Louisa reading a book curled up in a lounge chair before the fire. James slept in his cot beside her. This was cot number two, his other stood in his parents' bedroom.

The SM kissed his wife's head. 'Why aren't you in bed, Mrs Miracle?'

'Because we must always see in the New Year together.'

He removed his coat and cap and examined his sleeping son. 'Do you call one year a tradition?' She smiled. 'Tea?' he asked.

'Yes please; I'll make it. You can read the introduction to my book.'

She returned with the tea and a plate of home-baked biscuits made by one of their mothers. There were so many goodies it seemed the grandmothers were competing in a sweetmeats' competition.

'I think it's interesting,' she said referring to her book.

George stopped reading. 'It is ... and sad.'

She handed him his mug and sat beside him on the settee.

'George, my darling, I know I'm going on and on about James but I can't stop being worried. This book talks about how and why babies develop and I think our boy may have one of the conditions it mentions. I know you love James more than anyone or anything else in the world but not talking about him possibly being ill is not good for him or for us.' She stopped and waited for George to speak.

'You're right of course. What can we do?'

She took heart needing him on her side. 'I've been keeping a diary of what James tries to say and do. If we show my notes to the paediatrician in Lynn, it may help him diagnose James.'

George nodded. 'I'll make a copy and post it with a covering letter.'

She took his mug of tea and placed it on the tray. She sat beside him, lifted her head and kissed him. They hugged one another and kept on doing so as the fire faded and the grandfather clock in the hall flexed its muscles preparing to sound its Westminster chimes to ring in the New Year.

What will it bring? thought both the Miracle parents.

Chapter 22

One significant event in February 1926 involved the philanthropist, Sir Jerome Hamilton-Weir. He died. A peaceful end, he expired quietly in his sleep. His nurse brought him his morning cuppa which went cold; a bit like the hearts of his twins.

In late February, George, Louisa and baby James set off for King's Lynn. The paediatrician received the notes from Louisa's diary and asked the parents to bring James to see him again.

The Wolferton porters knew their SM worried about his boy and didn't hesitate to cover his shift.

The trip to King's Lynn began with the weather biting-cold thanks to winds direct from Siberia making the waiting-room in the West Norfolk and King's Lynn Hospital a jolly warm place to be.

'Come in,' said Professor Reid welcoming the family Miracle. They sat in his consulting-room as their worry-level rose further.

'I must congratulate you both on your record-keeping with young James. I found it most helpful. If only all my parents were so dedicated and efficient.'

The compliments helped a little. George explained. 'My wife created the notes, Professor. She deserves all the credit.'

'Well, there are those who care for the little ones and others who keep the trains running,' he said with a grin.

He didn't grin again that morning. He placed James on the bed and examined him. The boy cried briefly, whimpered and gave what his parents reckoned to be a laugh.

The nurse picked up the infant and left. The professor explained. 'I would like one of my colleagues to examine James. It won't take long. Please stay here and we'll be back in a few minutes.

The few minutes became several then many. The parents did little talking and a lot of hand holding. Their love for one another was never stronger and they took comfort simply observing one another even if their smiles were forced.

They sat taller when the nurse entered carrying James and Professor Reid followed. The nurse placed James in a cot and waited beside him. The adult Miracle hearts raced at a dangerous pace.

'My colleague examined James and we agree your son has most likely acquired a condition known as cerebral palsy.'

Louisa stifled a scream and couldn't stop tears appearing. George squeezed her hand and willed himself to remain calm. He spoke first.

'When you say most likely, Professor, do you mean you're not certain?'

'Because James is so young, accurate diagnosis is difficult. But our examination together with the notes taken by Mrs Miracle, suggest his brain is not functioning in what we consider a normal way.'

Louisa wanted facts. 'Will he die?' she asked in a polite but blunt fashion.

'Let me explain what we know about cerebral palsy.' The paediatrician explained using words the Miracles could understand. 'It's a condition, a physical disability which can affect movement, posture and speech. It lasts for the patient's lifetime but does not necessarily become worse and is caused when the brain is injured either during pregnancy or soon after birth.' He stared directly at Louisa. 'It is definitely not anyone's fault and certainly not the mother's. At present there is no known cure.'

George and Louisa both wanted to ask questions and by the time the explanation ended, their minds were racing as their hearts began to shatter.

They left for home with notes, instructions and a determination to give their son the best possible chance to live a long and happy life despite his probable disability.

George wanted Louisa to talk about something else or if about James, to discuss the activities they would undertake for their boy. The journey seemed to take forever although it was only the short distance from King's Lynn to Wolferton, about 9 miles.

Two porters moved to open the carriage door when they spotted the Miracles. They were clever men. Rather than ask how the trip went, or about the condition of wee James, they pushed other topics.

'Welcome home Mrs Miracle,' said Lennie Greene.

'All trains on time, sir,' reported Sam Mason although we heard about a minor accident with a cow on the line the other side of Heacham.'

George wanted to stay and check paperwork in his office. He found himself being politely pushed away.

'Len and I have matters covered here, sir. You run along home and enjoy a good fire. We'll see you in the morning.'

'Good night, Mrs Miracle,' called the porters touching their caps. George gave his porters a grim but grateful smile and whispered, 'Thank you, gentlemen'. He carried James home and relief flooded the body of both parents when they closed the kitchen door.

Louisa continued her diary about James. She took on the main task of massaging the infant's arms and legs. Using a list of words well-known to infants and toddlers, she spoke these words again and again, pointing and smiling and encouraging the lad. She became both a physiotherapist and a speech therapist untrained but determined to help her son develop.

Telling their mothers the sad news hurt both teller and listener. Connie became depressed not knowing how she could help in a practical sense with Emily expecting her second.

Rowena offered to move to Wolferton and take over the domestic duties. For now, her kind offer was politely declined. George and Louisa spent ages talking about their new roles as parents giving hope and strength and skills to their possibly seriously disabled child.

'We need professional help, my dear,' said George. 'All your efforts are brilliant but what James needs are experts in building muscles and in teaching a child who has trouble even shaping his words.'

'Can we afford professionals?'

George took in a deep breath. His wage covered normal living expenses for an average family, but the Miracles faced extraordinary expenses. And what if they chose to have another child or children? Could they afford the extra expense?

Rowena wrote again offering to help whenever needed.

'My mother wants to become an unpaid housekeeper,' said Louisa.

'She's the best grannie in the world,' said George feeling confused and depressed the more he considered the situation. His SM duties kept calling and without his job he couldn't support his family.

The couple thought it rude to continue refusing Rowena's on-going offer and she arrived, moved into the downstairs bedroom at the back of the house and told her daughter to forget about the shopping, cooking, washing and cleaning.'

'It's *my* role, Louisa, you concentrate on helping James.'

Louisa spoke to people who knew about cerebral palsy, read anything she could find on the subject, and again discovered there was no known cure for the condition. She kept that from her mother.

Life went on; George ran the station with his usual efficiency but at times became irritable if events didn't run smoothly. Porters and others spotted his temper albeit noting it to be always under control.

Everyone knew about his son's health problems and either kept an eye on Mr Miracle or kept out of his way.

After a week living with the Miracles, Rowena sat for a discussion with her daughter and son-in-law. While extremely grateful for Rowena's tireless efforts, George became uncomfortable. He knew his wife shared his discomfort. Refusing Rowena's love caused angst.

They decided to hire professional therapists to come to the house and work with James. They drew up a budget. Things were tight.

Having hand delivered a letter to the father of her child informing him of their daughter's marriage, Rowena wondered if she would be asked to vacate the Foxton cottage. Ignoring that possibility, she made an offer she might not be able to fulfill. 'I have the answer. I'll rent my cottage and put the funds into an account for James.'

George and Louisa protested. 'No, Mummy, you mustn't do it.'

'We can't ask you to give up your cottage, your life with your friends and your church to become an unpaid housekeeper.'

'Why not? It's my life and why can't I help my family, the people I love?'

A silence landed in the station master's house. The young couple wanted to raise their family on their own. They would normally welcome any offer of help but this seemed way too generous.

'Let's sleep on it,' said George, 'and we can discuss it tomorrow.'

Next morning, before his wife and her mother were even out of bed, George was hard at work at the Wolferton station. People often saw him throwing himself into his work but now his dedication reached new heights. Many wondered if the pressure would harm him.

A Down train arrived from King's Lynn. A middle-aged gent in a suit, coat and hat alighted carrying an umbrella and briefcase. He spoke to a porter who pointed at George who saw the man approach.

'Good morning, sir' said the SM. 'How can I help?'

'Mr George Miracle?' asked the passenger.

'I am.'

'Is your wife the former Miss Louisa McClaren?'

'She is,' replied George intrigued.

Who is this man and why is he asking such questions?

'My name is Ashcroft and I have business with her.'

With the pressure caused by his son's condition, George became a coiled spring, a powder-keg. He snapped. 'What sort of business?'

'I'm afraid I can only discuss the matter with your wife, sir.'

Struggling, the SM told Sam Mason he would take the passenger to the station house and return as quickly as possible.

A buzz ran around the station as George escorted the gent. They entered through the back door, as always, to find Rowena making breakfast for herself, Louisa and James.

'Louisa, this gentleman wishes to speak to you.'

The atmosphere caught fire. All Wolferton adults were fascinated.

'Good morning. Are you the former Miss Louisa McClaren?'

'Wait a minute,' said George interrupting. 'Who are you and do you have any identification?'

'I do sir, but I don't wish to explain my business until I am sure I am speaking to the right person.'

'I used to be Louisa McClaren but now I'm Mrs George Miracle.'

The gent remained polite. 'May I see some identification please?'

This was frighteningly unusual. George recovered first. 'Our wedding certificate, Louisa,' he said.

When she returned and showed the paperwork, the gent relaxed. 'Thank you. My name is Ashcroft. I'm a private detective working for a firm of London solicitors.' He opened his case and removed a folder containing several pages. 'I'm instructed to hand you this document. It states you are a beneficiary in the estate of the late Sir Jerome Hamilton-Weir.'

Chapter 23

In Eaton Square, Sophronia and her twin brother Enoch were no longer mourning the death of their dear pater. The period of their grief, complete with crocodile tears, could have been measured in minutes if at all. Now their anxiety kicked in. What's in the will?

Having threatened their father while he lay seriously ill in hospital, and been told by his solicitor's clerk their father's will was changed soon thereafter, the twins were dead-set keen to get their hands on the cash; all of it with none of this sharing with that bastard half-sister.

Being given the title deeds to this glorious London mansion as well as the family country seat in Cambridgeshire was a given. In addition they wanted all the cash sitting in the old man's account; or did they mean accounts plural? Oh, and the healthy portfolio of his shares too.

'Slip a pony to the solicitor's clerk you bump into at the races and have him give you the details of the new will,' said Sophronia already planning on spending big. 'Tip him well.'

'There are no races for at least a fortnight.'

'Damn, well I'm not going to turn up at some rundown suburban solicitor's office and ask for the will. How cheap do you think I am?' She turned on him. 'You're good at groveling. You go.'

He hated groveling. 'Surely they have an obligation to contact the beneficiaries once probate is granted.'

She flared, suspicious. 'Once probate is granted? What do you mean and how do you know legal jargon?'

'I'm not just a pretty face, sister dear. These wills take time.'

She stared and glared at him thinking. *Don't even think about cracking jokes.* 'You'd better not be trying to do me over, Enoch. Try it and I'll have your dangly bits for Christmas decorations.'

'I told you I read the *Wills Act* of 1837.'

Sophronia fumed discovering her brother showed initiative and intelligence but before she could explode, the twins were interrupted by their father's valet holding a tray on which rested two envelopes. 'Mail for you sir, madam,' he said holding out the tray.

The twins tried hard not to run. Each grabbed their envelope, moved apart and tore at the item to discover the contents. The servant departed being glad to do so.

Sophronia read fast and reacted faster. Screaming, she discovered oaths and curses she never knew she possessed. 'I'll kill him,' she spat. Of course killing a deceased person would be a first for science. 'We'll appeal and have the whole thing thrown out.'

'You need to read the attached letter,' said Enoch who remained calm although furious. 'I think Mr Shakespeare referred to it as "Hoist with his own petard".' He continued reading.

The oaths kept coming from big sister. It took her an age to (a) understand she'd not been given what she expected and (b) discover her late father used her blackmail threat against him to prevent her and her brother from ever challenging the revised and final will.

Downstairs, the domestics spoke in animated voices.

'I'm not staying here,' said the butler. 'I'll never work for those spoilt, evil brats.'

'And go where?' asked the cook. 'I heard they've been given the poisoned chalice.'

'What's the poisoned chalice?' asked the chambermaid.'

The butler shocked them all. 'Why don't we all just up and leave?'

'What?' exclaimed the women as one.

'Imagine their faces when no-one responds to their bell-ringing so they storm downstairs and find the place deserted.'

He grinned and the females joined in. That *would* be worth seeing.

Louisa took the folder with an expression best described as stunned. With mouth open, she stared at her husband and mother. They too found speaking difficult. The visitor started the conversation.

'I require you to sign and date this letter. It's a receipt acknowledging you have received the documents.'

He held out the letter, George stepped forward, took and read it. 'It's okay,' he assured Louisa. The private detective held out a fountain pen. Louisa signed and dated the letter returning both items to the visitor.

'Thank you for your time,' he said and turned to George. 'What's the fastest way back to London?'

'Come with me,' said George and led the man outside.

The mother and daughter stared at one another with questions and answers ready to go when James began to cry. Without hesitation both women left the room and George returned to find it empty. He spotted the document, picked it up and read.

The women returned with James in his mother's arms.

'This cannot be true and if so will one of you please pinch me,' he said indicating the document.

'Is it a mistake?' asked Louisa.

'Not unless there are two women called Louisa Gillian McClaren of Tudor House, Hampstead born on the same day as you, my dear.'

The shock lingered. Most people have at least one major even catastrophic event happen to them in their lifetime. Giving birth to a baby with a lifelong, life-changing physical and/or mental condition is certainly a major event. But to receive an inheritance from a person you've barely even heard of, for Louisa makes it two major events.

'What does it mean?' she asked rocking her son.

George again studied the document. 'Well if I've read this correctly, you now own a seven-bedroom house in Eaton Square, Belgravia, London complete with all furnishings, plus cash and shares to the value of more than a hundred thousand pounds.'

Shockwaves bounced around the room followed by stunned silence. Heart rates took off.

George turned on his usual so-called sense of humour. 'And you think I married you for your beauty.'

His wife didn't laugh. 'I can't believe it. There has to be a mistake. They've picked the wrong Louisa McClaren. Why would this man, this stranger give me so much money? I met him once for five seconds, said hello and he was gone.'

In the silent pause, the only person who knew the answer began to cry, silently at first but with small, ever-increasing sobs. Stunned, even scared, George and Louisa stared at her waiting for her to speak.

'Because he's your father,' said Rowena and her tears exploded. Later, her reaction doubled in intensity when she discovered she too was a beneficiary as the Foxton cottage now belonged to her.

'I can't believe this,' fumed Sophronia. 'The illegitimate bitch scores the cash, the shares *and* this house and we're stuck with the country seat and not a penny.'

'It's worse,' added Enoch moving away from his sister in case she took out her rage on her sibling; the one in the same room.

'Worse? What the hell do you mean?' she snapped.

'He's left a cottage in Foxton to the woman he impregnated.'

'What!' screamed Sophronia scanning the document for details.

'We do get the country seat but there's a catch; it's mortgaged to the hilt so we're stuck with a massive debt and to pay it off, we'll have to sell the property meaning we'll each finish up with fifty per cent of sod all.' Sophronia froze. 'The old man's re-mortgaged the Cambridgeshire property to punish us.'

Sophronia wanted an object to throw. Enoch continued.

'And as we have next to nothing apart from the mater's pathetic bequest, we'll have a roof over our heads in the sticks but with no staff to cook and clean and no income to repay the mortgage.'

'This is a bloody outrage!'

'You could always find a job, sister dear.'

Now she did throw an object and Enoch warned her.

'Stop that! The will stipulates nothing, large or small, apart from clothes, shoes, personal jewellery given specifically to either of us, and toiletries and underwear, may be removed from this house.'

She hissed. 'Underwear? The bloody will stipulates underwear?'

'I think in this case, we can assume the pater is taking the piss or crapping all over us or both.'

Sophronia made a sort of growling sound as she turned red and clenched her hands so tight her eyes ached.

Louisa and George stared at Rowena. Her distress shocked them and her comment flattened them.

'He is my father?' gasped Louisa. 'But you said my father's name was Richard McClaren and he died before I was born.

'I lied, what else could I do?' said Rowena and sobbed.

George took control. 'Come and sit down, all of us.' They did and even James became quiet. His frightening future prospects were now seen in a new and vastly different light. His mother, and by virtue of marriage, his father were now instantly wealthy, fabulously rich.

Once settled and Rowena mopped up her misery and fear, she explained. The Miracles heard how the then Mr Hamilton-Weir seduced a young servant girl who became pregnant. The gift of the Foxton cottage and the upkeep of his daughter, Louisa, were to be kept secret and had been until now.

George re-read the documents. 'He has two legitimate children and they will hardly be happy as you get pretty much everything. They may well appeal and win,' said George not understanding the blackmail wording designed to prevent the will being challenged.

The three of them sat there, flabbergasted. Their lives would never be the same again. Or would they?

Sophronia reckoned she'd worked it out. 'Dickie Carrington hates us. He failed to fix the bitch, missed out on a big pay day, suffered terrible injuries and to get back at us, he's gone to the pater and blabbed about his attempt to kill her under our instructions. The pater changed his will to punish us and reward the bitch.'

'Carrington wouldn't confess to anything because if he did he'd be up at the Old Bailey on a conspiracy to murder charge,' added Enoch.

Sophronia screamed in frustration and anger. She connived. 'We may be a soft target but he's softer. He needs to suffer.'

Enoch despaired. 'Oh for Christ's sake, Sophronia, stop all this bloody revenge. We were shafted because we went after the old man's little pet. If we'd left her alone we'd be seriously comfortable with a third each and set for the rest of our lives. Face it, woman, we blew it.'

The thing Sophronia hated the most was the fact her brother spoke the truth. 'No problem,' she said. 'I'll slip into Plan B.'

'Which is?' he asked curious and yet understandably afraid.

'I'll marry into money.'

He thought about saying his next speech but went ahead anyway.

'Sorry, sister dear, but wealthy old men want youthful virgins and dashing young chaps want wealthy old hags. You ain't either.'

That was a seriously powerful insult albeit the truth. He fled before she could scratch out his eyes.

Over breakfast the next morning in the Wolferton station master's house, the adults did what they always did but with limited conversation. George and Louisa were instant millionaires but still incapable of fully comprehending the news.

Louisa's father died a knight of the realm. Super rich, he bequeathed the bulk of his estate to his illegitimate daughter.

She tossed and turned during the night remembering the luncheon she attended in his spacious Eaton Square home; the home which now belonged to her. She recalled the brief meeting when by accident she met the man who owned the property—her father.

Louisa kept re-living the few words they exchanged, his appearance, his children who are her siblings, and found it impossible to be excited about her stunning slice of great fortune. It was too much to handle. Her poor mother lived for years with a huge secret. Louisa's father built a reputation as a generous philanthropist and apparently mixed with Royalty at many charitable occasions.

He knew the recently deceased Queen Mother. Her son proposed a toast at Louisa and George's wedding. Did Louisa's father know of this event?

He certainly did as the private detective hired by Sir Jerome kept him abreast of most events, certainly important events such as the marriage of his youngest child and the Royal connection.

Talk about mind-boggling.

That morning, as George left for work, he spoke to his wife and mother-in-law.

'I think for the immediate future, we should say nothing about our unbelievable news; tell no-one, and I mean no-one.'

'I agree,' said Louisa.

'I'll not breathe a word,' said Rowena still in shock at the bequest and having her secret finally revealed.

'I'll go to London, visit the solicitor and ask whatever questions we need to ask. Telling anyone about this fortune will be like opening an extremely large can of worms. You don't need me to tell you how people will react. Are we agreed?'

The women nodded. 'Yes, my dear,' said Louisa and her mother cried again. He left for the station.

Chapter 24

The Domino Effect took off after World War 1. Germany lost and from the Treaty of Versailles found itself required to pay massive war reparations. Many German soldiers were incensed including one born in Austria, an obscure, mustachioed corporal named Hitler.

Struggling to pay its debts, Germany was offered a deal allowing it to pay in cash or kind and so offered coal as part payment. 'Thank you,' said France and Italy. Cue the dominoes.

If Germany was giving it away, why buy British? This created a coal-mine-size hole in the British budget, one of the world's leading producers of coal. The country lost export income and the LNER lost too with much less coal to transport.

In 1923, France, annoyed at the slow reparation payments, laid claim to the Ruhr. The price of the black stuff collapsed. Less coal came from British pits and with depressed prices, the mine owners saw profits plummet. Their solution was to cut wages by nearly 50% and, to rub salt in the miners' wounds, increase the hours men had to work. You can imagine their reaction; more hours for less pay.

Exhausted, miners limped home to their miserable, malnourished children. Life for thousands of families became unbearable.

The unions reasoned with the mine owners and achieved nothing. The Trades Union Congress decided; they must strike.

But the TUC reckoned miners striking alone would have little impact. Far better to have as many unions as possible join them. They invited their comrades to strike, including those in the railways.

George Miracle worried because he felt obliged to run his station, his child struggled with serious health issues, a mammoth windfall needed tackling and now, he faced the choice of going on strike. What did his employer have to say about it? And remember, George sported a tattoo, "I'm a company man" on his heart—he was in fact two men; Mr Loyal and Mr Hard-Working.

Talk of a general strike filled the newspapers with the government using the press to warn of dire consequences should such a strike take place. Paperwork continually landed on the SM's desk. One memo from the LNER grabbed his attention.

It stated, "Striking railwaymen would be regarded as having acted in breach of contract".

Right, thought George. *We all know what the company thinks.*

He chatted with his Wolferton colleagues. The men on the footplate, in the guard's van, and those operating signals were in the hot seat. If they joined the strike, the trains wouldn't run and their jobs could be over.

'I'll leave it to you, gentlemen. You decide to strike or not.'

Amidst all this public frenzy of threat and anger, George wanted answers to questions about Louisa's inheritance. He went to London.

If George reckoned the news of the bequest to Louisa would remain a secret, he'd made a basic mistake. There were several possible leaks. Louisa's siblings, although furious, could blab. The solicitor's clerk who'd sell his soul for sixpence leaked like a sieve. Were there other beneficiaries? His mother-in-law was one. Anyway, the cat escaped.

In London, George made his way to the office of the solicitor who handled Sir Jerome's will. Without an appointment, he could have a wasted journey but took the chance. The SM slipped ever closer to paranoia thinking about such fantastic wealth. He travelled in his SM's uniform and found himself in a solicitor's office.

'We know who you are, Mr Miracle,' said the solicitor handling the estate. 'Through his agent, Sir Jerome told us of his son-in-law.' This rocked George who'd been told Louisa's father died decades ago. 'No doubt you have questions,' smiled the man wearing a bow-tie.

Many answers later, the solicitor broached another subject. 'The country property in Cambridgeshire, bequeathed to Sir Jerome's other children, is for sale. You and your wife may wish to purchase it although I suggest using an agent acting on your behalf. We would be happy to act for you should you choose to make an offer. I am confident a reasonable figure would be accepted although there is a mortgage to be repaid. However, having studied your wife's bequest, I am sure it will clearly be possible.'

Half an hour after he arrived, George ended his chat with the man who knew Louisa's father as well as anyone. 'If your wife would care to ask me about Sir Jerome, I would be happy to tell her all I know. If acceptable, I could call one afternoon to your humble abode in Eaton Square.'

His eyes sparkled and George struggled to behave normally. He walked to the station as if tipsy, and passed a newsstand with a poster declaring the words, **General Strike**.

Despite the threat of a nationwide strike, life continued and the King and Queen rejoiced when a new granddaughter arrived. The Duke and Duchess of York produced a daughter, Elizabeth, to be known within the family as Lilibet.

The General Strike began on May 3, 1926. Britain never saw anything like it. The government ordered the army to perform certain tasks. Volunteers drove buses. Men who crossed the picket lines and continued to work needed police protection. Thousands marched filling the streets of major cities with union banners on display.

The Monarch of course was above politics but George V did show his colours when he said, 'Try living on their wages before you judge them'.

George Miracle kept working. His life changed. If he joined the strike and was sacked, his loss of an income would mean nothing. Millionaire became his new status, his middle name.

Some miners used the railways to try and make the strike successful. The well-known LNER locomotive, *Flying Scotsman*, was not the same as the train, *Flying Scotsman*. Near Newcastle and with 600 passengers on board, the train was deliberately derailed. Only one passenger was hurt but the LNER suffered serious delays. The eight miners who sabotaged the track were caught and jailed.

Thousands of railwaymen did go on strike but the government tried everything to keep the trains running. Bank managers lived out a boyhood dream when charged with firing locomotives. Young chaps in plus fours waved a green flag or drove on the London Underground, one by reading instructions in the cab on the job.

The government stood firm and introduced legislation making coming out on strike in sympathy illegal. This became an example of a government able to change the law in next to no time if they put their mind to it. Of course this new legislation helped the mine owners and hammered the unions.

A few unions supporting the miners got cold feet. If they continued their support, they would be heavily fined. They weakened. After 9 days, the General Strike ended. Many men kept striking but the little money the union could pay them eventually ran out.

The unions lost, the mine owners won and the children of poorly paid men working underground continued in misery. Some families suffered more than others as mining accidents and fatalities were an all too common occurrence. Compensation, what compensation?

Six months after the strike ended, about 25% of railway employees who went out were yet to be re-employed. And there were now half a million capable vehicle drivers in the country. Stand by your lorry.

The twins cut their losses. Of course they couldn't pay the mortgage on the Cambridgeshire property and any money raised from its sale would at least put a little folding stuff in their pockets. They agreed to sell. With no choice, and wallowing in shame (Enoch) and anger (Soffy), they retired to a cottage their mother left them which was rented ever since her death. It reeked of ordinary with a dying garden and a leaking roof. Sophronia once described it as a broke fisherman's hovel. Now it became her home. Enoch joined her with plans to abscond as soon as anything better appeared.

They were so desperate and cruel they forced the long-term and elderly tenant to move into the decrepit shed in the back garden reducing his normal rent by a measly ten per cent.

Oh my, how the once mighty twins have fallen.

When the Duke of Fakenham heard the gossip, he laughed so much and for so long, neighbours thought he suffered apoplexy.

George, Louisa and Rowena sat for a serious discussion. He told them all he learnt when in London including the possible purchase of the Cambridgeshire property.

'*More* property?' gasped Louisa.

'We can easily afford it,' he said.

'But why and what will we do with it?' demanded Louisa. 'We don't even need the London mansion and as you work every hour God sends, we'll never go there. And think of the upkeep.'

'It could be an investment,' suggested Rowena. Her comment stopped the others. They needed an explanation. 'Your father became a philanthropist by helping needy causes. Louisa, you could follow in his footsteps.' The intrigue increased.

'Mummy, I have no idea what you're talking about.'

'You could use the Cambridgeshire property to help people in need. Hire a manager to run a charity in the house and grounds. Your father would be so proud.'

Talk about a shock. They currently lived in a spacious and lovely station house owned by the company, a perk of George's job. Overnight they joined the Midas Club to be confronted with choices they once could never even dream about. George ran with Rowena's suggestion.

'Could a mother who alone raised her daughter be involved in a charity for single mothers?'

Another conversation-stopper bounced around the room. This life-changing bequest affected all three of them and all three knew it would affect a fourth member, young James. George continued.

'This money, the properties and shares can be used to hire people to help James. We can give him the therapy he needs and give him the chance to grow and reach his true potential.' The women cried.

George contacted the London solicitor and arrangements were made to purchase the property in Cambridgeshire. The twins never knew the identity of the new owners. Being professional hagglers, the sale didn't happen overnight but their desperate plight saw them buckle.

George and Louisa hired a housekeeper allowing Rowena to return to her cottage in Foxton. Miss Ruth Halfpenny lived in the Wolferton village with her sister and brother-in-law. Ruth cared for her elderly parents for years until they died. Her cooking skills were superb, and she loved being able to walk back to her family home once a week for a meal and a chat.

Finding physio and speech therapists proved tricky because living so far away meant travel for young James would be a tremendous time-consuming exercise. Nothing came of it. The Miracle isolation became a second disadvantage for James. Wolferton was a small village. When the station opened in 1862, there were 200 villagers.

Medical specialists tend to live in the big cities. For James to receive constant professional care, big changes were required.

With gossip on the rise about the Miracle good fortune, George went on the front foot. He rang his friends George and Valerie Carruthers. He lied about being in London on railway business and could they meet him for coffee before he rushed back to Wolferton. They happily agreed and George asked them to meet him at a coffee house near Eaton Square.

After their warm greeting, George broke the news. 'I want to show you something and ask your advice.'

Intrigued, the couple were led into Eaton Square and stopped outside a certain house.

'I have news I wish to share.'

'This is not like you, George,' said Lady Carruthers. 'Coffee in Belgravia; have you come into money?

George spoke in a calm, unemotional way. 'As a matter of fact, we have.' The Carruthers were all ears. 'We've been told Louisa's biological father is the late philanthropist, Sir Jerome Hamilton-Weir. She is his illegitimate daughter.' His companions gasped. 'A few days ago, we discovered the wealthy man has died and left most of his estate, not to his legitimate children but to Louisa. Part of his estate includes this house.' He indicated.

Lord and Lady Carruthers stared at the front of the magnificent property, at George and back at the house. They knew about his sense of humour but not for a second did they consider this a joke.

'I don't know what to say,' said George 1.

'Good for you, George and well done, Louisa,' said Valerie.

'Shall we go inside?' asked George 2 and led them to the gleaming black front door.

He unlocked it and the trio entered the magnificent entrance hall with its black and white tiled floor. The fully furnished house was impressive. How could it not be? After a brief tour and a surfeit of exclamations, they settled in the front drawing-room and the SM made his pitch.

'I need help, George. I need financial advice, legal advice and how to avoid making a terrible mess of our new windfall. Your uncle, the politician, gave me advice once but this seems to be seriously difficult and requires an expert. You are my best friend and I trust you entirely. Please, will you help?'

Louisa found specialists who could work with James to help him become even remotely mobile and speak even if that meant refining his undecipherable sounds. But these professionals lived in London, Cambridge and Birmingham, and they were the ones closest to Wolverton. The distances seriously handicapped the chance of regular treatment for James. Louisa made two decisions.

George arrived home, kissed his wife once, his son twice and collapsed on a chair. Mind you he spent half an hour at the station when he alighted at Wolferton even though he'd taken official leave.

'I think we have the answer,' he sighed sipping his tea.

'Yes, but what's the question?' she asked. 'There are so many.'

'George Carruthers knows a man, a great friend of his poor father, the Lord who was murdered.' Louisa hung on her husband's every word. 'Oh and George and Valerie send their love to you and James.'

'How are their children?'

'Fine but please, let me finish. Crispin Webb is the man's name; he's a solicitor and accountant, semi-retired and who works from home in London. George rang him and I spoke with him briefly. He sounded perfect, *is* perfect. He could help us set up a trust fund for James, a Miracle family company dealing with the income from the properties, and we continue as before living here and raising our boy.'

'No,' said Louisa with force and shocking her husband. 'James needs specialists, and travel to see them is exhausting which would undo any good he receives.'

Right now, George loved his wife even more. He worried though thinking she wanted to move into the Belgravia mansion.

'What should we do?' he asked.

'Buy a small flat in London and once a week or two, with a nanny, we'll take James to London for his treatment.'

'You're brilliant,' said the SM. 'So how do we find a nanny and whereabouts in London would you like to live? I can recommend the Noel Park Estate in Wood Green.' It was the only part of London he knew well having lived there when he worked at Liverpool Street station. But was it handy to medical specialists?

167

Chapter 25

The Miracles drew up a list of topics with questions. Crispin Webb came to Wolferton, stayed the night, and the meetings with George and Louisa established the business side of their new lives. They purchased the Manor House in Cambridgeshire anonymously. Imagine the reaction of the twins if they discovered the "bitch" had bought their country seat. The Miracles searched for a flat in London where Louisa could stay with James for his treatments. They would lease the Eaton Square property, fully furnished, and use the income to fund a charitable activity in Cambridgeshire.

But they would continue to put down roots in Wolferton.

George loved the last decision. Being a station master flowed through his veins. He wrote to his mother revealing their new-found wealth without giving specific details. He struggled to imagine her response. 'Please pass on the news to Em and Bert,' asked George and reckoned they'd be over the moon. His mother's reply worried him. She sounded thrilled and yet confused. Connie grew up in strained circumstances and thus couldn't grasp the size of the inheritance.

A mansion in the heart of London! What would your father say?

George and Louisa discussed sharing their wealth with those they loved. Naturally Louisa didn't consider her half-siblings. George wondered about Emily. They decided to wait on those matters.

For now their top priority became finding treatment for James.

Crispin Webb found and purchased a two-bedroom Mews cottage in Maida Vale not far from Regent's Canal and arranged for his niece to furnish it giving the Miracles their London base. Now they needed a nanny.

Louisa once worked as a nanny for the Carruthers, which serendipitously was how she met her husband. Louisa knew a nanny's duties and chose a local, middle-aged widow whose husband was killed in the Great War. Beatrice "Beau" Twain, small, tough as old boots and with a heart of gold could, George reckoned, have been the daughter of Daisy Woods now residing in Whittleton.

Childless, Beatrice saw the task of dealing with the special needs of James as a personal challenge. A bond between child and nanny developed. In time, he called his nanny what sounded like, 'Yanee'.

They followed a routine. James, Louisa and Beatrice set off for London on Tuesday mornings catching the 09:03 Up at Wolferton. In London, there was a speech therapy session at 3pm and physiotherapy appointment at 10am on Wednesday morning. Overnight they stayed in their Maida Vale cottage. The travelling trio arrived back at Wolferton by late-afternoon with the station master always there to greet them.

Living with their boy, it was hard to see any progress. His physical behaviour seemed static at best, his speech mostly unintelligible. But when Rowena, his maternal grandmother came to stay, she couldn't believe the change in her grandson.

'His movements are so much better and his speech is wonderful.'

'Wunafool,' mimicked the child stunning his parents and grandmother. He took to this parrot-like behaviour where he would seize on a word he heard and repeat it. His diction meant syllables ran into one another producing what sounded like gibberish or as if the boy was drunk. Mind you, James knew exactly what he was saying.

By now the world and its mother knew the Miracles were rich. Of course the story changed from one telling to the next with extraordinary exaggerations flying around. One reckoned George bought the Royal Station and was charging the King and his family to use its facilities.

It matched that apocryphal tale where King Edward VII and his cousin the future Tsar of Russia were not believed by a ticket inspector who claimed to be the Archbishop of Canterbury.

The porters and other staff members at Wolferton treated the SM as if nothing had happened. They did so because George didn't change. He didn't know what airs and graces were, and treated the passengers and his colleagues in the same professional, friendly way.

'It hasn't changed him a bit,' was a common expression heard in the village.

He enjoyed his talks with the Reverend Attwood and there was a standing invitation for the rector to come to the SM's house for coffee after the last train on Sunday evenings once Evensong ended.

In the colder weather they settled inside in the snug but in summer, the back garden became the place to be. The scent from the blossom tickled their sense of smell, and even the insects treated the two friends with respect.

Miss Halfpenny's shortbreads went down a treat. Both men dunked them in their coffee although the rector produced a wee flask and topped up his drink with a splash of single malt. He long ago gave up on persuading the station master to join him.

'So how is your young lad coming along?' asked the priest.

'He's having regular therapies in London and my mother-in-law who hasn't seen James for a couple of months reckoned he's making big strides.'

'Good to hear. I reckon all my parishioners are praying for you and your family, George.'

'Thank you,' whispered the SM.

Kenneth paused before speaking. 'Do you think the Almighty gave you a windfall to make up for the problems taxing your boy?'

George struggled. He thought it a strange, even cruel question but knew the priest could never be described as your average theologian. George knew him to be a decent man who cared for others. Kenneth helped him.

'When I finally meet God, one of my first questions will be about how He chooses which child is landed with a terrible disability or disease or both. I'll ask, "Is it a lottery, Heavenly Father? What's your modus operandi on the selection of children with cancer"?'

George studied his guest. 'Do you say those words to anyone else?'

He chuckled. 'Good heavens no; only to you and my bishop.'

'Your bishop?' gasped George struggling to believe the rector.

'He's like me. "Of course it's all nonsense, Ken", he once said. "But the art, architecture, poetry and music; those glorious, magnificent gifts alone make maintaining the faith essential. Oh and we must give hope to those who *do* believe and rely on their faith".'

'I don't believe you. I think you're making it up.'

Kenneth pretended to be shocked. 'A man of the cloth bearing false witness? What is the world coming to?'

George didn't have an answer so changed the topic. 'I need your help, sir.' The rector heard about the purchase of the manor house in Cambridgeshire and a proposal to use it for charitable purposes. 'We know our benefactor was a philanthropist and wish to continue his good works. My mother-in-law suggested a respite home for parents with children who have a disability. What do you think?'

Kenneth's heart pumped faster. 'I think it's absolutely marvellous and if I can help in any small way, I'd love to be involved. Let me ask a few folk working in that area.'

The priest was nothing if not a man of action. Within a few days he called at the station master's house brimming with excitement.

'I've spoken to people in different charities and they all reckon Mrs McClaren's respite home idea is perfect.'

His response thrilled George and Louisa and when Rowena was told, her heart beat faster. Before long, the dream took flight and the project was off and running.

Using advice from Crispin Webb, the property in Eaton Square was let to an ambassador from a European country, and the funds placed in an account to maintain and run the proposed charity in the Cambridgeshire property. Louisa suggested the venue be called Hamilton-Weir House and Rowena couldn't wait to become involved.

Crispin arranged for a reputable Cambridge builder to visit the property and his recommendation set the project in motion.

Apart from the huge home, there were several outbuildings and the builder suggested they be turned into self-contained flats. With the house and renovated outbuildings, the property would become a place of respite for parents with disabled children and even the children themselves. It could offer respite for the whole family. No visitor would be charged with all services provided free.

Rowena volunteered to become the live-in unpaid housekeeper with plans for resident nurses and a local doctor on call.

George and Louisa were over the moon. They knew about the strain when raising a child with serious health issues. To be able to use their windfall in such a practical way gave their hearts a serious serve of deep satisfaction.

Rowena took delight in seeing how her sad start to life as a mother now became an experience of great joy. Having a personal involvement with her grandson meant she couldn't wait to start.

Life at Wolferton continued as it had for decades but in Cambridgeshire, the new charity went ahead in leaps and bounds. Rowena rented her cottage in Foxton and moved to Cambridgeshire finding a space in the main house while sending written reports of building progress to Wolferton.

It took months of hard work before the property was ready to open. Rowena became the unofficial and accidental project manager. She knew nothing about building regulations and struggled to hang a picture but lived on site making tea for the tradesmen and adding her homemade carrot cake definitely improved the work rate and camaraderie.

Crispin Webb established the charity's legal status and George and Valerie Carruthers and George and Louisa Miracle became trustees.

Rowena kept in close contact with her "partner-in-crime", the Reverend Kenneth Attwood who wholeheartedly supported the project. When Rowena came to Wolferton for a few days mainly to see her grandson, she and the rector put their heads together.

'We're only weeks away from opening,' said Rowena, 'but how will we attract the people who need the service?'

'Let's start with the churches in Cambridge. I'll contact the priests in and around the city explaining what we can offer. In such a large city, there will be mothers in need who will make ideal guests.'

'Mothers only? Surely there are widowers or single fathers with a child in need.'

'Forgive me, Mrs McClaren. Of course we must offer the service to every needy parent, not only in Cambridge but the whole county.'

'And what's happened about finding an administrator and a matron to oversee medical needs.' Rowena's passion preceded her.

The rector was highly impressed with her attitude. 'I love your enthusiasm, madam. I'll go back to the same clergy in Cambridge to help us find the appropriate people.'

Rowena turned serious. 'And remember, we must pay them.'

'Of course,' replied Kenneth; 'the housekeeper, cook, everyone.'

They made a good team, the rector and the grandmother.

Finally, Hamilton-Weir House's opening drew nigh. Rowena and the rector interviewed several applicants for the post of administrator and recommended a Cambridge woman, a retired bookkeeper. A matron took control of matters medical and three nurses were to share shifts with at least one in attendance at all times. The charity was ready to receive its first guests.

'Should we have an official opening ceremony?' asked Rowena.

'Should we invite my father's other children?' asked Louisa who wished she'd remained silent.

Ideas went back and forth until Kenneth asked Rowena a question. 'What do you think Sir Jerome would want us to do?'

'Nothing fancy,' said Rowena.

'I don't believe he went in for grand gestures,' said his daughter.

'Well let's honour the man with you two ladies unveiling a modest plaque in the foyer.'

The women happily agreed and Hamilton-Weir House was open for business.

Chapter 26

Months ticked by and James kept growing. Another birthday, another Christmas and James loved being pushed around in his pram but lying down frustrated him so extra cushions enabled him to sit up and watch the world go by. It also helped his speech as he would point and announce, in his unique way, the name of the object he could identify. His speech became busier.

Life for young James dominated life for the Miracles. He grew, his therapy sessions happened every fortnight in London, the charity in Cambridgeshire helped more and more needy families, and the station at Wolferton ran smoothly under its dedicated station master.

Emily Culpepper made her mother doubly happy by giving birth to another grandchild; Connie's third, making it three boys in a row.

On his latest trip to London, James wiggled around in his pram and the physiotherapist recommended a wheelchair.

'I should have suggested it earlier. It'll also help his mental development and self-confidence.'

When the wheelchair arrived, the boy's eyes fairly gleamed. His father thought it terrific and took the boy for a walk around the garden and along the road to the signal box. Cluffie came out and waved to the boy who thought he was Christmas, slapping the arms of his new wheelchair and grinning incessantly.

'Why did we wait before buying a wheelchair?' asked George.

'Because we thought it would be too much for him,' replied Louisa. 'He loves it; we'll never get him out of it.'

On sunny days James was always with his nanny in the garden but this day Beatrice suggested a trip. 'How about a walk to the station, James?' she suggested.

He slapped the arms of the chair and cried, 'Wains, wains.'

When they arrived on the platform, George was busy dealing with a late train, a disgruntled passenger and a farmer wanting to arrange the transport of his chickens.

'Let me handle this, sir,' said senior porter Sam Mason.

Surprised, George studied him. *Why is he interrupting me?* Sam nodded behind George who turned and stared.

In his new wheelchair being pushed by his nanny, his son was bowling along the platform. The boy wanted to show off his conveyance and in so doing made his father cry; not as would a bawling baby but in silence with tears rolling freely down his cheeks.

George moved to James. The boy held out his right hand as if trying to touch his father from twenty yards away. Beatrice brought the vehicle to a smooth stop and the SM knelt and grasped his boy's hands. In a garbled diatribe from his son, the father copped a solid serve of criticism about crying when he should be happy.

Locals waiting for their train on both platforms knew about the SM and his disabled son. All were transfixed at the sight of Mister and Master Miracle meeting at Wolferton station.

That trip to the station in his wheelchair gave young James a taste for future visits. Now, provided the weather behaved itself, James pestered his nanny to be pushed to either of the platforms. In his fourth year, the boy's intelligence seemed to belie his years. His speech continued to improve and watching him, one could see the effort he put into making sense. His face would contort as he forced his words to become intelligible.

Although his physical disability stood out, it quickly became clear his mental ability suffered no such impairment. Smart, even intelligent best described James Miracle. He would be seated on the platform with Beatrice beside him being greeted by porters and passengers with his father both worried and roaring with pride. It didn't take the child long to twig how certain trains arrived at certain times on certain platforms.

'Own,' he would say pointing to the Down platform. In mid-morning when they first arrived, he knew the 11:08 would pull in heading to Hunstanton. He requested being settled beside a certain station bench so he was opposite the locomotives when they stopped.

The enginemen on the footplate knew the kid in the wheelchair, his relationship to the SM, and always waved and called out to him. A few called him Jimmy which at first upset the child with him calling back, 'Ames, I'm Ames.' But he found it delightful loving his own special name. He told his mother about it, she who insisted the boy must always be called James.

Louisa soon weakened seeing how much her son reacted to people who clearly cared about him. She never called him anything other than James, apart from Darling and Dear, but she loved the drivers and firemen christening her James Jimmy.

On the platforms, James would wave as best he could and couldn't wait for the trains to leave. Without fail, each driver would, against all regulations of course, give the whistle a short toot or occasionally two toots sending Master Miracle into a paroxysm of delight. He bounced in his wheelchair, grinning without restraint and waved as the trains departed.

At first, the station master asked his porters if such an action should be discontinued and each man politely mocked their boss. 'He loves it, sir,' said Sam Mason, 'and if you try to stop it, you'll have a mutiny on your hands, here and at your home.'

George told Louisa about James and his latest station visit which she knew already thanks to Beatrice. The parents agreed to make an appointment with the specialist who first diagnosed James and now operated from rooms in Harley Street. Could a seriously disabled child have a clever even brilliant brain smarter than many adults including his parents? On their next trip to London, they included a visit to the specialist.

He explained how intelligence was not necessarily linked to physical disability and at times the two were miles apart. It could definitely be possible James was highly intelligent. After examining the patient, he confirmed his opinion. The nanny wheeled James into the waiting-room leaving Louisa to speak to the specialist.

'His speech and mobility are definitely improving, Doctor,' said Louisa, 'but is there anything else we can do?'

'Maintain the therapy but I would recommend splints on his legs.'

Louisa gasped. 'But if he's confined to a wheelchair, what would be the point?'

'Who said he must be confined to a wheelchair?'

Louisa froze. 'You mean James might one day be able to walk?'

'There are no guarantees but you'll never know if you don't try. With one leg being slightly longer than the other, he would need special footwear but if you're willing, I'm sure James will respond. He has an eye-catching enthusiasm for life.'

She struggled to stop the tears. 'Thank you, Doctor; I can't tell you how happy that thought makes me. My husband will be so pleased.'

He calmly warned her about keeping expectations under control, and gave her an appointment to return with James for a fitting of the splints. The journey home seemed to take forever.

That night in bed, Louisa told George about the possibility of James being able to walk. For at least a minute, the SM couldn't speak.

When the Queen Mother died in 1925, her son, King George V, moved from York Cottage into the much bigger main house at Sandringham. His Majesty had a real soft spot for the Norfolk estate.

The station master always received official notification prior to a Royal visit. This day the Royal Train arrived and the SM stood ready. By now the two hard-working Englishmen appreciated the other for the work they did.

'Good day to you, Mr Miracle.'

'Your Majesty,' said the station master bowing without fanfare.

'I trust all is well at Wolverton?'

'Trains on time, sir and all passengers delivered safe and well.'

The King smiled enjoying a few words with a person he admired. 'How's your boy coming along?' The King knew what it was like to have a child suffer having lost his son to epilepsy when Prince John was 13.

'Thank you for asking, sir. He's doing well. Next week he's having splints on his legs.'

'My son, Henry, wore splints when he was young; did him the world of good. Please give my best to Mrs Miracle.'

The King turned and left the station. George nodded his bow. 'Thank you, sir,' he said as the Monarch strode away.

The porters and passengers studied the station master admiring how easily he dealt with the King while never making a show of it.

During his late supper, with James asleep and Beatrice having retired, George told his wife about the Royal visit and how the King of England wished to be remembered to Mrs Miracle.

George and Louisa were never smug or blasé about their dealings with the Monarch and rarely told anyone about Royal conversations.

The SM surprised his wife when he told her about one of the King's sons once having to wear splints.

'Are you sure?' she asked.

'His Majesty said it did his son the world of good.'

There were smiles all round as Miss Halfpenny served one of her spectacular stews.

'If it's all right with you, Mr Miracle, I'll be away to my sister's for lunch on Sunday.'

'Of course, dear lady, but don't you dare even think about not returning safe and well.'

This became a regular spot of repartee. She smiled and said goodnight. The Miracles talked about James and his proposed splints, about the rector working on new ideas for the Cambridgeshire charity, and about the visit of George's mother and stepfather in two weeks. George wanted to talk about a new farmer in the district with the potential of boosting the station's goods and perishables traffic but knew it to be of no interest to his wife.

They retired and kept discussing family matters. In their darkened bedroom, Louisa struggled with upset stomach symptoms. Mentally, her health became equally as bad.

'George, I need to tell you something.'

'Don't tell me you've been left *another* king's ransom.'

She paused. 'I'm scared, George.'

She sounded scared and George dropped his well-worn teasing routine. 'What's happened? What's the matter?'

'I don't want to give birth to another disabled baby.'

He put his arm around her. 'Now my darling girl, we've talked about this many times. We worry about events *if* they happen and not before. We both would love another child but let's wait until something happens.'

Her soft voice sounded crystal clear. 'Something *has* happened.'

It took him a few moments to comprehend her statement. In the darkness he stared into her eyes and saw her smile.

'It's the best news ever,' he said and she returned his kiss and hug with interest.

Chapter 27

Connie and John Beckwith arrived by train to be greeted by a smiling station master who never did come to grips with his stepfather's name. Calling him Da, Dad, John or Mr Beckwith all seemed wrong. He settled for sir.

Louisa admired and enjoyed her in-laws, and Connie and John were thrilled to see James again and the improvement in his speech and movements. They loved pushing him in his wheelchair.

Beatrice and Miss Halfpenny both took a few days off with Connie stepping into her old role at Whittleton despite being told Louisa could manage.

The visitors were stunned when Louisa told them about her pregnancy. Connie purred on the outside but privately worried hoping the baby would be perfect. Emily's two sons were fit and thriving on their farm.

Connie's visit gave everyone a boost and James was sad to see his Grandma Miracle go. She used her Miracle name as it was the name James knew.

Louisa's pregnancy continued and she suffered the worst of morning sickness. With a nanny and housekeeper living with the Miracles, at least the mother could call on help. George spent as much time as possible with his wife, encouraging and reassuring her. Trips to London for James were suspended for the foreseeable future.

Life at Wolferton continued with VIP visitors arriving for a stay or a visit to Sandringham. There were Royals from other countries and politicians needing to discuss matters of state with the King.

During a quiet moment, George would compare his two SM positions; Whittleton with its failing branch line, and Wolferton with its aristocratic clientele. The locations were like chalk and cheese.

Apart from running his station to the highest standard, he never stopped thinking about the health of his son. He wondered how on Earth he and Louisa would have managed without the unexpected and massive bequest she received from the father she never knew.

Louisa grew ever bigger. The unspoken tension in the station master's house edged ever higher thanks to the issue of the new baby. James would soon have a brother or sister and his parents both desperately wanted a "perfect" child. It became walk-on-eggshells time.

George thought about asking the Reverend Attwood if he might pray for the health of Louisa and the new baby but wondered if an atheist asking a Doubting Thomas priest would embarrass him. He saw the chance to ask when Mr Attwood arrived at the station en route to a meeting in King's Lynn.

'Good morning George; how is your good lady?'

'She's due next week, Rector,' said George.

'Please give her my best and tell her I'm thinking of both of you and eager to hear your wonderful news.'

His handshake and smile gave George a feeling of strength. Kenneth's train left and George answered the phone in his office.

'Mr Miracle,' panted the housekeeper, 'she's had her baby. It came all of a sudden like.' George froze. 'The midwife delivered the little 'un and the doctor's on his way. You might want to come home, sir.'

You might want to come home, sir! Was that the understatement of the century? Still George struggled to speak.

'I'll be right there,' he gasped and went to hang up. 'Are they both all right?' he blurted struggling to deal with the shock and surprise.

'Mother and daughter are both fine, sir.'

In the background, he heard the sound of a baby crying. *I have a daughter.* In a daze, he hung up and raced out of his office.

Porters Greene and Mason were on the other platform. George called. 'Gentlemen, I need to go home. My wife's had a baby.'

'Congratulations,' called one.

'Boy or girl, sir?' called the other.

In a tizz, George rubbed his hands. 'It's a girl. James has a sister.'

He seemed stuck to the spot. 'Off you go, sir,' yelled Sam. 'We'll expect you when we see you.'

George ignored his dicky hip and ran home. He burst into the kitchen and Miss Halfpenny pointed. 'They're in the sitting-room.'

The doctor arrived after George but with the baby nestled safely in her mother's arms, both father and medical man were not required. The midwife fussed around the settee which became the birthing bed, the doctor checked mother and baby, and Beatrice popped her head around the corner asking if James could meet his sister.

'Of course,' said George who wanted to thank his wife, greet his daughter, help his son meet his sister and rejoice.

'I thought you hated being late,' said Louisa.

He laughed aloud. 'You look wonderful,' he said, 'and well done once again.'

'Mrs Blakeney was due to call in to check on me and thank goodness she did.' The midwife smiled. 'As soon as she arrived, my waters broke and little Miss Impatience here arrived.'

'And you're okay?' asked George.

'Good as gold and ...' Beatrice gently pushed James towards his mother. 'James, come and say hello to your baby sister, Victoria.' They had agreed on the names Victoria or Kenneth.

The boy leant forward and stared at the tightly wrapped bundle. 'ello, Victoria,' he said and moved his head from parent to parent.

'She has your mother's beauty, James, so let's hope she has your brain,' said the station master.

Other than Victoria, they all laughed with none more excited than the boy in the wheelchair.

This became a new era for George Miracle and his family. The arrival of a new baby impacted their tiny world with a bang. But when you add young James, desperate to improve his speech and mobility, and passengers, freight and VIPs using Wolferton station, well life was never dull.

The Reverend Attwood celebrated the new baby by conducting a christening after one Sunday morning service with Beatrice and Miss Halfpenny being joint godmothers and the rector himself doubling as celebrant and godfather.

The priest and the station master maintained their Sunday evening coffee get-togethers. 'What do you plan to do about schooling for James,' asked the priest.

'We haven't discussed it. We're so busy with Victoria and re-starting therapy sessions for the boy, finding a school for students with special needs has been lost in the traffic.'

'He's old enough for school, George, and bright as a button. Why can't he begin formal learning at home?'

'Of course he can, and we can afford a private tutor but where can I find one?'

'In the village.'

'In Wolferton? Are you serious?' The rector nodded. 'Who?'

'Mrs Galbraith is a member of my congregation. Last century, her parents ran a school in Peterborough where she worked as their assistant. I know she'd love to still teach and James would be the perfect student.'

'That's brilliant news, Kenneth. What should I do?'

'Let me ask her and you could talk about it with Louisa and the boy wonder. I'll tell you what Mrs Galbraith says.'

'She must be paid a salary,' insisted George.

'The labourer is worthy of his hire,' replied the rector as they raised their coffee cups and toasted the new teacher in waiting.

Louisa was feeding Victoria and struggled to contain her excitement when George told her about James being schooled at home.

'Here, lessons at home? '

'Kenneth will ask Mrs Galbraith and if she agrees, James can learn to read and write.'

Their joyful anticipation became infectious. Having inherited vast wealth was important, life-changing but their first priority always involved the love and attention they gave to their children.

Mrs Eleanor Galbraith, a widow in Wolferton and parishioner at St Peter's, suffered an attack of joy when the rector asked her about teaching young James Miracle.

'I'd be delighted, Rector. I've kept most of the teaching material from my parents' school. When can I start?'

And so began a perfect marriage made in Wolferton Heaven. A hungry James became a sponge, eager to absorb and master the tools of reading, writing and arithmetic to go with his brain being desperate for knowledge.

Three mornings a week, in the sunroom, Mrs Galbraith would sit beside James in his wheelchair and, using an improvised blackboard, ancient and out-of-date GER notebooks, all of which were scrounged from the back of a cupboard in the station master's office, and a box of pencils, young Master Miracle began his formal education.

Whether his physical disability boosted his mental ability, no-one knew but his hunger for learning impressed his family and especially his teacher.

Once James grasped reading, he wanted books. Mrs Galbraith would beg, borrow and reel in anything she could to feed his voracious appetite. She played it well. Finding a subject which intrigued the boy saw her find books on his favourite topics and away went the reader.

Eleanor couldn't believe the boy's progress. When Beatrice took the lad to the station, Mrs Galbraith chatted to Louisa and Miss Halfpenny about the boy's stellar progress.

'I've never seen a student absorb so much and comprehend the way James does. He may well require a properly qualified teacher soon as he needs to be challenged. I'm running out of topics and skills to teach him.'

Louisa nursed baby Victoria while finding her heart begin to sing.

Beatrice sat on a bench on the platform, reading a novel, while James watched for trains. The SM always found time to come along and say hello. He'd seen his son attempt to draw on paper and watched how particular he became in creating images usually of people and engines, of locomotives. Today he saw his son writing. 'What's this, James?' he asked intrigued by the numbers listed on the page.

The boy didn't hesitate speaking with drawn-out vowels. 'These are my engine numbers, Dad. Stop pretending you don't know.'

George couldn't speak. He studied the data. As station master he knew all the locomotives which travelled on the line between King's Lynn and Hunstanton and here were their loco numbers, one for each line on the notepad with an A and a D and a time beside each letter.

'What are the letters A and D for, James?' asked his father struggling to believe his son not only grasped the concept of a sort of timetable but could record the results.

'A is Arrival and D is Depart, Dad. You should know that.'

He challenged his father who again cried. The tears welled in the father's eyes as he put his hand on the train spotter's shoulders and squeezed a tad too firmly. He bent and kissed the boy's head before walking back to his office.

'All right, sir?' asked porter Mason.

'My boy's a train spotter.'

The porter laughed. 'Didn't you know?' George became confused. 'He saw a couple of lads from Dersingham taking numbers about a week ago and asked them what they were doing but I don't think they understood his speech. A couple of us explained the practice and next thing, there he is, Wolferton's leading train spotter. He'll be after your job next, Mr Miracle.'

Sam laughed and George returned to his office his heart aflame.

At night he told Louisa. 'I thought you knew,' she said. 'He asked me if Dad would like him doing that.'

'The boy can't walk, has trouble speaking clearly and yet here he is creating his own railway timetable.'

'And Mrs Galbraith reckons she'll have to stop teaching him.'

'What!' exclaimed George in despair. 'Oh but why? She's doing a marvellous job.'

'No, she means he knows the basics so well, he needs a more experienced teacher to take him further.'

Both parents reckoned this to be a wonderful problem.

While the progress made by James thrilled his family and all who followed his progress, a sharp eye was kept on baby Victoria. Did she react in the way an able-bodied infant would be expected to respond? Having seen how their son as an infant failed to perform various simple, basic tasks like kicking and rolling over, George and Louisa often watched their daughter in silence although their chatting to her and playing with her using toys and reading stories never ceased.

George received the usual correspondence with details of the latest Royal Train coming to Sandringham next Saturday afternoon reaching Wolferton at 2:47. The SM advised his team.

'Gentlemen, the Duke and Duchess of York are arriving this weekend with their two daughters, the Princesses Elizabeth and Margaret. I'm told Princess Margaret is still a babe in arms.'

The staff knew the routine and their roles in treating each arrival with professionalism and courtesy. With Longevity the middle name of the porters, they were rich with experience in dealing with Royals.

Beatrice brought James to the station where he took up his train-spotting position. In his early train-spotting days, he found it hard reading the station clock, so his father found an old fob watch he used as a porter at Liverpool Street. James adored being able to tell the time with a watch he kept in his jacket pocket. His father taught him how to read railway timetables, and Mrs Galbraith taught him about world time zones using a globe given to him by his step-grandfather, John Beckwith.

The train arrived with George ready to greet the Royal Family. The Duke of York, the second son of the King and Queen and next in line to the monarchy after his older brother, Edward the Prince of Wales, stepped from the carriage. George bowed his head.

Complete with nanny, an equerry, and two Welsh corgi dogs, the Royals stepped from the train to be greeted by the SM. George met the Duke and his family for the second time, last Christmas being the first with Princess Margaret asleep in the arms of her nanny.

'Good morning,' said the Duke with a slight hesitation in his speech.

'Good morning, Your Highness,' said the SM. 'Welcome to Wolferton; station master George Miracle at your service.'

'Are you the chap who held his wedding breakfast here at the station?'

George smiled with restraint remembering with fondness the happy day.

'I am, Sir, and my wife and I were granted the great honour of your father the King kindly proposing a toast to us as the bride and groom.'

The Royal parents were amused. 'And so he should,' replied the Duke. 'My father mentioned the occasion. He takes a keen interest in all members of staff at Sandringham and surrounding districts, and particularly returned servicemen and women.'

The Duchess took an interest. 'Do you have a family, Mr Miracle?'

'Yes Ma'am, we have two children.' He turned and indicated. 'Our boy over there is recording engine numbers.'

The members of the Royal Family turned towards the child in the wheelchair with the Duchess particularly interested.

Her interest piqued. 'May we see his work?' she asked.

'Of course, Ma'am. Let me show you.' He led the three Royals along the platform. 'James, this is their Royal Highnesses the Duke and Duchess of York and their daughter, Princess Elizabeth.'

In his slow, broken but beautifully constructed sentence, James said, 'How do you do, your Royal Highnesses,' and bowed his head.

The Duke stepped forward. 'How do you do, young man. My father, the King, is a great collector of stamps but your father tells me you are a collector of engine numbers.'

'Yes, you are correct, sir,' said James turning his notebook so the Duke could see his latest information. 'Today the 10:04 Hunstanton Down arrived one minute late.'

The Duke stood there stunned. He loved the way the boy overcame his speech impediment and became genuinely shocked at the technical information from such a youthful train spotter.

'Come and see, Lilibet,' said her father and the Princess, even younger than James, peered at his notebook.

'Your handwriting is very neat,' said the young Royal.

'Thank you,' said James. 'If you work on the railways, you must always be acc ... acc ... accurate.'

James dug in determined to pronounce the word he wanted.

'Well spoken, young man,' said the Duke, smiling at the boy.

George sensed the Royals needed or wanted to depart. 'Your car awaits, sir,' he said indicating the gate leading to the area where horse-drawn carriages used to pull in to convey Queen Victoria on her trips to Sandringham.

Princess Elizabeth smiled at James. 'Goodbye and thank you for showing me your work.'

'Goodbye,' said James and again bowed his head.

As the Royals departed, Beatrice stepped forward. 'I'm not so sure about you, James Miracle. Next you'll be helping the King with his stamp collection.'

The grin on the boy's face extended from ear to ear.

Chapter 28

Wolferton station was but a tiny part of the London and North Eastern Railway. The huge LNER, second only in size to the LMS, the London Midland and Scottish, ran trains from London deep into Scotland and elsewhere. There were great contrasts between the various lines. The distance between the two major cities of London and Edinburgh was well over 300 miles; the distance between King's Lynn and Hunstanton was a mere 16 miles.

Over at Whittleton, years after George Miracle left, the Crabbie limped along, unheralded and unloved. On weekends, Freda and her beau, porter Fletcher Drum, living in sin on Freda's farm with Rufus, still ran her jam and chutney stall for those curious enough to learn about the Druids. Like the branch line, her business was small beer.

The LNER ignored Crabbwell and other small lines throwing its energies into freight, especially coal, and passengers travelling between the main cities from which the railway did make money.

The company struck it lucky when appointing its Chief Mechanical Engineer, Nigel Gresley. He was born in Scotland when his heavily-pregnant English mother travelled to Edinburgh—before the LNER existed—to visit a gynaecologist, and whilst there gave birth.

Nigel served an apprenticeship and worked for other companies but became a star when appointed CME at the LNER. A young Mr Gresley found himself recommended for the job—a bit like George Miracle in that it's not what you know but who—and over 20 years designed an array of steam locomotives which to say the least were eye-catching, his most famous arguably being the *Flying Scotsman*.

Gresley's improvements thrilled the LNER. He allowed the footplate crews to change shifts en route by designing a walkway within the tender, allowing the second driver and fireman to walk onto the footplate and take control of the train without it stopping. To this development Gresley further improved his Pacific class locomotives making their non-stop running possible. Shorter travel times allowed the company to boast their LNER train made the England Scotland journey in under 8 hours; a great selling-point.

During the 1930s, Nigel Gresley designed locomotives which could travel at speeds previously thought impossible. In 1934, the A4 Class Locomotive *Mallard*—named after a breed of duck—reached a top speed of 126 mph. Against its great rival, the LMS, the LNER boasted of the appearance and world-record-breaking speed of its locomotive. Lady Wedgwood, wife of the LNER's chairman, sent a telegram to Gresley: "Three cheers for the *Mallard*. LMS out for a duck."

Gresley spent his early years designing carriages and trucks and to his swish locomotives he added sumptuous carriages giving the LNER the ability to offer dining in style for its passengers.

But heavier carriages meant a heavier load and Gresley found ways to improve his locomotives. Overall efficiency was key and he made extensive use of articulation still widely used a century later.

And all this created newspaper headlines for the main lines but meant far less publicity, in reality no publicity, for those smaller lines.

Sam Taylor brought a newspaper into George's office. 'Have you seen what the company is putting on the mainlines these days?' George read the article. 'When do you think we'll see one of those Gresley monsters whizzing through Wolferton?' asked the porter.

Raising his eyebrows, George returned the paper and gave his colleague a certain stare. 'I'm guessing when Hell is covered in snow.'

Baby Victoria went from crawling to walking in what the district nurse described as record time. The young girl's good health was an ongoing source of joy for her parents who rejoiced as much in the relationship between their children. James took it upon himself to teach his little sister the importance of avoiding the fireplace, sharing her toys with others and caring for their pet cat.

It took Louisa an age to agree to have a cat worrying it might scratch James. When she finally agreed and Victoria was a toddler, the little girl took responsibility for grooming Socks, a black moggie with white feet. He surrendered when the little girl carried him outside.

'This is where you go to the potty, Socks,' she explained and of course the meticulous feline learnt the routine and complied. Inside, Socks preferred James' lap because the boy hardly moved.

With the arrival of Victoria, and by concentrating on her, helping James to walk was not their only priority. Of course he was still showered with love and attention but the wearing of splints worried his parents if their son could never walk. What was the point?

Clearly his speech improved. People meeting him for the first time struggled to understand but his family and the station staff could now converse with him with relative ease.

But the outstanding, unfulfilled quality remained his inability to walk. Louisa and Beatrice resumed London physiotherapy visits for James, and his mother told the therapist about the specialist's comments on James attempting to try and walk unaided.

'I agree,' said the therapist. 'If you're willing, Mrs Miracle, I suggest we jump in at the deep end and aim for the stars.'

Louisa struggled to speak but nodded and whispered, 'That would be wonderful.'

The therapist massaged the boy's legs and feet. The boy liked the man who'd worked on his body for ages while the therapist saw James as one of his greatest challenges.

'Right, young man, come on, let's have you standing.'

His mother worried but the patient wanted to try anything and, more importantly, wanted to succeed. Using his assistant, the therapist helped James with his splints guiding him to stand. Both adults were ready to catch the lad if he needed help.

'Now, James, which is your right leg?'

He slapped it. 'This one, silly,' he said causing the adults to smile.

'I want you to move it forward, please.'

Shock hit the child and the boy's expression spoke volumes. With perfect understanding and a fiery spirit, he faced his toughest task. Despair dominated because the harder he tried, the harder it became.

'I can't,' he cried with a pathetic sob in his voice, and Louisa stood, wanting the exercise to stop. Beatrice felt the same.

The therapist had treated James for nearly three years and knew the boy well. He tried a tactic which might backfire and harm the child's mental condition, his spirit.

'I think you're not trying, James,' he said in a neutral tone of voice. The boy stared at him, part frightened, part angry. More attacks were heard. 'I think you want to spend the rest of your life in that wheelchair.' He pointed at the equipment.

You could cut the atmosphere with a knife. James stared straight ahead. The seconds ticked by. The two professionals each held one of the boy's arms. The adults fell silent. Louisa held her breath when it happened. James Miracle, cerebral palsy sufferer who never once in his life walked, took a step. It was a shuffle but who cares, he moved.

Mind you it should be put in context. The distance his foot travelled was miniscule but at the same time massive. The therapist whispered. 'I don't believe you can move your left foot.'

Again silence filled the room and after a pause, James Miracle took his second step; this one a good half inch longer than the first. Still being held by two strong adults, they neither propelled nor carried him as he took those two tiny steps of his own accord.

Now the therapist changed tactics becoming positive. 'Brilliant, James but don't stop now. Step forward on your right again.'

Encouragement boosted the boy. He made a slightly longer step. 'And again,' urged the therapist. James took a step on his left foot.

Now the patient needed no further instruction. He took tiny steps. If the adults either side of him let go, he would have collapsed in a screaming heap with his mother producing the loudest scream.

'Walk to the bed, James,' urged the therapist. It stood three yards away. His tiny steps became longer and the time between each step shorter. Of course he could see the target and now aimed for it. He drew closer, his mother's heart pounding.

Close to the bed, the therapist glanced at his assistant, nodded, and they let go of the boy's arms. He pitched forward, fell against the bed and clung to the sheet. The therapists applauded, showering him with praise. His mother ran, weeping and hugged the mobile child. Beatrice cried without restraint. What a visit, what an achievement.

As the assistant and Beatrice helped James back into his wheelchair, the therapist took Louisa aside. 'Mrs Miracle, you've seen what your boy can do. He wants to be able to walk. All the time and effort you've put into James may one day pay off.'

'Thank you, Mr Eastern, thank you so very, very much.'

'He needs to walk daily even for only a few minutes. In your home set up a handrail, a ballet barre. And he needs proper footwear. They must be bespoke because of his different leg sizes. I recommend this gent. He's made footwear for several of my clients.'

Louisa accepted a business card and before going back to Maida Vale, all three went to a bootmaker in Silver Street.

The trip to Wolferton became unlike any other. After previous physiotherapy sessions, James would be tired and Louisa and Beatrice chose to keep the conversation low-key. Now the world changed. James walked for the first time in his wheelchair-bound life. Yes, strong adults held him but didn't lift him. The boy, his mother and nanny dared to dream. Could he ever walk on his own, unaided?

Louisa kept a lid on her emotions. 'You should be proud of yourself, James,' she said squashing her joy. The boy sparkled.

'Will you tell Dad or will I?' he asked.

The passengers in their compartment heard James as he found it difficult to speak in a soft voice. Pronouncing his words proved tough; whispering was a whole new level of expertise.

Louisa fought to keep emotion out of her voice. 'We'll both tell him. Now are you going to try and spot locomotive numbers?'

His excitement turned to a mild anger as he reprimanded his mother telling her that proper train spotters collected numbers while stationary on a platform or a bridge.

The Wolverton station master knew the carriage in which his family was seated. He helped his son in his wheelchair onto the platform.

George nodded to the guard who gave the driver the all clear.

'Welcome you three. Did you say hello to London for me?'

George kissed his wife but froze as James spoke.

'Dad, I walked today.'

The shock on the SM's face surprised his family. Thankfully the wind didn't change direction. He stared at his son and couldn't speak.

James reckoned the truth should be told. 'Only little steps and the ther-a-pist held me. Two people held me.'

George recovered a little and gripped his son's face. 'You are brilliant, my boy, absolutely brilliant.'

Both parents shed tears and instantly hugged one another.

'Oi, oi, what's all this?' asked a smiling Sam Mason.

'I can walk, Mr Mason,' said James and the jovial porter froze.

'Blimey, Jimmy, that's fantastic.' The local grapevine caught fire.

Chapter 29

James Miracle's parents put wooden parallel bars in the school room and each day his mother and Beatrice helped James stand between them, steadying them as he exercised. Wearing splints, James practised walking. Progress took forever but progress it was.

Therapists explained how wasted muscles might take years to "come alive", remain useless forever or only develop a small percentage of their capability. Louisa adopted the philosophy of "slow but steady wins the race". The one source of undiluted joy remained the sight of little Victoria running freely around the house chasing Socks and loving life.

By now Hamilton-Weir House had helped more than a hundred families with a long waiting list of people hoping to gain a place. George took a back seat pleased his wife and particularly his mother-in-law were so involved. He kept more than busy with the number of politicians and Royals arriving at Wolferton en route to the Sandringham Estate.

Like his predecessor, Harry Saward, George found his hands full with kings, queens, emperors and others from a number of European countries. One unusual visitor, the Russian mystic Rasputin, is reckoned to have arrived demanding an audience with the King at Sandringham. Aware of the possible visit, the Monarch, Edward VII, issued the SM specific instructions.

'Don't let him anywhere near the estate, Harry. I hereby give you permission to send him back whence he came.'

George wondered if he'd ever have to deal with famous or infamous visitors and play the role of policeman or bodyguard.

Christmas drew closer and son James needed a teacher who could introduce the boy to more difficult and challenging subjects.

As usual, the Royal Family would spend Christmas at Sandringham and George studied the instructions for their movements, dates and times, sharing these with his porters and signalman.

'I've heard a rumour, gentlemen,' he said. 'There is going to be a special broadcast on the radio from Sandringham.'

This idea grabbed their attention and they wanted more details.

'From Sandringham you say?' asked Sam Mason.

'For the first time the King is going to speak to the nation from his Norfolk home. If you're on duty, I'll have the radio broadcast the event here in my office. If you haven't access to a radio, you're welcome to pop in here and listen.'

Everyone buzzed.

The week before Christmas, Louisa and Beatrice took James up to London, not for a therapy session but for a fitting. The bootmaker, having measured young James for a pair of boots, completed the task.

The Miracles entered the shop, James sat waiting and his new boots appeared. You should have seen his eyes sparkle.

The skill of the bootmaker became evident. He'd made the boots a little larger to allow the young boy's feet to grow into them. The right boot with a built-up sole helped tackle the boy's lopsided stance with one leg being a little shorter than the other.

With the boots on the boy's feet, the bootmaker gently squeezed them for comfort and fit.

'How do they feel, young man?' he asked.

'They feel good, sir,' replied James, 'but I need to test them.'

Louisa and the bootmaker stared at one another. Both moved to help the boy.

'Thank you but I can do it,' he said. He tried to stand but failed.

'Let me help, son,' said his mother and he yielded.

Once standing he couldn't move. His mother held his arm. The adults waited remaining silent. Inside his head, James spoke to himself. Then shaking his arm free from his mothers' grasp, he opened his arms like wings and using them as a means of balance, he stepped off his left foot; a small but definite step. He tried another.

'I'm fine, Ma, you can step back,' he said not watching his mother.

She hesitated and waited. After what seemed like an age, James took another step and another. He wobbled and both the adults grabbed an arm each. James Miracle loved his new boots.

The King's broadcast proved a huge success. Written by the poet and author, Rudyard Kipling, His Majesty spoke clearly and with affection. People up and down the country wondered if he might repeat the event next Christmas. Despite being described as a tyrant king, George V received tremendous admiration from his people.

The other George, SM Miracle, arranged the Wolferton roster enabling him to take his family to church on Christmas Eve. James sat tall in his wheelchair with Victoria rugged up, holding her mother's hand. The rector grinned with pleasure his teeth shining bright.

'This is my favourite Christmas present, the family Miracle and all so cheerful and resplendent. Merry Christmas to you all,' he beamed.

The children were in fine form. The decorations, the ceremony, the music and the joy on the faces of the people grabbed George's attention, especially in light of the fact he knew both the rector and his bishop privately regarded religion, as in belief in the supernatural, as invented by humans, in fact nonsense.

Grandmothers Connie and Rowena were not at Wolferton. One found her hands full with her grandsons in Whittleton, and the other worked tirelessly with several parents and their disabled children in Hamilton-Weir House. There the highlight of the celebrations occurred on the faces of smiling parents as their delighted children received a gift from a surprise visitor in a big, red suit.

George and Louisa discussed the education of their children. Louisa came up with a gem of an idea. Mrs Galbraith admitted James needed a teacher with more expertise and urged his parents to find someone else. But losing Mrs Galbraith seemed such a shame.

'Why doesn't she stay on and teach Victoria?' said an excited Louisa. 'Victoria's too young to start school but learning at home like her brother would be perfect.'

George grinned. 'And here I am thinking I married you for your beauty.'

Mrs Galbraith's face came alive. 'I'd love to teach little Victoria to read and write,' she said.

'And count,' added George.

'And count,' she said smiling.

That was one problem solved but a new teacher for James still needed to be found. His parents talked about advertising in the local newspaper. They worried possible teachers might have to travel a long distance to Wolferton.

George pondered arranging free or discounted travel for a tutor.

Victoria loved her "schoolroom" where big brother once studied with Mrs Galbraith. Now the girl was the special student.

After the last Sunday train, George came home for his coffee 'n chat with the rector. The clergyman knew when George would be home because he heard the last train arrive and depart.

The men sat by a fire enjoying their afters. George brought up the issue of finding a new teacher for James and went into detail about advertising, travel required, and finding the right person who would relate well to a lad with cerebral palsy. Kenneth said nothing waiting for George to finish. When he did the rector spoke in a quiet voice.

'I'll teach him,' he said and George's mouth opened.

'You?' gasped the SM.

'If you'll have me. I mean my Cambridge degree has been wasted on writing sermons the content of which I seriously struggle to invent.'

George wanted to hug the visitor. 'Kenneth, forgive me. Why didn't I think of you in the first place? Having you teach James is perfect. The boy will be over the moon.' He turned serious. 'Now we must pay you of course.'

The rector scoffed. 'Don't be absurd. I'll derive enormous pleasure from teaching the lad and we'll go on a journey, a wonderful adventure together.'

'I want to wake James and tell him now. And Louisa will be so excited.' She was, they both were. James showed impatience busting to know when his lessons would start.

It became an exciting time in the station master's house. The children worked hard at their education, loving their teachers and lessons. Louisa and Beatrice kept giving James his physical exercises and George ran the station loving every minute.

Spring arrived and with it came warmer weather and blooming gardens. Walking the short distance to the station, George saw annuals flaunting their wares reminding him of his former station at Whittleton. His mind buzzed with memories of the gardens created by the elderly Horace Gardiner. The otherwise basic platforms became a miniature Kew Gardens. Those were happy days and George often thought about the branch line to Crabbtree wondering how it managed to survive.

His children were thriving in their studies, he found working at Wolferton a joy and thoughts of moving never entered his mind. He could see himself remaining there for the rest of his career.

With the 11:35 due in a few minutes, he came out of his office and wandered to the end of the platform to inspect the station and its surrounds as was his wont. A few passengers gathered on both platforms and his usual, "Good morning" to locals took place.

He heard a voice calling and turned to see his son enter being pushed by the rector. They were a good thirty yards away.

'Hello Dad,' cried James waving.

George waved wondering why his son wasn't in school but thought it might be an outdoor lesson or the teacher taking a break.

Then the station master froze. The rector locked the wheelchair and to be doubly sure, held it in a vice-like grip. James appeared to be trying to stand. He struggled. George wanted to move and help his boy but a force or thought or whatever made him stay still.

Using all his strength, James pushed upright and used his arms like wings to keep his balance. He swayed. Passengers stared. George stared, spellbound. He'd often watched James at home but always using the wooden parallel bars. There were no bars on the Wolferton station.

Using his flailing arms, James thrust them back and forth across his chest as he took steps; proper steps. James walked in his unique way, a sort of leaning forward and waving his arms routine. Porters stopped and gasped. The expected train could be heard approaching.

The boy might well be thought to be drunk. His head and torso were ahead of his lower limbs but still he kept going.

Driving the 11:35, Ernie Cruickshank enjoyed a perfect view of his favourite train spotter, the boy who lived in a wheelchair but now was haring along the platform towards the loco and his father whose arms were as wide as the standard gauge tracks. The driver saw no need or reason to sound the loco's whistle other than history being made on the Wolferton Down. And my, did Ernie give that whistle some welly.

George's heart exploded with joy but as James drew ever closer, the SM worried. His son seemed headed for a fall and began leaning evermore forward as he walked, his built-up boot dragging. Falling flat on his face became a real possibility. As his father moved towards the travelling offspring, James overbalanced but lunged forward and collapsed into his father's arms.

More train whistle sounds were heard as was excited applause from both platforms with cheers as well. Nobody cared as George Miracle openly wept.

The fireman, Buster Mitchell, leapt off the footplate and lifted the boy aloft. All firemen have muscles on their muscles. 'You little champion, Jim boy,' cried Buster and James adored the experience.

Persuading the youngster to return to his wheelchair became a struggle mainly because the recently mobile but exhausted lad wanted to do it all again.

They convinced him to try again tomorrow and the boy departed with his teacher pushing and everyone on the platforms waving and cheering. The station master continued to weep.

Over supper at the station master's house, the conversation overflowed with the exploits of James the travelling train spotter.

Chapter 30

Wolferton was called the Royal Station because of its regular patronage by the Royal Family. Once the King began broadcasting a Christmas message from Sandringham, the estate's fame increased. Everyone sat around a radio as the weather kept people indoors. Who else is at Sandringham, asked the public?

The health of the Royals attracted great interest. But an unwritten agreement existed between newspaper barons meaning intimate details about the Royals would receive little if any publicity. Of course, European and American papers ignored said agreement.

When the King's father, Edward VII, found himself in potentially scandalous situations, such as being called as a witness in divorce proceedings, the fourth estate found itself under pressure to not report or, if necessary, subtly cover the matter. Of course such a sensational event received widespread coverage. Thank goodness His Majesty appeared as a witness and not as the respondent.

One of the first lessons George Miracle learnt having arrived at Wolferton involved never gossiping about VIP passengers. Naturally rumours about Royalty would always abound and the Wolferton station master found himself in a perfect position to collect tittle-tattle. He ignored the idle chatter, said nothing, and ran the station.

King George V's oldest son, Edward, the Prince of Wales, seemed to be a chip off the block of his late grandfather. Both Edwards were keen on the ladies and the younger Edward gave himself a certain freedom by becoming the first member of the Royal family to obtain a pilot's licence. Forget the railway; a visit via Wolferton station became redundant as the Prince landed and took off at Sandringham.

Flying didn't endear the Prince to his father. The King reckoned his son would make a terrible monarch. 'Heaven help us if Edward ever becomes King,' he was reported to have said. More Royal gossip.

On their latest Sunday evening coffee and cake chat, George and the rector discussed politics. 'What do you make of this chap, Hitler?' asked George.

'Ambitious and seriously dangerous,' replied the clergyman.

'I can't believe we'll have another war. I saw enough of the horror in France and please God it never happens again.'

'Please God?' queried the Reverend Attwood. 'That's a strange expression coming from a non-believer.'

'Figure of speech, sir,' replied the grinning railwayman.

The visitor paused. 'I have news, George.'

'Oh and good news I hope?'

'I'm getting married.'

'What!' exclaimed George thrusting out his hand. 'Congratulations my dear fellow. My, you're a dark horse. Who's the lucky young lady?'

'Her name's Catherine and like me she's no longer in the first flush of youth. We met at university twenty odd years ago. I asked her to marry me then but she chose another.'

George fell silent needing time to think. Kenneth explained.

'She's divorced, George, which means I'll be leaving Wolferton.'

'No!' exclaimed the SM knowing the popularity of the rector and particularly with James. 'Why? You leave because you marry?'

'I'm afraid the good old C of E doesn't take kindly to divorced persons re-marrying when the ex remains alive, and when a priest is involved, well, rules are rules and the quality of mercy is most definitely strain'd.'

'James will be devastated. What will you do? Where will you go?'

The rector shrugged. 'My wife-to-be has a house in Cambridge. I'll probably teach. Now listen, my friend. When I told you I was serious about your boy sitting for a Cambridge scholarship I meant it. He's still far too young but in a year or three, he should definitely have a go. He has the brains, obviously not from his father, and he would thrive in a robust academic situation. He could live in halls and spend weekends with his grandmother at Hamilton-Weir House. Please allow me to push the idea when the time is right.'

The SM could hardly refuse. 'Thank you, Kenneth, you're a champion. I'm overcome by your kindness and my boy's intelligence.'

The rector gambled. 'If James moved to live with Mrs McClaren, we could continue his education. He could come home on weekends.'

In bed, George told Louisa everything about Kenneth Attwood leaving Wolferton and his offer to continue teaching their son in Cambridge.'

'He'd love it,' she said. 'Mummy will be thrilled to bits.'

'Beatrice will be shattered.'

'She said last week that James didn't need help as much anymore.'

They fell silent, thinking. 'We're getting old, Mr Miracle. Our disabled son may one day go to university and our daughter started school able to read and write.'

'We're not the only ones growing old,' replied George. 'I heard today the King is poorly. When he last came to Wolferton, to me his face showed a marked deterioration.'

'You didn't say anything about his health.' He sighed and she realized. 'Of course, silly me, you're trained to *not* speak of matters Royal, even whispering to your wife in bed with all the lights out.'

Pauses slipped into their conversation. George asked a question.

'Have you ever done anything you think or know is wrong and never told anyone about it?' asked George.

'Whatever brought that on and what on Earth are you talking about? Now's a fine time to tell me you're related to Jack the Ripper.'

'The rector told me about his first proposal of marriage being rejected and it set me to thinking about my past.'

'What's wrong with proposing marriage? Oh, hang on, Mister. Don't tell me you once proposed to another woman and she said no. So who is she, this mysterious first true love of George Miracle?'

He sighed. 'You are my first and only true love, Mrs Miracle.'

'So you say,' she said, leant in and kissed him. With her back to him she spoke. 'You know your worst sin, George Miracle, is your *lack* of sin.'

The rector told the bishop of his intention to marry a divorced woman. His Grace reluctantly agreed to accept Kenneth's resignation. 'Damn stupid rules,' he muttered. 'Archaic beliefs will drive more people away. You might be better off out of it. What will you do?'

'A spot of teaching I think. I've been tutoring a disabled boy and when he's of age, would dearly love him to apply for a Cambridge scholarship.'

'Is he up to it?'

'He has cerebral palsy which affects his movements and speech but his brain is inspiring. In a few areas he knows more than I do.'

'You're doing a Thomas Tighe.'

The rector pondered the name. 'Might he have been the Irish clergyman who tutored Patrick Brontë and helped him win a Cambridge scholarship?'

'The same and the best of luck to you and your young man. So when do you plan to resign?'

The men discussed the future with the rector being urged to delay news of his nuptials until as late as possible. Besides there was much more tutoring needed in the station master's house.

The people didn't know their King had suffered poor health for several years. During the Great War on one of his visits to troops on the Western Front, George V fell from his horse and the injury affected him for the rest of his life. His constant smoking brought on bouts of bronchitis and his chronic pulmonary disease as well as pleurisy meant his doctors recommended rest. The people of Britain knew little of their monarch's health issues.

He continued the Christmas Day messages from Sandringham and people eagerly awaited the broadcasts as a must-listen activity. The station master became a well-known face when the Royals alighted.

'Good day, Mr Miracle,' became a regular refrain when the Windsors stepped from the train. One visit saw the winter weather unusually mild and James came to the station to update his train journal. His method of travel, certainly on such a short journey, involved using his legs. He'd park himself on a station bench, still marked with a GER symbol, and wearing his coat and scarf, would note the arrival and departure times of trains.

This Christmas, the Duke and Duchess of York arrived with their daughters and the youngest, Princess Margaret, now an active walker.

George greeted the family and they shared a friendly conversation. About to depart, Princess Elizabeth spotted James.

'Isn't that young boy your son, Mr Miracle, the one who collects engine numbers?'

'Indeed he is, Your Royal Highness.'

The older Princess spoke to her sister. 'You should see his work, Margaret.' Elizabeth addressed the Duchess. 'May we go and see his work, Mummy?'

Before the Duchess could reply, George made a suggestion.

'Sir, Ma'am, he could come to you if you wish.' The Royals stared at the station master. They didn't speak so George called to his son. The Duke and his family were stunned as the boy they'd only ever seen in a wheelchair, rose and in his unique style, walked towards them. He stopped and bowed his head.

The Windsors paused and turned to George who explained. 'James has been studying and working hard and has now mastered walking.'

The Duke of York stepped forward and offered his hand to the boy. James needed to swap his diary to his left hand before shaking the hand of the second son of the King of England.

'Heartiest congratulations, young man; you are a credit to yourself and your family.'

'Thank you, Your Royal Highness,' said James bowing his head.

He proudly showed the Princesses his handiwork before the family said goodbye and, wishing everyone a Merry Christmas, departed for the car waiting in the yard beside the station.

'You have a tale to tell the family tonight,' said the SM, and the two Miracles shared a massive grin.

In bed, George and Louisa luxuriated in discussing the story of their boy walking to the Duke and Duchess of York and their two daughters, and explaining his handiwork to the young Princesses.

'They're a lovely family,' said George. 'I think it's a pity the Duke is the second son and not the heir to the throne.'

For the first time ever, George Miracle broke the rule about Royal gossip and raised the topic of a certain Royal romance.

'You know the Prince of Wales is keen on this American, Mrs Simpson. She's a divorcee and still married to her second husband.'

'Do you think they'll ever marry?'

'Not while His Majesty is still alive. I heard the King exploded when he discovered the romance and forbade Mrs Simpson coming anywhere near Sandringham.'

'But George, if they're in love, why can't they marry?'

'If the rector is forced to quit over marrying a divorcee, imagine the reaction to the future King doing the same. It's not so much the head of the Church of England marrying a divorcee, which the King, Prime Minister, parliament and the people oppose; it's the couple being sympathetic towards the Nazis and their leader, Herr Hitler. If we go to war against Germany again, how will it appear if our future King is pals with the enemy?

The King gave his annual Christmas message which again touched the hearts of his subjects up and down the land. He spoke clearly albeit with a spot of throat clearing. As the people listened, no-one knew it would be his final Christmas broadcast. His Majesty took to his bed and a few weeks later died.

He timed his passing perfectly thanks to a couple of injections from his doctor who said, 'The King's life is moving peacefully towards its close.' By dying at five minutes before midnight, it allowed *The Times*, the King's favourite newspaper, and not those dreadful tabloids, to be the first to announce the tragic news.

The funeral befitted a monarch. His body rested in St Mary Magdalene Church on the Sandringham estate, and from there was to be moved to Wolferton station. Having already handled the King's mother's funeral a decade earlier, the station master knew the procedure. The funeral train included a carriage with a locked section for the coffin and additional carriages for the guard of honour and officials. The station master never missed a beat standing ready to send the train on its way to London for the ceremonial gun carriage cortège and service.

The locomotive pulling the Royal Train waited patiently hissing quietly. The footplate crew checked and double checked the steam pressure. Only rarely did you drive and fire a train carrying a deceased monarch. No-one attempted the old joke about being late for your own funeral.

George checked his watch. He wanted his part of the process to run smoothly. His lookout porter spotted the hearse coming along the road from Sandringham. He signalled to the signal box who signalled to the SM. George received the word. The King is on his way.

The SM checked his attire—coat buttons correct, top hat straight, black armband and tie perfect. As he walked onto the platform, his phone rang. He would deal with His Majesty in a moment.

He answered the phone. 'Station master George ...'

'George, come home!' The voice of his wife screamed fear.

'What's happened?'

'Victoria's gone!'

'What do you mean? Gone where?'

'We don't know. She's missing.'

'She's probably hiding.'

'We've searched everywhere; the house, the garage, the garden, she's not here. Is she with you?'

'Of course not. Didn't Mrs Galbraith come to help with revision?'

'Victoria waved goodbye to her at the front gate and Mrs Galbraith said she saw a car waiting on the road to the church. George, she's been kidnapped!'

It felt as if a knife had plunged into George's heart. Memories of his mother being grabbed by armed robbers exploded in his mind. He gasped. The thought flashed that because he and Louisa acquired great wealth, someone would one day try and steal their money. A ransom for a precious child became an obvious scenario. Now it had happened. Now it was real. Sam Mason stepped into the office.

'Hearse pulling in, sir,' he said and froze. The porter stared at his dumbfounded boss whose face screamed panic.

'What's happened?' exclaimed Sam, moving to hold the SM who started to collapse.

'My daughter's missing; they think she's been kidnapped.'

'Jesus,' whispered Sam. 'I'll call the cops.' He grabbed the phone and dialled.

'But the King,' said George and tried to straighten up, smarten up.

'Bugger the King. He's dead. Vicky's alive and we have to find her.' He spoke into the mouthpiece. 'Hello, is that the police?'

To be continued

The Miracle Terminus – The Stationmaster Miracle Series – Book 4

George Miracle - Books 1 and 2

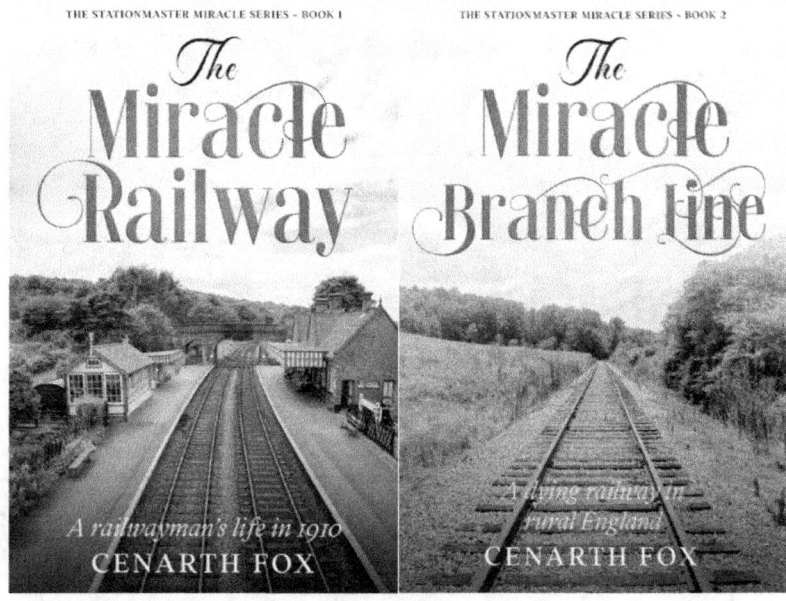

THE STATIONMASTER MIRACLE SERIES - BOOK 1

The **Miracle Railway**

A railwayman's life in 1910

CENARTH FOX

THE STATIONMASTER MIRACLE SERIES - BOOK 2

The **Miracle Branch line**

A dying railway in rural England

CENARTH FOX

Meet George Miracle; born London, England, 1898. In 1910 he starts work as a station lad at one of the biggest and busiest railway stations in the world—Liverpool Street in London. George rises to lad porter and then porter before he's conscripted. He survives the Great War although a German soldier gave him a permanent reminder of his time in a French trench. Back on the rail he is arrested for murder. He gets about a bit does George. He moves to the sticks to a small station where its even smaller branch line is due for the chop. As the youngest station master in England, he faces the sack for fraud, falls madly in love, and deals with a crazy murder plot and an armed robbery. His life may have you laugh out loud and even make the hairs on the back of your neck get busy.

It's like someone from the times telling us their experiences.
It's a pleasure to read.
Twitter July 2022

The Detective Joanna Best Mysteries

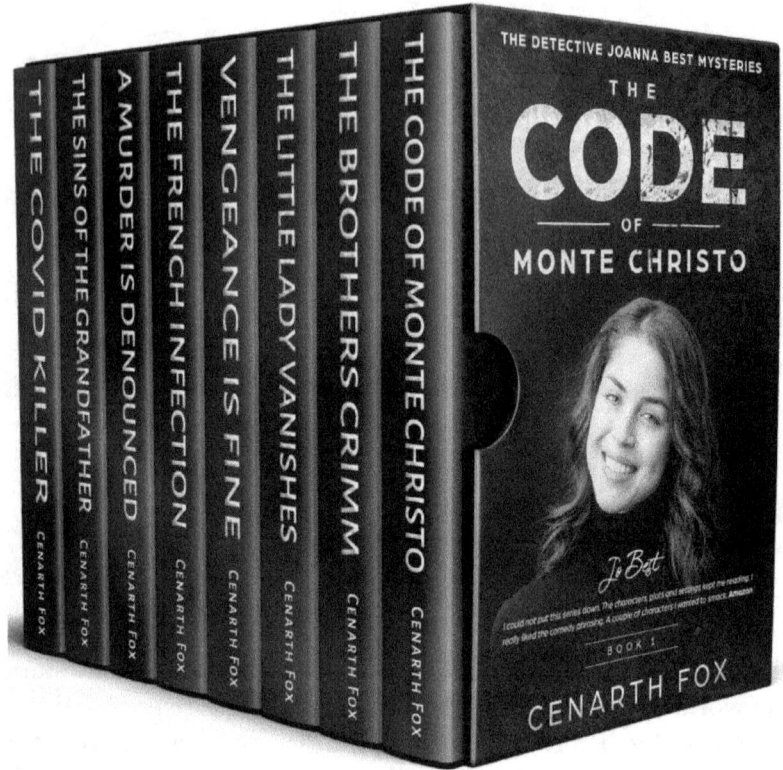

www.cenfoxbooks.com

Joanna Best is the youngest homicide detective in town. Smart, feisty and gorgeous, she's brilliant at cracking cases and rubbing people up the wrong way. Some jealous colleagues are desperate to undermine her. Certain criminals want her dead. Juggling a career with Victoria Police, having three men madly in love with her, and a strange family, Jo Best's adventures will drag you in. Her second banana is an Australian born Chinese IT guru who makes computers sing. Her best pal is a female 60ish police surgeon, a forensic genius and chocoholic.

I could not put this series down. The characters, plots, settings, kept me reading. I really liked the word comedy phrasing. A couple of characters I wanted to smack. **Amazon**

Sherlock Holmes

The great man is soon to retire. On his last night at Baker Street, the loyal landlady drops a bombshell. Holmes is staggered. Mrs Hudson has done what!? Sherlock Holmes never panics—until now. Dr Watson arrives and is stunned. It's their greatest challenge. Sir Arthur Conan Doyle is furious. A famous author turned WW1 counter—intelligence spy is on the case. *The Strand Magazine* smells a scoop. Inspector Lestrade from Scotland Yard plans revenge, and at stake is the brilliant reputation of the world's most famous consulting detective. His only hope is to 'play the game'.

www.cenfoxbooks.com

A delightfully imaginative pastiche. Recommended. **Peter Blau BSI**
An extraordinary book, one of the most enjoyable pieces of Holmesian fiction I've read in a long time ... a complex, ingenious and deliciously funny story of intersecting realities, and the conclusion is entirely satisfactory. I love it! **Roger Johnson**
Commissioning Editor: *The Sherlock Holmes Journal*

A Sweeping Saga

Born in a London slum and sent on a hellish voyage to a bloody war in Australia

A SWEEPING SAGA

broke, bullied, betrayed—but alive in Van Diemen's Land

CENARTH FOX

Jonathon Sweeping became Oliver Twist before Dickens was born. In a London slum, his young parents battled poverty, disease and heartache. Forget schooling. Shove the child up a chimney. Make young Sweeping a sweep. Threaten him, injure him but under no circumstances pay him. No wonder death and stealing dominated society when even children fronted the Old Bailey. What hope for the boy? Jonathon moved from prison hulk to convict ship to the other side of the world where Van Diemen's Land with its stunning natural beauty became a war zone. It was kill or be killed as genocide exploded. The boy became a man fighting injustice, cruelty and bushfires. He started a family and together they lived, loved and built a new nation in what became Tasmania. This is Jonathon Sweeping's sweeping saga.

A combination of fine scholarship and effective prose make A Sweeping Saga a great pleasure to read.
Emeritus Professor Michael Roe University of Tasmania

Agatha Crispie

She was Agatha Miller, Agatha Christie, Agatha Mallowan, Mary
Westmacott and Dame Agatha. She is the Queen of Crime.
Her writing output is Guinness Book of Records material.
After the Bard, she's the most popular author.
At first, publishers rejected her manuscripts.
Where are those publishers today?

In Agatha Christie's novel, *The Body in the Library*, one reads the
name Dorothy Sayers.

'Very few of us are what we seem.'
'The best time to plan a book is while you're doing the dishes.'
Agatha Christie 1890—1976

*I enjoyed this book a lot it is extremely funny I would recommend it
to anyone who is a fan of Agatha Christie.* ★★★★★ **Amazon**

Three World War Two Thrillers

Louise Beatrice Wellesley, nicknamed Plum by her big brothers, is a brilliant and beautiful English actress studying at Cambridge in 1939. She's recruited as a spy for the Secret Service and soon is on stage in a Parisian nightclub wearing a costume to shock her mother. Sharing a dressing-room with Edith Piaf is never dull. War begins and in Paris, Louise fights Nazis, the French police, part of the Resistance, and a British traitor. Back home at Windsor Castle, she joins a group of actors and stars in *Cinderella* before the Royal Family. When the IRA kidnap a Royal, the leading lady carries out a Girls-own rescue and so impresses Winston, he demands she join the SOE. Plum plays the role of a nun in Lyon, is captured and tortured by the Gestapo, fights an archbishop, climbs the Pyrenees and, back in London, uncovers a mole in Baker Street thanks to someone who knows Sherlock Holmes. Go girl.

I have read 100's of books on WW2. I can honestly say this trilogy will go down as one of the most enjoyable. All 3 books were riveting. I adored her and can't recommend these books enough. **Amazon 5★**

A Plum Jewel is the third in the series about a beautiful young actress turned spy. In the opinion of this reader it may be the best. Cenarth Fox has loaded this tale with so many twists and obstacles the reader may feel the need to take notes. Mr. Fox's knowledge of the working of wartime Britain and France is remarkable. The reader is right in the middle of the action. I can't recommend this book strongly enough. **Scott Skipper 5 stars**

The Plum Trilogy – www.cenfoxbooks.com

Meet the Author

I always enjoy hearing from readers with their questions and/or comments. I have a free newsletter (Foxy's Follies) with news about my latest books, plays and musicals. If you'd like a copy, please send a request by email. I never share the email address of my subscribers.

cen@cenfoxbooks.com
writer@foxplays.com

And if you'd care to post a review of my books on Amazon or Goodreads, I'll be most grateful.

Happy reading

Cenarth Fox
www.cenfoxbooks.com

P.S. The scripts of my stage shows can be read online at
www.foxplays.com

www.ingramcontent.com/pod-product-compliance
Lightning Source LLC
Chambersburg PA
CBHW070607120726
47909CB00007B/2471